TUSK
AND
STONE

Also by Malcolm Bosse

THE VAST MEMORY OF LOVE
MISTER TOUCH
STRANGER AT THE GATE
FIRE IN HEAVEN
THE WARLORD
THE MAN WHO LOVED ZOOS
THE INCIDENT AT NAHA
THE JOURNEY OF TAO KIM NAM

For Young Adults

THE EXAMINATION
DEEP DREAM OF THE RAINFOREST
CAPTIVES OF TIME
THE BARRACUDA GANG
ORDINARY MAGIC
(*originally titled* GANESH)
CAVE BEYOND TIME
THE 79 SQUARES

TUSK
AND
STONE

MALCOLM BOSSE

FRONT STREET
ARDEN, NORTH CAROLINA ◆ 1995

FOR MARK
with love

We gratefully acknowledge
the translation by William Buck,
from *Mahabharata*
(Berkeley: University of California Press, 1973), p. 337

Library of Congress Cataloguing-in-Publication Data

Bosse, Malcolm J. (Malcolm Joseph)
Tusk and stone / Malcolm Bosse
p. cm.
Summary: After dacoits attack his caravan and he loses his identity
as a Brahmin, Arjun resigns himself to his new life, becomes
an elephant driver, and searches for his kidnapped sister.
ISBN 1-886810-01-4 (alk. paper)
[1. India—History—324 B.C.-1000 A.D.—Fiction.
2. Brothers and sisters—Fiction. 3. Soldiers—Fiction.
4. Elephants—Fiction.]
I. Title.
PZ7.B6494Tu 1995
[Fic]—dc20   95-23448

The Earth quaked as though to shake him off;
all the trees and animals in the world trembled,
and fear shook the sea.
There was a harsh grating noise—
Arjuna had strung the Gandiva bow and stood on the Earth.

—THE *MAHABHARATA*

Note   INDIA'S SOCIAL SYSTEM, which has survived for three thousand years, can be confusing to the Westerner. Four classes or "varnas" dominated ancient India: the priestly and scholarly Brahmans, the military Kshatriyas, and the shopkeeping and farming Vaishyas. They were born again through rituals that allowed them to wear sacred threads. The peasant Shudras, who were not twice-born, constituted the fourth and lowest varna. There was also a fifth group, the Panchamas, who became known as the untouchables because they lived outside of the orthodox religious system. They could not enter temples, draw water from public wells, or cook food for other people.

In medieval times varna was balanced by another way of making distinctions among people. This was jati or caste, a division based upon specific occupations and rigorously observed social customs. In modern times caste has assumed more importance than class. There are nearly two thousand jatis, each with its own rules and traditions. If this sounds complicated, it is—and becomes far more so in actual practice.

The thriving seaport I refer to as as Mamallapuram is now a rather shabby town called Mahabalipuram. Nearby hills contain world-renowned sculptures carved from stone more than a millenium ago.

One minor point about spelling. Ś and Ṣ in Indian pronunciation both sound much like sh in "shed." Consequently, I have used Shiva rather than Śiva or Ṣiva, which are sometimes found in books about India. I have followed the same method for spelling similar words.

Preface

THAT ERA IN WESTERN CIVILIZATION between the fall of Rome and the rise of city-states has been called the Dark Ages. Exhausted by a turbulent past and comforted by a changeless present, Europeans experienced little variation in their way of life.

Elsewhere, however, the world was buffeted by wars of conquest and challenged by new ideas in the arts and religion. Think of the Near East and China. Think of medieval India. Today we have a few stone monuments as visual testament to the excitement of living in seventh-century India. Upheaval and renewal went hand in hand there. Few times in world history have people embraced so much tumult and change at the service of living to the fullest. It is a pity we have such fragmentary evidence of their daily lives. And yet—what if we viewed that distant land at a remote time through the eyes of a boy approaching manhood? If we looked, say, through the eyes of Arjun . . .

TUSK
AND
STONE

PART ONE

✦ I ✦

BEFORE ENTERING THE PATHLESS FOREST, Arjun looked over his shoulder at the clearing. His glance took in the exhausted porters sprawling against tree trunks, their pack loads stacked beside them; bullocks, unharnessed from spoke-wheeled carts, bending wearily to graze in wild grass; merchants and caravan drivers milling around their campsite, cursing the heat; a few women balancing water jars on their heads as they returned from a nearby stream.

After that glance the boy turned and hurried off. Arjun had had quite enough of this creaking, groaning, rattling caravan for one day. He wanted to be free of it a while. Until it entered the forest, today's road had meandered, under a pounding sun, across one dusty hill after another in a seething glare that brought tears to the eyes. A wagon had broken down. After much squabbling its owner had been left behind. From eating something spoiled, an old merchant had vomited all over his mule. Two drivers had spent half the day yelling insults at each other from their carts. The caravan's leader had shouted orders as if he were Lord Shiva looking down at mortals from Mount Kailasa. "Don't lag, don't stop for anything!" But people paid little attention to him. They stopped to drink, to rest, to rearrange their packs. Segments of the wagon train dotted the hot countryside at increasingly distant intervals until the leader at its head could not be heard or even seen from the rear. Arjun, positioned about midway in the ragged column, wished for the freedom to go forward alone, quickly. He'd like to get the day's march over with, instead of shuffling along like a sleepy cow. He found it hard to believe that he'd joined the caravan only two weeks before. It seemed so much longer!

That's what Arjun was thinking when he turned his back on the clearing and moved rapidly into the forest. Soon out of earshot of the noisy camp, he began to shed the memory of a long, dreary day. This morning Uncle had told him they would reach Kashi in a month if all went well. And if all didn't go well? His question had made Uncle smile. There were still floods to consider. After all, the rainy season had ended just recently. Water from the monsoon continued to pour down the mountainsides, pushing silt into the rivers and choking their channels. Maybe a river along the way would overflow its banks and keep the ferries ashore. But, of course, that would mean nothing more than a delay in crossing. How long? Uncle pursed his lips. A week or two or—three. Another possible source of delay was armies. They were always on the move somewhere. Perhaps the caravan would have to step aside and let war elephants, horses, and bowmen use the roads first. "You must be courteous in dealing with armies," observed Uncle, tapping his cheek thoughtfully. And then dacoits were sometimes a hazard. Patting Arjun's arm reassuringly, he added, "No cause to fear, though. We have a well-armed caravan.

Dacoits are cowardly fellows. Unless they have a clear advantage, bandits will never attack." But Uncle didn't seem convinced by his own argument. With a gloomy sigh, he muttered, "Well, you never know. Surely it's possible they might creep into camp at night and cut loose a few sacks of goods. Lord Shiva protect us." He cleared his throat as if clearing his mind. "All in all, it is my judgment we have nothing to worry about. The worst I expect is the journey taking longer than we hope."

Arjun was actually hoping that it would take longer than Uncle expected. Although he didn't like traveling in a caravan, Arjun did like the idea of delaying their arrival in Kashi. Once there, he'd be turned over to a Brahman schoolteacher. Everyone knew what that meant: hours of reciting prayers every day and studying Sanskrit grammar and astrology and treating the master like a god. But Uncle, who always tried to help and often made things worse, had suggested to Father that a course of study with one of Kashi's renowned teachers would do the boy good. Uncle traveled to Kashi every year to exchange brass figurines, cast in the village, for muslin goods, the softest in India. So he claimed to know all about the scholars who lived in the City of Light.

Perhaps Arjun's father let his eldest son go because his only daughter was going as well. Gauri was nine, five years younger than Arjun. The family hoped that one of the holy men there would find a cure for the poor girl's affliction.

So Arjun was bound for Kashi, sacred to Lord Shiva, home to countless holy men and prison to young students like himself. For Arjun the journey might as well take forever, if only he didn't have to spend it on a hot road among sluggish oxen and betel-chewing porters.

What Arjun really wanted was to see the ocean—not

the Ganges River, where Kashi was located—but the vast ocean, a stretch of water so wide that you couldn't see across it. He felt that any boy of fourteen should have seen the ocean. Where Arjun lived, it was dry and dusty following the monsoon. Beyond the village walls there was nothing to look at but rice paddies and bean fields. People raised chickens, milked cows, dug in their vegetable gardens. That's what they did day after day after day. So he was glad to leave the village, even though it also meant leaving his family. Mother had cried bitterly when he left. His two younger brothers gaped at him from bewildered, awestruck eyes. And Father spent half the morning giving him all sorts of advice. Arjun, do this. Arjun, don't do that.

Although a Brahman, a member of the highest social order, Arjun's father had never been successful. He had inherited land, but a lifetime of battling poor health, especially lung trouble, had kept him from taking an active role in the cultivation of his fields. He depended on stewards who cheated him and laborers who rarely worked hard except for what they could steal. Even so, Father was looked upon as the head of the village's most important clan. He made the decisions, not Uncle, and that made Arjun proud.

He was doubly proud that Father trusted him with Gauri. "You are her big brother," Father had told him, holding up a finger of warning, "so you must look after her always. Uncle is there to help, but you, Arjun, must protect and oversee her, both on the journey and in Kashi."

This was a heavy responsibility, but Arjun was ready to accept it if he could leave the village and go on an adventure. Every morning during the monsoon, he got up impatiently hoping that the rains would end. No one ever traveled during the rainy season. Not even god-men dared to venture from temples or caves while the monsoon swept across India from west to east. During the rains everyone suffered, especially Father, who had always been prey to coughs and headaches caused by such weather. For three whole months the rain streaked every wall and muddied every floor and left mildew on every piece of clothing. Arjun's youngest brother, only five, developed an itchy rash in spite of rubdowns with oil, and whimpered fearfully at night when jackals, restless in the driving rain, howled from surrounding fields.

At last, in a path curving northward, the monsoon winds whirled beyond the village and left the steamy land to dry out. When the next caravan came through on a cloudless day, Father allowed Arjun and Gauri to join Uncle on the journey to Kashi.

Arjun recalled his final look at the family before the caravan took them from view: Father tall and frowning; Mother dabbing at her teary eyes with the tip of her shawl; one brother holding a stick as if it were a sword; the younger gravely sucking his thumb.

Arjun saw the four of them vividly in his mind's eye. He had a gift for remembering what he saw. Although he'd been walking quite a while now through unfamiliar forest—denser than the woodland of home—he was not afraid of getting lost. He might be thinking of his family, but his eyes were remembering each tree and bush along the way.

Arjun halted and from a little pouch took out some sandalwood paste and rubbed it on his throat. This repelled mosquitoes. It also cooled his skin in the dank heat of a forest too thick for much sunlight to shine through. He wore a dhoti, a skirtlike length of cotton cloth; the front end of it was drawn between his legs and tied in the back to a waistband. Looped over his left shoulder and curving around his right hip was the three-stranded circle of cotton thread that signified his initiation into the Brahman order. His head was shaved, with the exception of a topknot that was never cut.

Having rubbed the paste into his skin, Arjun felt cool enough to continue his walk. Should he return to camp now? He had nothing to do there until mealtime. Gauri had fallen asleep after riding a mule all day, so she didn't need him. Uncle would be swapping stories with drivers and smoking one of his mixtures of cardamon, resin, and banyan bark. Arjun had often seen him grind these ingredients into a paste and coat them thickly around a finger-long stick. After they dried in the shape of a tube, he twisted the stick out and smeared ghee, clarified butter, on the aromatic roll before lighting it. Uncle claimed that such a smoke was able to strengthen teeth, cure a cough and ear pain and laziness. Arjun didn't believe him, though, because Father argued that the smoke only made a cough worse. Many of Uncle's ideas were rejected by Father. Arjun felt it was a miracle that the two brothers had agreed on his going to Kashi.

Was it time to return to camp? Although the caravan had halted early that day because of the good location near a stream, the afternoon was already half over. When the light started to fail, retracing his steps might prove difficult. And who knew what was out here? Looking down, Arjun saw a trail of ants. He remembered that the black bear considered ants a delicacy. He had never seen a black bear, but someone once told him that it had a white, curved marking on its chest, a huge appetite, and a bad temper, and it always aimed for the face when attacking a man.

Arjun was thinking about black bears as he entered a swampy part of the forest. The fetid ground was covered by sedge grass as high as his waist. Tangles of tree branches and broad leaves made it hard to keep erect as he squirmed through the dense undergrowth. Just as he decided to go back, Arjun heard a rasping noise from behind a stand of reeds, then a following rush of sound as if some kind of animal was taking in a great gulp of air. Arjun halted. He had never heard anything like it before. Then it came again—deep and resonant in spite of its short duration, almost like a sigh. Following it came another rasping intake of breath. Around the boy it was abruptly still. No bird called, no insect buzzed, no leaf fronds ticked against one another. It was deadly quiet, as if the air and every living creature had suddenly turned to stone. What could make such a terrifying sound?

There wasn't time for Arjun to wonder. Just then a large swamp bird rose out of the sedge, its black wings beating with the heavy report that women make when they slap wet laundry against a rock. The bird's squawk that trailed its rising roused Arjun to action. Stepping forward, with a single impulsive swipe of his hand, he bent the reed stalks ahead of him to one side and peered into a small clearing.

He was staring into eyes no more than six strides away from him.

Great yellow eyes in a yellowish brown head.

Arjun took it in all at once: the massive fawn-colored body, striped transversely in black, sprawled on a bed of broken reeds; the tufted ears twitching; prominent white spots on the broad, thick forehead; and a wet black nose.

He had never seen a tiger until now. He had hoped

never to see one, surely not this close. There was no chance of escaping. If he turned and ran, the great beast could reach him in one easy spring. Arjun still gripped the parted reeds. He was afraid to breathe for fear of annoying the beast, who had just been interrupted while eating a meal of sambar.

The deer's carcass lay between the tiger's paws. Its three-tined antlers had the look of a small tree, and the hair on its neck stood out like a mane. But its tan belly had been ripped completely open, exposing the entrails not already eaten. The sambar's head, turned toward Arjun, was a sooty brown color, and its round, glassy eyes seemed to stare balefully at him. Arjun had seen sambar deer in the woods at home. They liked to roll in mud, then bathe in the river, snorting in their pleasure.

The tiger yawned, showing gouts of bloody flesh on its long yellow fangs. The great creature's eyes blinked sleepily. Its ears wiggled, agitating a cloud of hovering flies. It belched.

Such lazy indifference told Arjun there was still a chance to get away. The tiger must have fed long and fully. Satisfied, it felt no desire to attack anything. Perhaps it would soon waddle into the undergrowth for a nap.

Arjun let the bent reeds slip slowly back into place. Taking a deep breath, he turned and put one foot forward. His heart pounded hard before he took another step. When nothing happened, he moved again, inching away from death. He took a few more steps, hearing behind him the glutted beast wheeze as it inhaled rapidly.

Arjun stopped again, touching the sacred thread for luck. If only his heart would stop pounding, he could hear better what was behind him. Another step. Another. When his foot snapped a fallen reed, he winced. Another step, and another, until at last he found himself at the edge of the swampy ground.

Once beyond the sedge and reeds, he broke into a wild run and kept running until his breath gave out. Throwing himself to the earth, Arjun stared up at the sunlight slanting through the trees.

His breathing eased, his mind cleared. What had just happened was a sign. Such encounters did not happen by accident. Perhaps the gods were favoring him in some mysterious way. Surely his escape from certain death was their doing. He touched the sacred thread. Ever since his initiation into the Brahman order, Arjun had felt there was a purpose to his life, unknown to him though it was. Perhaps his mother had put that idea into his head when she told him, "Arjun, do you know why your father named you for a Pandava hero of the Great War? Not because he thinks you'll be an archer like Prince Arjuna. Your namesake was far more than a warrior. He was a man who spoke with the gods, who saw into the life of things. Your father sees in you that sort of promise, though you're filled with mischief and not interested in learning. We both believe in your destiny."

Arjun sat up. He could see, at this very moment, his mother's face as she spoke those words. The light shining in her eyes had almost frightened him.

 2

As HE GOT TO HIS FEET, Arjun glanced around to orient himself. Recognizing a bush between two wild fig trees, he felt sure of his direction and began to walk rapidly forward. He could reach camp before dusk. His step was light and confident, the outcome of his miraculous encounter with the tiger. When the village priest bestowed upon him the sacred thread, the ritual had been called a second birth. Now he knew a third.

Should he tell Uncle? Uncle would only smile wisely and suggest that a holy man ought to decide what it all meant. After which Uncle would offer his own interpretations, one after the other, each piously based on quotations from the Vedas, and none of them convincing. He might suggest that the tiger had been Lord Shiva in disguise because the Great God wore tiger skins—Uncle was a staunch follower of Shiva. So the fallen deer must have been Vishnu—Uncle disapproved of the rival Vaishnava cult. But then, likely as not, Uncle would scratch his head and mutter, "Well, you never know."

Arjun did wish to tell Father, who never explained what he didn't understand. How would Father react? He might ask something reasonable. "Was it a big tiger?"

Arjun had a flashing memory of the great mouth when it opened wide to yawn: the thick drool, the bright pink gums, the shreds of flesh clinging to yellow fangs, the huge slab of pulsing red tongue. And at the same moment he was looking ahead at something on the forest floor.

A man, face down, was lying there.

Rushing forward, Arjun knelt beside him. Seeing no movement, Arjun gingerly began to turn him over. He stared at a twisted mouth, at open eyes that reminded him of the sambar's glassy look. Arjun recognized the dead man. He was a wagon driver from the caravan.

Arjun felt wetness on his hands. Blood was still pouring from a large wound in the man's stomach. A zigzag line of crimson through the woods told Arjun that the driver had staggered some way before bleeding to death.

Arjun got up and cautiously followed the bloody trail. Almost immediately he heard a clamor of voices not too far away, then cries of pain and terror.

Crouched, he moved steadily toward the noise. The screams terrified him, yet he kept going until he saw, through gaps in the forest greenery, men rushing back and forth. Edging close to a thick-trunked banyan tree, he lay flat and from this protected vantage point studied the clearing he had left earlier that afternoon.

It was hardly recognizable. Bodies and goods were scattered everywhere. Turbaned men with drawn swords were shouting at one another gleefully while chasing people of the caravan. An old merchant was run through as he tried to escape. Goats bleated and mules jittered as they strained at tethers, and from somewhere beyond the clearing a woman's piercing scream rose again and again.

Arjun rolled back behind the tree and looked up at the sky as if to anchor himself in a world he knew.

Dacoits.

Dacoits! Uncle had been wrong as usual. There were not that many of them, perhaps no more than twenty, and yet it seemed they had taken the caravan almost without a fight.

He peered around the trunk again. There were at least a dozen bodies on the ground. Only one wore the turban of a bandit. The caravan had been unprepared for the attack. Most of the drivers and merchants must have tried to run away.

Where was Gauri?

He stared frantically at the scene. Whoever didn't lie dead or dying was being herded into a group of cringing prisoners. No women were in sight. From the under-growth emerged two dacoits with a merchant who cra-dled one arm in the other, whimpering in pain. A few bandits were trying to calm the snorting bullocks, whose eyes were rolling. Other raiders were bent over the dead, rifling through their money pouches.

Arjun watched as a dacoit tethered a goat to a small tree, then pulled the rope taut, cinching the animal's neck against the trunk. Another dacoit yanked hard on the goat's tail, forcing it to stand spread-legged in response to the pressure. A third dacoit lopped off its head with a sin-gle blow of his curved sword. One of them began to skin the animal, while another fashioned a cooking spit out of a tree limb.

Gauri! Where was Gauri?

The woman was still screaming piteously from beyond the clearing. Then Arjun heard the cry of anoth-er woman from the opposite direction.

Where was his sister? Where was Gauri?

Again the screams of women. A driver was dragged into the clearing by one foot, then, as he pleaded, was skewered by a lance. Arjun turned away from the scene and retched. Did the raiders hear him? Did it matter? Where was Gauri? On a wild impulse he rose behind the banyan and prepared to rush out and wave his arms and shout his sister's name. Then, just as abruptly, he sat down. A strange calm enveloped him. It was as if nothing were wrong. He was home, drying off after riding a vil-lage buffalo in the water tank. Looking across the tank, past the buffalo and other boys at play, he saw a rice paddy where a counterpoised sweep was lifting water from the channel of one field into the channel of another. Everything was as it should be. He was waking from a nightmare. He had fallen asleep beside the tank and was now awake.

But noises beyond the banyan tree told him there was no nightmare to wake from. In sudden panic he began crawling away toward the undergrowth. Crawl, crawl! Run, run, run! Run for home! Get out of here!

He stopped and studied the dried blood on his hands. Those men out there would cut his throat in an instant if they found him. He must run. In a week he could reach home. He'd travel fast and live on berries.

And when he got home?

Ah, when he got home! Could he look into Mother's eyes while explaining how he'd abandoned her only daughter, his only sister? Could he face his father and find an excuse? "Yes, Father, I ran to save my life. As for Gauri, I never saw her, so I don't know if she was alive or dead when I ran."

Arjun turned and crawled back to the tree and peered around it. The scene had changed rapidly. The animals were already calm, even the goats. Prisoners had been prodded against a wagon, where lashes of rope secured their hands and feet. Thrown on the ground, they lay like sheep trussed for market.

Uncle was not among them.

Two spitted goats were turning now above a large fire that held back the shadows of dusk. Many of the dacoits were settling around it. They drank from earthen jugs and chewed quids made of betel nut wrapped in areca leaf and smeared with quicklime. The narcotic of the quids was having its effect. Smiling happily, they bragged of their good fortune in discovering a caravan laden with brass and barrels of honey and iron bars.

Two of the bandits, frowning and grave, sat off by

themselves. Abruptly, the bearded older one shouted at the men lounging around the fire. There was still work to do before those goats were cooked, he told them. His men looked sheepish and grew silent. He ordered them to bring up the prisoners one by one.

There was a shriek from beyond the clearing.

"And leave those women alone!" he yelled at the bushes. He turned to his companion and muttered, "We'll have nothing to sell if they don't stop it." To another dacoit he called out, "Bring the women here and tie them there." He pointed to a nearby wagon. "If any more happens to them, I'll have your throat cut out."

Coming up and kneeling beside the leader, a bandit spoke too softly for Arjun to hear.

"Where?" asked the leader, looking around.

The bandit got up, hurried off, and quickly returned from the undergrowth with a frail-looking girl. She wore a blue sarong. Tied around her shoulders was a gray shawl. Her hair was pulled back severely into a bun.

Gauri.

Arjun leaned dangerously forward to get a better look at her. The gold bangles on her arms were missing; the dacoits must have taken them. But a small anklet remained on her slim left foot. Mother had placed it there the day they left the village with the caravan. The tilaki mark on the girl's forehead had been smeared, but otherwise she seemed unharmed, even though her hands were tied behind her back.

Gauri. Her name meant the Brilliant One. The goddess Gauri was the source of the world, Mother used to say. She was what the universe had been before creation sorted out the individual things.

The bandit who fetched Gauri pushed her only

slightly, but it was enough to send her sprawling in front of the seated leader. He stroked his beard and studied the wan, frail little girl for a while.

"Too young to sell for pleasure," his companion observed.

"Can you cook?" the leader asked Gauri.

The girl stared at him from great round eyes.

Arjun had never felt more helpless in his life. He wanted to rush out and say, "My sister doesn't talk. We're taking her to Kashi for the holy men to see. But she can sing!" He thought of that—when her voice lifted in wordless song, the girl brought tears to the eyes of listeners enraptured by the clear, thin, haunting sound.

"Can you sew? Sweep?" the leader persisted.

Gauri looked at him as if he were nothing more than a tree.

The leader seemed both startled and intrigued by her indifference. Then he shrugged. "Where you're going, you'll learn soon enough to be useful. I know just the market for you." To the bandit who brought her he said, "Keep her apart. And take that off her foot," he added with a scowl, pointing to the anklet. "Are we so rich we can ignore a loop of gold?" He glared contemptuously at the circle of bandits who awaited their meal of roasted goat.

Pushing Gauri down against the wheel of a wagon, which obscured Arjun's view of her, the bandit joined others in bringing male prisoners one by one to the campfire. The leader looked each one over and decided his fate. Some were taken off to the right, past the clearing, and their short, agonized cries made their fate plain enough. Others were led back to the wagon and thrown down. It became clear to Arjun that it was the younger, stronger, unwounded men who were being kept alive.

Then the women were brought into the clearing. Arjun couldn't look at them, but their wailing would enter his mind often in times to come.

He sat back against the banyan, smelling the pungent odor of cooked goat, then heard the cries of delight as the dacoits began their meal. He listened to the slurping and grunting they made and the laughter of good fortune and the belching that ended their feast, reminding him of the tiger.

He never moved, but sat hunched over, too saddened and horrified and worried about Gauri to notice his own hunger.

The moon came out, the dacoits muttered fitfully, and the sobbing women, trussed and huddled together, grew quiet. Arjun never stirred until the sound from the clearing became an occasional groan, a whimper, a cough within sleep.

At home in the ebony night the old bullfrogs would be croaking heavily. During the monsoon season a strange thing always happened. Tiny brown frogs appeared out of nowhere, crawling on everything, a squirming, hopping mass of wet little bodies. They were thick as the rain itself for a few weeks, then they vanished, not a single one of them to be seen. Later, when the monsoon ended, their little leathery corpses filled the ditches like leaves. He had forgotten those tiny mysterious frogs. Perhaps he had forgotten many things about home. But home was where he should be right now, and Gauri too, and Uncle. They should never have left.

With a sigh he inched to the edge of the banyan and studied a trio of guards seated around the glowing camp-fire. If he tried to circle them and reach Gauri, what might he do then? Untie her and get her out of there? The wagon that she had been thrown behind was not ten paces from the wary guards. He had no chance of moving silently enough. And so he must wait.

Time passed somehow. But how could the gods let it pass at all, let it move forward beyond this terrible moment? Time ought to stop here. The gods should roll time back and rearrange the world before the attack, then let the moments start again. That would be what the priest called divine mercy.

As for himself, he would not sleep. Even the thought of sleep was impossible. He must stay awake until the nightmare of today had finally ended. He'd never sleep again unless today was only a bad dream.

Yet he slept.

The next morning, awaking with an abruptness that had him gasping, Arjun stared out at a thick ground mist that bathed everything in liquid gloom.

The dacoits were already at work. He heard their leader shouting orders, urging them on. "Tighten those girths! You! Don't forget that pack over there! We didn't come so far and work so hard for nothing! I want every piece of brass, every iron rod! Load them up! That's what they're still alive for!"

Peering around the banyan trunk, Arjun saw that the leader was referring to the caravan survivors, who were going to carry packs and also the goods that had been stowed in the wagons. The dacoits went around cutting the throat of every bullock and mule. Then they pushed all the wagons into the middle of the clearing and made a bonfire of them. The dacoits were taking loot, but their leader must have decided to leave behind the unwieldy trappings of a caravan. Surely he wouldn't mind if some of his captive bearers dropped dead from exhaustion. Rewinding their turbans and sticking their swords in waistbands, the dacoits formed a column with Gauri and the women in the middle of it, along with a small herd of goats. The bearers came next, prodded forward by the lances of the rear guard.

Arjun watched the column as it left. Fog was churning around legs and arms until they vanished from the clearing like bushes lost from view in a monsoon storm.

So for now, he thought, Gauri is gone.

Then silence. Total silence enveloped him. Through veils of mist he saw the dead where they had lain on the ground since the day before, their postures stone-like in the gloom.

Arjun hadn't seen Uncle in the column this morning or among the prisoners last night. He must be somewhere in the clearing or just beyond it, where the bandits had cut down anyone fleeing.

Waiting until he was sure the dacoits would not return for something forgotten, Arjun stepped out into the clearing. He turned over the corpses one by one. Finally he stood beside the ashes of last night's fire. The sight of a bone with shreds of goat meat clinging to it affected him like a sudden blow. Arjun realized how hungry he was. Picking up the bone, he ripped the meat off with his teeth, swallowing rapidly until he gagged.

The edge of his hunger dulled, Arjun looked around at the lifting fog. What must he do? First, find Uncle.

It did not take long. Just beyond the clearing, opposite the banyan tree behind which he'd hidden, Arjun found the body.

The aromatic roll, charred at one end, was still

clutched in Uncle's hand. He must have been smoking when the dacoits appeared, and in his haste to escape he forgot the burning roll and held it tightly until his death. Uncle used to say, "You mustn't smoke while angry. You must sit erect, take three puffs at a time, inhale through your mouth but exhale only through your nose. The gods are pleased by this, because, you see, it helps you enter the spirit world. Now there's a sloka in the Rig Veda, an instructive bit of verse, that reminds me—though I can't remember which sloka . . ."

Arjun knelt and sobbed brokenly. When at last he looked up, the fog had lifted.

People lay dishonored on the ground. He couldn't build a fire big enough to burn them all. A communal grave would take a couple of days to dig, and where would the dacoits be by then? The leader might intend to sell Gauri at a slave market close by.

There was also the problem of handling the dead. As a Brahman, Arjun would be rendered impure by disposing of corpses himself. Even so, this was a special circumstance. Surely the gods would not be displeased with him. What would Father say? "Do something, boy. Honor them somehow."

Yes, Father would expect that of him. But time was passing, the dacoits could be expected to move swiftly wherever they decided to go. Arjun made a thorough inspection of the camp site and beyond. There were thirty-two bodies in the vicinity. The sight of so many calmed rather than agitated him. Clearly, what he did for a few must count for all.

He dragged four bodies close to the ashes of the campfire. Then he pulled down some palm leaves, enough to cover the corpses. One was an old woman, the only woman whose body he found. Another was a boy not much older than his own brother Nakula. He discovered the boy with his head wedged into the declivity of a tree trunk, as if by concealing his face he might avoid a lance in his back. Arjun paused to study the dead boy. The last time Arjun had seen Nakula, he had been clutching a stick like a sword. Nakula would have fought the dacoits, but with the same result as this boy.

The third body was that of a middle-aged man who had rarely spoken to anyone in the caravan, although everyone knew he was the agent of a Chalukyan prince. The agent had been going to purchase gifts in Kashi for the prince's forthcoming marriage. The Chalukyans, who held sway over most of western India, would be furious when they learned their agent had been murdered on the way.

Last, Arjun hauled the body of his uncle into the clearing and placed it beside the other three. Laying the palm fronds across the bodies, he stepped back and steepled his hands and tried to think of a fitting prayer that would apply to all of the dead.

He had not yet pronounced the first word when a voice merrily called out, "It's a waste of time, you know, to put those leaves on them! Before the sun goes down tomorrow, the vultures and wild dogs and ants of this forest will have picked their bones clean!"

 3

A SKINNY LITTLE MAN stood at the edge of the clearing. He wore a dhoti and a dirty shawl hung around his narrow shoulders. There was no sacred thread across his chest, so he didn't belong to one of the twice-born classes. He was either a Shudra from the lowest class or an outcast Panchama. But he lacked the usual servile timidity of a Panchama. He stood there grinning, as if this scene of death amused him.

Having studied him, Arjun waited for the little man to say more.

Pointing to the covered bodies, the man called out in mock fear, "I hope, boy, this isn't *your* work!"

Arjun said curtly, "Our caravan was attacked."

Nodding, the little man took a step forward. "Dacoits these days are as thick as centipedes in a log. Thicker." He spread his arms wide. "They roam these hills and forests because this is a main caravan trail. They live by robbing poor innocents like you and selling them." Coming closer, he glanced critically around. "Nothing left here." Bending to inspect a dead body, he reached his hand out, then drew it back. "Bad days, bad days," he murmured. "Only yesterday I saw a one-eyed woman walking down the road. A bad omen. Well, then, go on and do what you were doing."

Arjun said a hasty prayer for the dead, beseeching Lord Shiva to grant them good fortune in their next lives. Opening his eyes and turning self-consciously, he saw that the little man was squatting in the shade, for the sun had come out.

"Good for you," the man said with a wink, "a dutiful, spiritual boy." His bloodshot eyes reminded Arjun of a village blacksmith who drank too much wood-apple wine. "What will you do now?"

"Follow the dacoits," Arjun said without hesitation, feeling a surge of pride.

The man guffawed. "Follow the dacoits. What a strange idea!"

"They have my sister."

"Ah, too bad. How old is she?"

"Nine."

The man shrugged. "At that age she'll be sold for a servant in one of the markets. It's not so bad."

"I'll follow."

The man shook his finger at Arjun as if accusing him of mischief. "You Brahman boys. So strict with yourselves! I know why you'll risk your life." He waited, but Arjun did not ask him why. "You fear telling your family you ran away without learning what happened to her."

Surprised by the man's shrewdness, Arjun replied stiffly, "Nothing's wrong with that kind of fear."

"Not wrong, just foolish. But your life is your own, isn't it, until it returns to the gods."

"You said they'll sell my sister in one of the markets. Which market? Where?"

The little man pursed his lips; he had a few days' growth of beard, which made his cheeks and jaw look muddy. He carried a stout walking stick. "That depends on the direction they take. They like markets run by their own tribes or castes. Not that I know much about their ways," he added with a grin.

Stepping forward without another glance at him, Arjun said briskly, "I must start. Goodbye."

He crossed the clearing to study the dacoits' trail, then realized the little man was just behind him. Arjun felt uneasy but not afraid. Although only fourteen, he was strongly built and tall for his age, a match for many grown men.

The little man seemed to notice his discomfort.

"Don't worry, I'm not following you. But I'd like to come along for a while."

"Is this the way you're going?"

"Could be, could be. The entire world is my way. Yes, I'm going your way."

They fell into step together and moved through the undergrowth until they spotted a trampled path that led to a broader one heading north. This path widened into a road filled with footprints. Arjun fell into a relaxed rhythm of walking.

"Yes, it's true," said the little man as if continuing a conversation. "That woman with one eye was a bad omen. And then I heard drums beating in a village, and when I got there I learned a woman was about to commit sati. And for a husband twice her age. Have you seen it, boy? Sati?"

Arjun shook his head. Ritual suicide at a funeral pyre was not part of life where he came from.

"This woman sat on the woodpile with indifference. She might have been sitting in a bath."

They were startled by a chital that leapt buoyantly across the path, its antlers as long as Arjun's arms, its golden haunches spotted with white. Smaller than a sambar, it had the same look. Arjun had a glimpse of the left eye, limpid and round, as it swiftly passed.

"When they lit the pile, she put one hand on the shoulder of her husband's corpse. As if comforting *him*. Do you hear what I'm saying? As if comforting him. Then she never budged, not even when the flames reached her. And her hand stayed right on his shoulder until they burned together into one black lump." The little man chuckled ruefully. "No husband would ever show such courage. It's good only wives sacrifice their lives for husbands. It would never work the other way around. Are you hungry?"

"Yes."

The little man halted and stared gravely at Arjun. "I know how bad you feel. They took everything, didn't they? So when we reach a farmhouse, I'll buy us food."

Arjun tapped his side, where a small money pouch was concealed. "No need, but thank you. I can pay for my own."

The little man shrugged. "As you wish. But I'm quite prepared to help you. Not that I'm rich. I'm only a poor vedar."

Arjun studied him briefly. A vedar belonged to the caste of hunters. The little man called himself one, yet he carried no weapons. Even so, he chattered on about hunting. "When I hunt, I take a good dog and a net and a noose of deer hide for trapping birds and arrows with hooks on the side that turn backward and hold in the flesh."

"Are you coming from a hunt?"

The man said nothing, as if his attention was elsewhere. Narrowing his eyes, he regarded the road. "It could be your dacoits come from the north. That's where the great Harsha rules. They say when he travels, the road is lined with people asking favors of him, and he gives them gifts of candied sugar."

Arjun stared at the half-moon goat tracks and the heavy footprints of the caravan bearers, who must be drooping from their loads. "Would the dacoits head into Harsha's country?" he asked. "Wouldn't they be afraid of such a great king?"

"They should be afraid, of course. But dacoits can be fearless."

Arjun thought of Uncle calling them cowards. Poor Uncle.

"I hear King Harsha takes along a special pavilion when he travels. Not for himself but for his favorite elephant, Darpashata." The little man whistled in awe. "They say Darpashata can dance on three legs."

Then without warning he began to talk of fiends who fed on battleground corpses and planetary spirits who came to earth for no other purpose than to torment men. He claimed personal knowledge of kapalikas—devotees of Shiva who lived in graveyards and wore their hair matted and drank from skulls and carried strings of human bones around their waists. He described hermits who practiced terrible austerities in order to acquire magical powers from the gods. They lay on beds of spikes or hung head down from tree limbs for days or held their arms out motionlessly until they withered like vines.

Arjun heard only fragments of these vivid stories. His mind was on what he saw, and what he saw was footprints, some making deep indentations in the soft ground. They were leading his sister into the unknown.

Then the road emerged altogether from the forest into a stretch of flat land. In the distance it was blocked out in paddy fields. Shading his eyes, Arjun stared at the telltale depressions made by the file of dacoits and their prisoners.

"Come this way," urged the little man suddenly, pointing to a footpath going westward.

"But look, the dacoits went straight ahead."

"Of course they did. I'm not blind. Their tracks are as plain as an elephant's. But come along this way. I know some farmers not far from here who'll give us food cheap."

Arjun was tempted. He felt terribly hungry.

The little man regarded him curiously. "As a Brahman, are you ashamed to take food cooked by low people?"

"My father doesn't believe in strict observance. We take food with anyone. The village priest says we displease the gods, but Father says what displeases the gods is too much arrogance."

The little man nodded his approval. "Even so, I've heard it said a Brahman cook is the best cook. That way everyone can eat his food. What he touches is pure for the highest and the lowest. So you'll come and take food with me?"

Arjun still hesitated.

"First we take food, then go quickly on."

"You mean, follow the dacoits?"

"Yes, I mean follow them," the little man said with a broad grin. "I've decided to go with you."

Arjun grinned back. This was such a strange fellow. "Why would you do that?"

"To see if helping you will bring me favor with the gods."

Arjun and the little man arrived soon at the juncture of some fields where a half-dozen huts stood. They were made of mud and wattle. Vines had been trained to grow over their thatched roofs, giving them a vegetable look, as if they had sprouted weedlike from the earth. An old man sat crosslegged in front of one of them, combing a small boy's hair with his hand. A woman bent down at the doorway, spreading fresh cow dung around it to settle the dust. There was an open fire beside the next hut. A girl was making ghee in a pot by skimming the fat from melted butter. Three women behind her were straining to roll a huge grinding stone across spices laid out on a board.

The women, glancing sideways, gave Arjun's companion a faint smile as if they knew him. A group of farmers were coming from the paddy, their eyes red-rimmed from glare. A few wore long curving mustaches. They all had black teeth and bright red lips from chewing betel. One of them whispered something to the others, and they all grinned at Arjun in a way that made him uncomfortable. Turning when past them, Arjun saw them turning to regard him too.

"Why are they looking at me?" Arjun asked.

The little man didn't answer. "This is the place," he said, motioning to a hut off by itself. Drifting from it was the plaintive sound of a bamboo flute. The intricate trilling reminded Arjun of his sister's wordless songs.

He was thinking of Gauri when the little man, lifting a piece of dirty cloth at the entrance, gestured him with a bow into the dim interior. A young man seated in the corner put down the bamboo flute he'd been playing. A humpbacked woman continued to work the shuttle on a small loom in another corner. She was weaving a red and blue shawl. Both occupants gave the little man a nod of recognition but nothing more, not even the trace of a smile.

Their cool reception, however, had no effect on him. He sat down as if he owned the place and started talking. Effusively, with gestures and grimaces, he told his indifferent audience that this poor boy was starving, a Brahman boy too, which would surely displease the gods who looked upon Brahmans with special favor and so to appease Lord Vishnu and Lord Shiva and all the goddesses too and curb their wrath and win their blessing he had cast around for somewhere to take the hungry boy and so he had thought of their generous home filled with divine spiritual mercy and sweet buffalo curds and strong palm toddy and so he had brought the boy here for something to eat and would pay for it too, though not much because a vedar had little money after giving alms to the poor at a temple. Having finished his windy speech, he sat back and watched the humpbacked woman fetch two small bowls of toddy.

Arjun refused his. In his family strong drink was forbidden. Then the woman threw open the back door and walked two paces into a smaller hut, which served as a kitchen. It had a roof of thatch that could be raised and lowered by a rope; she lowered it now, making it dark inside.

The garrulous little man was now discussing bandits. Chortling, he knocked back some toddy. "Give him the best curds, not the ones you give me!" the little man commanded loudly. The humpbacked woman soon returned with two bowls and some hot pickles.

Scooping up curds with the fingers of his right hand, Arjun sucked the milky lumps into his mouth. Buffalo curds were usually sweet or mildly tart, but these tasted bitter. His surprise must have shown, because the little man laughed and reached out to touch his arm reassuringly.

"You don't know the curds of this region," he said, plunging fingers into his own bowl. "They have a spice here that's special. Play something," he told the young man, who picked up the flute as if responding to the command of authority.

Slurping toddy, the little man blew his breath out in contentment. "The people around here are musicians.

They harvest spices and play music. Nothing bad in them. But dacoits? Nothing good in them. They live off the misery of others. Perhaps your dacoits will have bad luck and meet evil spirits along the way. This region has plenty of them. They lurk in the top of palm trees. Sometimes they fly about in the air. Often they make themselves invisible. Have more curds, boy. You'll get used to the special taste. Yes, these spirits demand prayer and flowers and coconuts. Otherwise they pounce."

Otherwise they . . . Arjun couldn't follow the little man's words. Otherwise . . . coconuts . . . they pounce . . . They have a special taste. Well, it was. Bitter. Otherwise a bitter pounce. He felt sleepy. The last thing Arjun remembered was upending the bowl of curds into his lap and then falling sideways.

Opening slowly, his eyes looked blearily into the weathered features of a burly man who wore a tall turban and a mustache with two long tips. Seeing that Arjun was awake, the powerfully built man chuckled and shook his head. "Must have given you a good dose of it. You were brought in yesterday."

Arjun sat up and glanced around at a large room covered with straw like a stable. Men were stretched out on blankets, napping while sunlight streamed through gaps in the wall boards. "Where am I?" he asked drowsily.

"In the army, that's where you are," said the turbaned man, who was sitting crosslegged beside him. Arjun noticed that the man wore a leather scabbard and a sword. "This is a Chalukyan barracks. You've been sold to the army." He twirled one tip of his mustache and spoke softly. "I can see you never dreamed of such a thing." In a low voice, so as not to awaken his comrades, the soldier told Arjun that he'd been brought here by a little man and a humpbacked woman in a wagon. He'd been drugged, but that was common in the region. Villagers around here grew spices, some of which could put you to sleep for a long time. If you started to wake, they'd funnel more of it into your mouth through a section of bamboo. That way they might keep you quiet for days. "So you, boy, were carted here and sold to the army."

Fumbling weakly at his waistband, Arjun discovered that the money pouch was gone. The little man had robbed and then sold him. But that didn't account for a strange new sense of loss, as if something far greater than money had been taken from him while he slept. Sweeping both hands over his head, he discovered that his topknot had been shaved off. His Brahman topknot gone! Touching his chest, shoulder, and hip, he realized too that his sacred thread, the yajnopavita, was missing. At his Brahman initiation Arjun had been told by the priest never to remove it. The yajnopavita, a braid of three white cords, each woven from three strands of cotton, marked him for a Brahman, just as the sacred thread of red hemp did for the Kshatriya and one of brown wool for the Vaishya. Without his sacred thread, who was he? Nothing! Not even a Shudra. His essence had been taken from him. He was now as low as the lowest Panchama.

"My thread . . . my thread . . ." He began sobbing.

The turbaned soldier gave him a cool look. "The dom brought you here just as you are. If you really did have a thread, the dom would have cut it off. The army won't buy dacoits who wear threads."

"Dacoits?"

Again the soldier chuckled. "What innocence. Of course you're a dacoit. That's what the army buys."

"A dom brought me here?" Doms belonged to the gravedigger caste.

"A skinny little man."

"Always talking?"

The soldier nodded. "He's a dom or worse. Maybe a vampire. But famous around here for selling drugged bandits. Villagers cooperate with him because they get a part of his fee. He'd rather sell people like you than do a day's work." The turbaned soldier glanced at someone snoring loudly, then turned back to Arjun with a faint smile. "Lucky you're young and strong. Otherwise the army might execute you for crimes. I've seen it done when dacoits are brought into camp for sale. The little man and his people get paid something anyway."

"I'm not a dacoit!"

The soldier twirled his mustache in a jaunty way. "Not now you aren't. You're going to fight for Chalukyan glory."

"Dacoits took my sister."

The soldier frowned in a little show of sympathy.

Encouraged, Arjun went on. "The little man knows where they'd sell her."

"That's probably true," the soldier acknowledged.

"Where can I find him?"

"Probably out hunting for more like you."

"I've got to find him." Arjun sat up straight. "I've got to know where they've taken her."

The soldier regarded him sourly. "You want to follow them?"

"I must."

"Ah, but you can't. This is a stockade with one gate and it's guarded. Climb the wall and you'll have an arrow in your back before you take five steps."

Arjun let out a short cry, reached down, and grabbed his left foot. Circling the ankle was a loop of iron, its ends held together by two copper rivets. "What's this?" he asked fearfully, unable to yank it off.

"When the army bought you, they hammered the iron on. That way you're known for a Chalukyan infantryman. They put your destiny on your foot."

"I'm not a dacoit. I'm not a soldier. I'm a Brahman," Arjun muttered.

"You're a soldier, bought and paid for."

"My varna is Brahman."

The soldier shook his head in amusement. "Forget about your varna. Officers command, men obey. Here, that's everything. There's nothing more. But if it pleases you, my noble young fellow, to think of yourself in terms of varna, then let it be as a Kshatriya." Stroking the mustache, he added, "An army camp doesn't need Brahmans with their prayers and books and music. You'll do a lot better if you forget all that and learn to use a sword like a Kshatriya."

"Play at being a warrior."

"It'll be more than play on the battlefield. But yes, play at it."

"Lila," the boy muttered.

"What's that?"

"Play of the gods," Arjun said. The village priest used to say that lila was the reason for creating the world. The gods did it just to feel the pleasure of making something. Play was at heart of everything that was. Mysterious, aloof, unpredictable play.

Arjun wondered if it was true. He felt himself shaking.

The husky soldier seemed to understand. Reaching out, he gripped Arjun's shoulder roughly. "I don't know about the gods and their idea of play. I do know it's some-times good if people like you and me think of life as a game we're playing and nothing more."

"Why?"

"It can make things easier." Dropping his hand, the soldier gazed thoughtfully at the napping men. "You'll see."

 4

NOTHING THAT ARJUN would have called play—divine or human—entered his life in succeeding days. Notwith-standing what the burly soldier said, there was more to the army than soldiers obeying officers. As a newcomer, Arjun had to contend with veterans; they, not Kshatriyan officers, gave him his orders. Every day, at their com-mand, he swept out the barracks and cleaned the latrines—humiliating for a Brahman accustomed to hav-ing Panchamas do such work. He was given any menial task the veterans could think of. Get me this. Go there. Hurry. Not there. Are you stupid? Not so fast. Quick. Stop. Go.

Arjun found himself at the mercy of rude shoves, ran-dom pushes, scornful laughter. The burly soldier soon left for duty in the north, so the one man inclined to help him was gone. Nor was he even noticed by the palapati, a sergeant in charge of this forty-man unit called a pala. For a recruit purchased like a slave there was no court of appeal.

All the officers were Kshatriyas. They wore the red hemp thread of the warrior class. Not a Brahman was among them, not a Vaishya, not even a Shudra. In Arjun's peaceful village, there hadn't been a single Kshatriya, so his knowledge of them was scant. He did know that kings were chosen from their ranks. As professional warriors, they felt disgraced by dying peacefully in bed. They lived only to fight.

These swaggering Chalukyan officers wore bright red cloaks and saluted one another by extending the right arm at chest level, hand fisted. Troops saluted by bowing their heads and bending from the waist. Staying aloof from the troops, the officers communicated with their men through palapatis. Daily, on their own drill field, officers practiced the arts of war. They swung maces, battle-axes, and two-handed Khadga swords at wooden posts. At straw targets they sailed chakras, disk-shaped pieces of metal with serrated outer edges. The chakras produced a loud whirling sound when thrown, and on reaching the target they sank deeply into it to stick there like shining half-moons. When the officers held archery contests, they brought out special long bows of palmyra wood, overlaid with paintings of leaves and flowers. A contestant drew back the string of sinew with his thumb and loosed a metal-tipped bhalla at a painted circle on a leather shield more than a hundred yards away. Frequently an entire third of an arrow shaft went through the target.

Many of the officers drank heavily during the contest. Dozens of soldiers, among them Arjun when not working, became spectators for want of anything else to do. They stood by silently and listened to officers boast of their prowess.

Arjun watched, but usually his mind was elsewhere; it never strayed far from the terrible questions: What had happened to his sister? Was Gauri alive? Sold? Where was she? How could he have walked away from the caravan and left her unprotected?

He began to think of his present life as an expression of cosmic punishment. Through carelessness and lack of judgment, he had acquired for his soul a heavy measure of bad karma for which he must pay in this life or the next. It was a bleak idea. Yet it gave him the fortitude to go about his daily tasks without a murmur of protest. The law of dharma determined the future of each soul by adding up the good and bad actions committed in a lifetime. Accepting his miserable fate might well improve the karma his soul carried into the next life. So unlike the burly soldier, Arjun could never think of his present life as play; he thought of it only as atonement. Imbued with this grim but powerful vision, he worked with the sad patience of a dutiful slave.

Such compliance and humility was finally noticed by the sergeant. The weather-beaten palapati had no interest in the past history of recruits. Sometimes one of them, hoping for preferment, claimed to be a Brahman or Vaishya. He would complain and snivel and ask for better treatment because of his professed birthright. But most of them lacked a semblance of the sort of calm dignity the old sergeant would expect from a twice-born. This boy Arjun was different. And he'd been sold to the army by one of those creatures who prey on caravans. Under these circumstances, he might well be a twice-born.

To satisfy his curiosity the sergeant asked Arjun what he really was.

The boy replied, "I am a soldier bought and paid for."

Arjun's willingness to accept his lot impressed the sergeant. He decided to give this young recruit a chance to do more than toil away at the whim of disgruntled veterans. He was going to make the boy a real soldier.

So Arjun was sent to a drill field along with regulars who daily practiced their martial exercises. He learned the rudiments of handling a sword and a three-pointed lance called the trisula.

After watching him awkwardly wield the eight-foot-long trisula, the sergeant told Arjun to put it down. "You're not yet strong enough for such a lance. And if you were, you'd carry it in the rear because that's where the new troops march. Behind the elephants. Go work with the archers for a while."

In another week the sergeant came around to watch Arjun handle a bamboo bow. The sergeant nodded in approval. "In another year you'll be a good archer. Your eye's good, and you stand correctly and draw and loose the bowstring as you're told, and you already sight along the arrow. Do you want to be a bowman?"

"I'll be whatever I'm told."

"Well, better a bowman than a lancer. You march in front of the elephants. That's important in case they panic. When they do, they turn round before stampeding. Do you understand me? They turn *round*. They won't run over the archers in front of them. They'll run over the lancers behind them."

He liked this stoic boy who took so well to discipline and seemed so willing to learn. For protection while loosing the bowstring, the sergeant gave Arjun a fence of leather for his left arm and a leather guard for his right thumb. Now and then he'd draw the boy aside and explain the military life. "In the old days," he said, "it was grand to be a chariot driver because they led the charge. But chariots turn over easily and their wheels break. Now only generals use chariots, and they stay protected in the center. Not a place for real soldiers. Some boys entering the army want to be mahouts and ride elephants and feel high above everybody. But, believe me, elephants will go the way of chariots. They're skittish beasts and difficult." He paused thoughtfully. "I don't envy cavalrymen either, because they count on animals too. You're better off counting only on yourself in combat. That's why generals today want more infantry. They can count on foot soldiers. And on archers. There will always be a place, boy, for archers. Nothing can match an archer for killing the enemy at long range. Good. You're going to be an archer."

Arjun learned to bandage his stomach and groin with pads of heavy quilted cotton for protection against sword thrusts. Veterans often wore triangular aprons of leather around their waists. "Any advantage is worth everything in battle," they explained to Arjun. Now that the palapati accepted him, they were treating him less harshly. Soon they were helping the young recruit learn. They showed him dagger thrusts and the right way to grip a sword handle and how to use a heavy pike in a charge. They taught him the meaning of signal flags and various drumbeats and calls of summons on the conch shell. They gave him a lesson in making their war whoop. Each gulma of two hundred men had its own distinctive battle cry, so in a melee they could locate their comrades. Arjun practiced his own gulma's battle cry until he could shriek rapidly four times, then by using his hands as a trumpet give a long, loud howl. The listening veterans grinned their approval.

Then one of them, squatting on the ground, traced in the dust certain battle arrays, vyuhas, which an army used in combat. There was the snake, the crocodile, the club, and the circle formation. In each vyuha the infantry and cavalry and elephantry took up different positions. The soldier scratched an X into the dust. That stood for the senapati, who rode in a four-horsed chariot and commanded twenty thousand footmen, two thousand horsemen, and two hundred elephants.

"That's only one army," the soldier explained. "One sena. Sometimes two or even three senas go into battle. I have fought when a thousand elephants were in the field." He rolled his eyes. "Their thundering shook the earth. So many arrows darkened the sky you couldn't see the sun." He scowled at another veteran nearby who snorted at the extravagant description. "You think it's untrue. What do you know? You weren't there." Turning to Arjun, the veteran thumped him on the chest. "King Pulakeshin was not much older than you, but from his war chariot he commanded the whole attack. I know. I was not twenty feet away from him. That afternoon he defeated the rebels and killed his uncle in single combat with a battle-ax and became Lord of the Western Waters. The gods gave him a great victory."

The other veteran spoke up sharply. "Why not tell the boy what he really needs to know? Thousands died that day, many of them crying for their mothers. Why not tell him that?"

Laughing, the veteran winked at Arjun. "Ah, it's true. A lot did. They died crying for their mothers."

His hair was growing out. At home he had kept his head shaven, aside from the uncut topknot. Now he looked at himself in a bowl of water and saw thick black hair sprouting near his ears and across his forehead for the first time in his life. In full knowledge that a Brahman who wore his hair long had forfeited his standing as a twice-born, Arjun resolved not to cut it. Not unless something happened. Not unless he found Gauri and rescued her from a life of slavery. Until then, he must forget who he once was. He'd think only of obeying the gods by doing, without complaint, whatever fate gave him to do. He worked in the barracks quietly and learned the ways of war and waited for a sign of change.

That sign came one day when Arjun overheard some veterans mention a visiting officer. He was here to interview recruits for the elephant corps. Not one of the veterans was interested. Like the palapati, they hated elephants and horses. They were foot soldiers with powerful forearms and thick legs. Eating a mess of rice and beans cooked in milk, they sat around and joked about the fancy ways of mahouts and horsemen. They'd be ashamed to ride on an elephant or a horse, especially a crazy elephant.

But Arjun was interested. He learned that whoever was selected for the elephant corps would go north for training. That meant leaving this infantry garrison. From what he understood, this thousand-man force of foot soldiers would remain here on station until needed in a full-scale war. He might stay for years while Gauri languished in slavery.

Perhaps the gods were giving him this chance. For the first time since he had entered the army, Arjun decided to act on his own. He located the place of interview, a tent in the officers' area where ordinarily the troops were not allowed to go. At least a score of soldiers were lined up; most of them were young, not much older than Arjun.

When his turn finally came, Arjun couldn't see anything inside the tent after standing a long time in the sunlight glare. Then he made out a man in officer's red sitting crosslegged behind a small low table. The officer had corkscrew curls that hung down to his shoulders and a fringe of hair like a curtain over his pale, smooth forehead. He wore earrings of enormous loops of silver.

Because it was a formal interview, Arjun fell to his knees, touching the ground with his head. The officer drank toddy from a bowl on the table. Next to him sat a scribe at a smaller table on which lay dried strips of talipot palm that he could write on with a reed pen dipped in charcoal ink. Now, however, the scribe stared sleepily at the recruit and didn't raise his pen, as if sure there would be nothing to enter about this boy.

The office took another sip of toddy and studied Arjun a moment. "Why are you here?" he asked in a deep voice.

"I am a soldier, Shri Pati."

Shaking his head wearily, the officer said, "Yes, I know that. Why do you want to join the elephant corps?"

Casting around for a reason, Arjun used the one suggested by his sergeant. "I like to be up high." But when that brought a frown from the officer, he added, "And I like animals, Shri Pati. I used to spend a lot of time with buffaloes. I rode them sitting down and standing up."

The officer raised his eyebrows slightly. "Standing up? You have that kind of balance?"

Arjun nodded. It was true. He could stay on a buffalo when it was moving at a good gait. He could stay longer than any boy in the village, even the older ones.

"It just so happens we can can test your balance," said the officer with a wry smile. He pointed to a corner where a length of bamboo, set on grooved chunks of wood, stretched about a foot above ground. "Go over there and stand on it."

Without hesitation Arjun went over and stepped up on the bamboo rod, which was no thicker than his big toe. It bent and swayed wildly under his weight, but Arjun managed to stay on.

"Your name?" asked the officer curtly.

"Arjun Madva, Shri Pati." At last he slipped off.

The officer leaned over and spoke to the scribe, who then began writing on the strip of palm.

"What do you know about elephants?" asked the officer.

"Nothing, Shri Pati."

"You call me Shri Pati. Don't they teach you the right way to address officers around here? I am a vahinipati," the officer declared sternly. Arjun knew that meant the major led a force of one hundred elephants. "Well, answer me. What do you know about handling them?"

"Nothing, Shri Vahinipati."

"We want only the best. We're proud of that," said the major. "Anybody can swing a sword and learn to use a bow. Few can deal with elephants." He paused to look Arjun over. "You're very young. That's good. We want mahouts who grow up with the elephants—somewhat like brothers. And you have at least one other thing we want: good balance. A mahout on a war elephant needs it more than anything. Only two of you managed to stay on that rod. That's worth taking you for. But of ten men who go into training, maybe one succeeds. The others go back to infantry." The officer lifted his right hand, palm out, in warning. "Not in a quiet garrison like this, but up north on the border, where there's constant fighting. Well, soldier? Questions?"

"No, Shri Vahinipati."

"You don't look stupid, but you don't act like someone who could learn to be a mahout either." Pausing for a new appraisal of Arjun, he took another sip of toddy. "Why did you join the army anyway?"

Arjun briefly explained the attack on the caravan, his own sale to the army. That seemed to reassure the officer, although he didn't ask more about Arjun's history. Instead, playing with one of his corkscrew curls, he asked, "Why do you think we're so careful choosing our recruits? Why do you think a major in the Chalukyan army spends so much time on you? It's not rare for infantry to get recruits through buying them. They're just bodies filling space on a battlefield. Infantry think elephants are reckless and stupid. They also think a mahout does nothing but ride around. Is that what you think?"

Arjun said nothing.

"In the elephant corps we have a strange life. Exciting, hard, demanding, and far more dangerous than the life lived by *them*—" He waved his hand as if including the whole infantry garrison. "I don't want to bother with you if you're not sure of wanting the corps. Well? Be quick. Are you sure?"

"I am sure, Shri Vahinipati. I am ready."

The scribe wrote.

The next day Arjun was called aside by the sergeant, who regarded him sourly. "What have you done, boy? I told you about those beasts. I've seen mahouts shot in battle, many, many of them. Don't you want to know why so many? Because they make an easy target up there. And because the enemy knows that the beasts go wild without them." The sergeant gripped Arjun's arm roughly. "Crazy boy. Do you want to live with such monsters? One of them can be washed and fed by the same mahout

44 ◆ MALCOLM BOSSE

for years, then turn without warning and trample him. Stay here, be an archer. I'm giving you advice I'd give my own son."

Arjun could not be dissuaded. The gods had placed him on this path, so he must take it. Wherever it led he would follow and keep following and never stop following until somehow, somewhere, he found his lost sister.

 5

THE CHALUKYAN VAHINIPATI and his detachment of forty men had come up from the southern capital of Vatapi with ten recruits for the elephant corps. The garrison at Wadi supplied five more recruits, including Arjun. The detail was now heading northwest from Wadi, its destination a training camp near the town of Paithan. This journey through the Deccan Plateau should take about two weeks. Aside from the vahinipati and his young Kshatriyan aide, who rode big, strong horses, the soldiers traveled by foot through a flat, dry countryside. Cloudless, it was swept steadily by cool winds from the northeast. A small baggage train of three wagons pulled by oxen brought up the rear.

The vahinipati might wear long spiral curls and silver earrings—a display of elegance scorned by veteran foot soldiers—but he sat his horse expertly and gave commands with the brisk confidence of a true warrior. Arjun believed if such a man had led the caravan that fateful day, the dacoits would never have succeeded in their assault. Such a leader would have posted guards and his men would have fought valiantly.

As he walked, Arjun created a daydream of revenge against the men who took his sister. In his thoughts, that same reckless band of dacoits was attacking the Chalukyan detachment, mistaking it for another poorly defended caravan. Arjun imagined their surprise, then dismay, then horror, at the force of armed men they so foolishly set upon. Trembling from the vision, he thought of them falling under sword thrusts or running for their lives or begging for mercy.

These images of retaliation never satisfied Arjun, however, but left him queasy. He had felt the same helplessness while crouching behind the tree during the dacoit attack. Every night, when the detachment spread their bedrolls in the fields, Arjun lay awake a long time, staring at the stars overhead. He relived the despair of seeing Gauri, hands tied behind her back, pushed sprawling at the leader's feet. He saw it happen many times against the night sky until the hypnotic pattern of constellations at last lulled him to sleep.

During the first few days the contingent of Chalukyan soldiers passed among rice paddies that were almost ready for harvest. Sown in the rainy season, this was a winter rice called sali. Farmers from Arjun's region grew it too, along with kalama rice that ripened even later. Here, as there, buffalo skulls had been set on stakes to frighten birds away from the kernel-heavy stalks. He noticed farmers walking homeward through little clumps of brittle woodland. On cords around their necks they carried water jars covered with leaf corks. Every afternoon the landscape eased behind veils of dusk; the lowering light blended with the smoke of cooking fires from hidden villages. Old bullocks were swaying along the paths. They reminded Arjun of home. The timeless calm of sunset reminded him of Gauri, her sweetness and silence and sudden outbursts of wordless song that brought tears to a listener's eyes.

The landscape took on a sooty-brown hue as the cool arid winds of winter blew across the withering plain of the Deccan. At night the travelers slept on grass that was coarsely fibrous, and they shivered within their blankets. Had the dacoits traveled this far north? Arjun wondered. Did Gauri huddle too under a thin blanket somewhere, waiting for the winds to die down? Was she fed enough? Beaten? Terrible questions filled his mind like clouds filling the sky.

A few days before reaching camp, Arjun noticed that the people in this region had a different look. The men wore long cotton dhotis down to their knees. They had droopy mustaches and teeth blackened from chewing betel leaf. Their expressions were sullen as they regarded the soldiers, but every one of them, after first stepping off the road to let the vahinipati ride past, bowed respectfully from the waist. This part of the Deccan had always been ruled by ancestors of the present King Pulakeshin. Everyone, from child to farmhand, recognized the emblem of the Chalukyan boar emblazoned on a banner carried by the vahinipati's aide. Arjun felt a surge of pride in belonging with men who commanded such respect. It was almost as if he had recovered the sacred thread of his class.

The elephant training camp was situated in wooded hills that rose gently from the plain to encroach on the south bank of the great Godavari River. Proximity to water for the elephants was a chief reason for locating the camp there. Also, a hilly site in the coming rainy season would mean fewer mosquitoes; that meant less torment for the great beasts. So Arjun was told by one of the recruits. Most of them had little to say but walked stoically along. He realized that each didn't want to give the others an advantage, since few would be chosen for the corps. Three did admit they had some knowledge of elephants, but never revealed what that knowledge was. One young man confessed to having once ridden an elephant. To a circle of questioners eager to learn more, he merely said, "Oh, you'll see for yourself. It isn't that hard. It wasn't for me."

When they reached camp, the recruits were assigned to a long, narrow barracks of weathered timber scored with cracks that let the winds in. Mahouts and their assistants, called kavadais, shared a cluster of huts in the middle of camp. A few of the senior mahouts lived with their wives in stone-and-wattle cottages on a bluff facing the river. The vahinipati and other officers remained at quarters in Paithan. Elephants, their front legs hobbled by thick rope, were allowed to wander at night through the woods. Kavadais went out and gathered them in the morning. Arjun learned one thing about elephants his first night there: They liked cool brisk weather rather than steamy heat.

Training for Arjun and the others began the next morning with a lecture from an old mahout who no longer worked the elephants. Under the shade of a huge rain tree, the recruits crowded together and listened. They had no more than a fleeting glimpse of elephants moving among foliage in the distance.

The old mahout told them that the elephant, called gaja by handlers, had once been known as matanga—roaming at will. They roamed at will until the gods brought them together with men for mutual benefit. One god even had the head and body of an elephant. This was Ganapati, the wise son of Shiva and Parvati. Despite his potbelly, the god rode on a mouse because mice gnaw through any obstacle and so did he. Ganapati had only one tusk because he broke the other off to use as a pen. With it he wrote down the words of the great poet Vyasa. In the old legends, continued the mahout, elephants flew with ivory-colored wings. In other stories they supported the world on their backs. Where you found clouds, you also found elephants, for they both brought rain. Some people believed that the Buddha had been an elephant in a former life. "But we don't believe in the Buddha here," said the old mahout. "If you believe in him, don't touch our elephants. That would pollute them."

The mahout stopped talking long enough to place a betel quid between his lower lip and gum. Then he continued, "The gaja has poor eyesight but can smell out anything. And his huge legs are like the whiskers of a mouse. Through them he can feel the footfall of a tiger at a great distance. Some people call him hastin—the one with a hand—because his trunk is the most sensitive of hands. You will see how wonderful it is. No goddess has a more delicate touch. Anything you can pick up from a smooth surface, so can he. In a single day he eats enough fruit and palm leaves and grasses and roots and tree bark to make up the weight of six of you. But his skin is thinner than it looks, easily torn, and burns in the sun. Insects that bite him can make gaja squeal like a baby. He is fast enough to run a man down, yet he can jump no higher than your waist. Gaja shuffles and sways like a camel, yet he's nimble enough to climb mountains. His tusks can go through a wall of timber, but his teeth and jaws are even more deadly. Gaja is more forgiving than we are, though he always remembers an insult or bad treatment. If you don't truly become his master, some day he will turn, without warning, and kill you. If you give your life to him, gaja will be more loyal than any man you have ever known."

Finished with words, the mahout took the recruits out for their first tests. They were told to climb a tall tree and swing from a high limb by both hands, then by one only. Two recruits balked at climbing to such a height; one got dizzy when ordered to look down at the ground while moving higher; at least half of them made fumbling or futile attempts to get purchases on tree limbs and had to choose new routes upward.

Arjun scrambled up with alacrity, just as he did back home, when he used to climb the tallest rain tree in the neighborhood. Sitting crosslegged on a high limb, he'd receive the admiration of smaller boys gawking up from the ground. Now he climbed out on a branch so slender that it swayed under his weight, and remained there until the old mahout ordered him down.

Although they would be trained to handle elephants, the recruits were also soldiers, so they had to be skilled in the arts of war. Under the watchful eyes of a dozen mahouts, they showed what they could do with the lance, the sword, and the bow. One recruit knocked Arjun down with the shaft of a tomara, a long special lance used by troops from the backs of elephants. The other recruits smiled at his defeat, for clearly Arjun had been first in tree climbing. But he did manage to wield a sword with some dexterity, and only three others were more accurate with the bow.

Back in the barracks, where the recruits flung themselves down in exhaustion, one of them said bitterly, "What about the elephants? Aren't they why we came here? All day I saw only their backs going through the woods."

Nor did they see elephants the next day, but spent the morning at military exercises again and the afternoon at the river. A mahout explained that elephants sometimes helped to build bridges. They had to be bathed, sometimes in swift rivers, and their love of water required anyone living with them to feel comfortable in it too. So the mahouts ordered the recruits to swim across the Godavari. At their interview three candidates had claimed they could swim, yet they refused now to go farther out than their waists. They were not returned to the barracks that night. Arjun heard that they had been shipped off to an infantry unit by the irate vahinipati.

And that night the same critical recruit complained of not seeing a single elephant all day, though from the riverbank they had heard the beasts trumpeting far off. "We swim, we climb trees, we shoot at targets, but do we ever sit on gaja?"

Next day they did not sit on elephants either, but at last they saw one up close. Singly, each recruit was conducted through the trees to a small clearing where a large male was fettered by its left hind leg to a thick post.

When Arjun's turn came, he walked to the edge of the clearing and stared at the huge animal in the center of it. Arjun watched the lips of the long trunk move gently across the ground, curling daintily as they sifted through patches of dry grass.

"Go up to gaja," a mahout whispered in Arjun's ear, giving him a nudge.

"How close?"

"You decide."

Arjun reasoned that the hind-leg tether allowed gaja a movement of at least six feet away from the post. "What do I do then?" he asked the mahout.

"You decide."

So Arjun stepped into the clearing and went slowly forward, aware of the brown eyes watching him. They had long lashes and a gentle expression, but their gaze was also intent, purposeful. To match their concentration, the trunk raised into an S shape and Arjun could see bristly hairs at its entrance. They moved as if caught by a breeze when the great beast sniffed the air.

By now Arjun was no farther than a dozen steps away from six tons of living creature looming over him. He halted and stood there, looking up and up at gaja's massive head. This close, the elephant's eyes seemed exceedingly bright; a great slab of red tongue flickered at the V-shaped mouth; one leg raised imperiously. The giant ears began flapping with the cracking sound of a whole flock of egrets lifting off a pond. And then from somewhere within the immense body came a pumping noise as if the heart of the earth was pulsing heavily.

Gaja threatens me, Arjun thought, and for an instant he nearly turned and ran. But he stood his ground and waited. He commanded himself to stay. He willed his eyes to meet those of the beast, whose trunk was now circling the air in front of Arjun. Should he go closer? If he went too close, that wrinkled rope of muscle might flick out and wrap around his waist. The beast did not try to get at him, however, but remained as it was, meeting the boy's stare with its own.

Arjun was terrified. Yet he pushed the fear aside, as if it were the curtain to a place he had to enter. Then he walked into another region of himself where everything he had ever been suddenly fell away and revealed a new Arjun Madva, someone older and stronger and braver. In this strange place within himself his eyes met those of the great beast hovering above him. The two of them were together, linked by their eyes. Nothing else existed. Then slowly, deliberately, Arjun backed off, still facing gaja as he moved to the edge of the clearing.

Standing there, the mahout whispered, "Go."

Turning, Arjun walked into the woods a little way. Alone, he fell to his knees, breathing hard, feeling the fear leak out of his mind. Then he felt that a part of him remained in the strange new place where he was older and stronger. He recalled each moment of his encounter with gaja, and the memory brought a smile to his face and a feeling of joy. Then he got to his feet and located the other recruits where they all waited near the river. He went toward them as if nothing had happened.

Late that afternoon they returned to camp for latrine duty. A few of them spoke of their own encounters with the bull elephant. Three hadn't left the edge of the clearing. One, bragging of his courage, said he had walked forward with his hand outstretched, intending to touch gaja's trunk, but the beast swiped out and missed him by no more than the width of his hand. Another had taunted the old bull from a range beyond the circle of its movement. Most of the recruits said nothing, as if embarrassed by their performance or unsure of how it had gone.

Later, a kavadai came to the barracks with a list of six names. Silently the recruits named picked up their bedrolls and followed him. Those remaining didn't have to be told that their companions were being transferred to a unit of infantry.

Then another kavadai came to the door and shouted out, "Arjun Madva!"

Trembling, the boy got up and followed him to one of the central huts. Arjun waited outside until the kavadai stood in the doorway and beckoned. He was a few years older than Arjun, with a broad face and angry eyes. "Go in," he muttered, then left.

Inside the hut Arjun saw one of the mahouts sitting beside a charcoal fire. The boy remembered having seen him on the first day, a skinny man, shorter than Arjun and probably older than Father. The mahout had never spoken to the recruits but always stood apart and watched from narrow eyes lost in baggy flesh. In a barely audible voice he began asking questions, just as the vahinipati had done. Finally he said, "What do you know about gaja?"

"Very little, Shri Mahout."

"Yet you did the right things. You stood there without fear. You didn't torment him or try to make friends. You made yourself known, that was all. Was that all?"

"Yes, Shri Mahout. I just wanted him to know I was there."

"When he tried to frighten you, you never moved. Were you frightened?"

"Yes, Shri Mahout, very frightened."

"But you met his look." The mahout laughed, a rustling sound like wind through dry grass. "It was good. That old bluffer deserves such treatment. So tell me why you are here."

There was no sense in explaining it might be a roundabout way of finding his sister. Perhaps he could use the palapati's argument: Boys like to ride high above everyone. Arjun paused before answering. Then he said, "I want be be here because it is only for a few. Only for those who can live with elephants."

The mahout smiled faintly. "You want to be different? Most boys are born into a group and want to stay snugly inside of it."

"I want to do what I want to do," Arjun said bluntly. The truth was, until this moment he'd never given the idea of being different much thought. He belonged to the Brahman class and had always wanted that. Yet he had no interest in rituals of the studious life admired by Brahmans. He respected his parents yet had never been especially dutiful—less dutiful than most boys in his village. Perhaps behind a lot of his actions, hidden yet powerful, was this impulse to do something different, just as he had told the mahout. "I want to meet gaja again, eye to eye."

"Simply because you want to," said the mahout, making himself a betel quid from the leaf and areca nut and cloves that were spread out on a piece of cloth beside him.

"Yes, Shri Mahout."

He smeared slaked lime on the leaf, then deftly folded it. "You'll ride elephants because the idea pleases you. Is that it?"

"Yes, Shri Mahout. And if it pleases *you*."

"Shri Mahout this, Shri Mahout that. What a polite little nobleman you are," the mahout observed with a sarcastic smile. "I wouldn't be surprised if you're a Brahman."

"I used to be."

"*Used* to be."

"I was a Brahman."

"Had you said 'am' instead of 'was,' I'd send you out of here this instant." He tucked the quid into his mouth.

"I am a soldier," Arjun said, "bought and paid for."

"But you'd rather ride an elephant than walk." The mahout chuckled again. "So did I when I was your age. Hear me, boy. You must never call me Shri Mahout. My name is Rama."

Never in his life had Arjun called an elder by the first name. Yet the mahout's look was command enough. Reluctantly, the boy said, "Yes, Rama."

"To the elephants you are not a Brahman and I am not a Shri Mahout. I am old and they know me. You are young and they don't know you. To begin with, that's all you need to know."

"I understand."

"No, you don't understand. But stay with me and you will. You'll learn through elephants what honesty is and how to recognize the dishonest. I believe in elephants. Some people call them cowards and fools, but I say they're blessed by the gods. They think as much as we do and sometimes they feel more. So you want to work with them?"

"Yes, I do—Rama."

"Live with them? Some day you'll be assigned a gaja for life. You'll grow old with him though he weighs much more than sixty or seventy of you. You'll have such giants in your dreams. Do you want to live with elephants?"

For a moment in memory Arjun stared from parted reeds at the yellow fangs of a tiger. The merciful gods had chosen to save him from those fangs for some purpose. For what purpose? The steady gaze of the old bull gaja had challenged him to do something. To do what? He had not left the strange new place of courage, so Arjun said, "I want to live with them." He added, "I want to—" Arjun paused again, surprised by what he was thinking. "I want to know why I want to live with them."

Decisively, the mahout spit a stream of blood-red betel juice into a copper bowl. "All right, then. You're my new kavadai. Tomorrow we go to work."

 6

THE NEXT DAY, TO ARJUN'S SURPRISE, Rama gave him the same kind of work to do that he had performed in the infantry barracks. This time his major duty was to clean a hut shared by Rama and the older kavadai. But if Arjun labored like a Panchama sweeper, at least he came in daily contact with elephants. The mahout allowed the new kavadai to observe them as they grazed or trained with handlers until their habits became familiar to him.

When elephants met, they sniffed with extended trunks, tip to tip, and sometimes thrust their trunks into each other's mouths. They were noisy creatures who used an assortment of grunts and roars and barks and rumblings to express themselves. One old female put her trunk to the ground, stepped on it, and blew hard to create a high-pitched whistle. An angry elephant usually snorted by exhaling as it smacked its trunk against a tree; sick, it grumbled deep in its throat; startled, it squealed like a human child. Squeaking meant pleasure, purring meant contentment. Trumpeting, Arjun learned, was reserved for other animals an elephant wished to frighten off.

When free of their handlers, the elephants grazed most of the time. Sometimes, around midnight, Arjun would get up and walk out of camp into the forest where they slept. He'd crouch nearby, watching their great, shadowy bulks move gently as if small hills were trembling beneath the moon.

Ever since his confrontation with the old bull, Arjun felt attracted to these beasts. Of course, their size and power and strange appearance provoked everyone's interest, but Arjun was drawn to them by a more subtle curiosity. They seemed to hide in their massive heads and bodies a knowledge of something he needed to know.

He watched a young kavadai roughly tickle a half-grown tusker behind the ear with a pole, then dash away. Amazingly quick on its big feet, gaja whirled about so nimbly that it could easily have circled the mischief-maker with its trunk. All it really did was make a snapping sound of mild annoyance by flapping its broad ears. Arjun learned from this incident that the might of elephants protected them from an impulse to act violently. He decided that at heart they were gentle creatures.

What Arjun didn't learn by observation he gathered from listening to mahouts who sat around the fires in the evening. He discovered, for example, that the higher an elephant held its head the more excited it was. The two tusks of a mature bull were always of different length. The longer was rarely used; the other, more blunted, did most of the work.

Once he overheard a group of mahouts discussing elephant weaknesses. He was surprised to learn that gaja wasn't capable of carrying as much for its size as a man could—surely not as much as a horse. And the giants suffered not only from snakebites but also from too much sun, which was why they laid branches on their backs. They got rashes and eye inflammations and aching tusks.

But more often the handlers discussed elephants in a lighthearted way. Nervous members of the camp herd were referred to as "rockers" because they swung one front foot across the other for hours while swaying from side to side. One rocker was drolly called Nataraja, the name for Lord Shiva in the role of divine dancer. A young tusker was so shy that he turned and ran when a female approached. He was called The Lover. An ancient female used to rap her trunk across the backside of a haughty bull when he wasn't looking. They called her Old Sly Bones.

So Arjun sat in the shadows beyond the firelight and listened. His own master rarely addressed him except to bark out an order—clean this, do that, go there—just as the veterans had done in the infantry garrison.

After a few weeks, Arjun was moved out of the newcomers' barracks and given a corner of Rama's hut for himself. Here he slept and ate his meals. Aside from watching the elephants, he wandered in the nearby woods or stayed in the hut. He began to despair of doing anything else. Now and then Skanda, the older kavadai, would tramp in and turn as if noticing Arjun for the first time. The mahout must have told him about Arjun's heritage, because Skanda usually mumbled something about "troublemaking Brahmans" and shook his head in an imaginary conversation with someone who shared his dislike of the highborn newcomer.

One day, shortly after dawn, Arjun was roughly awakened by the mahout, who leaned over him and asked, almost fiercely, "Would you like to have some fun?"

For a moment Arjun hesitated, studying the skinny man. Rama already had a quid of betel in his mouth. "Yes, I would, I would like that," Arjun said.

Without another word Rama turned and left the hut with Arjun following. Skanda was still asleep.

As they walked through the forest, Rama said, "You make a good sweeper. A good sweeper is humble and patient. A good sweeper can make a good mahout."

Arjun did not reply but walked just slightly behind his master's right elbow.

Rama led the way to the bank of the Godavari River, where a herd of a dozen elephants and their handlers were gathered. Already a few of the beasts were in the water, along with their mahouts. "Come with me and don't be afraid," said Rama. "They're always friendly in the water. That's why I'll start you here."

The morning passed swiftly for Arjun, although the sun was nearly overhead by the time he and his master left the riverbank. It began with him watching the elephants sport around in the river, sucking water into their trunks, then expelling it into their mouths. Rama laughed at Arjun's wonder. "That's why some people call gaja the One Who Drinks Twice," he said. Some of the elephants sank beneath the surface, only their trunks snorkeling out as an S-shaped breathing tube. "They swim very fast," Rama said. "You have to paddle hard in a boat to keep up with them. Now watch me give that tusker a bath." He pointed to a gaja who was already lying on its side in the shallow water.

Rama had brought along a wicker sack suspended by a cord from his shoulder. Now he opened it and took out a pine cone from a pandanis tree. He waded into the river and began scrubbing the beast's side and back with the rough cone until pink skin showed through caked dirt and gray pigment. Then he proceeded to crawl over large patches of the beast, moving the cone in quick, hard, scouring circles. When the cone broke off in pieces, he took another from the sack. Then by tapping the old animal briskly on its ear, Rama got it to roll over so he could do the other side. Halfway finished, he paused and looked at Arjun standing on the bank. "Come out here," he ordered.

Without hesitation the boy entered the river and slogged to the elephant's side.

"Here," said Rama, opening the sack and taking out a cone. "Go to work."

So Arjun moved forward, took the cone, and leaned toward the great belly. He had never been this close to an elephant before. His nostrils filled with its loamy odor. Arjun felt as if he were smelling the deepest part of the earth, far below the soil, at the place where the longest roots of a rain tree were buried. He moved the cone lightly, tentatively, across a wrinkled portion of skin.

"Harder," commanded Rama, who was now washing gaja's feet with its five horny nails that were each almost as big as his hand.

As they worked, Rama told his assistant that frequent bathing relieved elephants of ticks and leeches. "Gaja knows you are doing something good for him."

Looking at the elephant's long-lashed brown eye so gently fixed on him, Arjun believed it.

"Feel his trunk," Rama said.

Rama felt the short, bristly hairs all along its length to the fingerlike end.

"Now blow into it." Rama backed up the order with a broad smile.

So Arjun took hold of the trunk, lowered his face, and blew hard into the tip. The leathery skin trembled a little, and he watched the brown eye blink.

"You see?" Rama chortled. "He liked that."

After their bath, the herd rolled around in mud along the shore and then showered their backs and flanks with gritty earth from the riverbank farther up. Arjun asked why they were allowed to get dirty again right after bathing. Rama made sense of it: Together with rubbing against trees and boulders and termite hills, this helped them shed old skin.

Once the elephants had finished dousing themselves with abrasive gravel, each handler found his own beast and led it away.

Arjun turned questioningly to his master when the tusker they'd bathed went with someone else. "Isn't that your gaja?"

"A mahout was sick, so I bathed his as a favor. I don't have one of my own." Rama found a shaded spot under some trees beyond the riverbank. Arjun sat beside the master while he prepared a betel quid. Rama explained that the lime came from sea shells that were burned on a bamboo fire, then heated in water until the liquid boiled away, leaving slaked lime. The areca nuts, loosened from husks, were dried, then also boiled until their seeds dropped out and were ground. "I like aniseed and cloves with my vitika," he said while deftly folding the betel leaf. Tucking it into one side of his mouth, Rama added, "Vitika keeps the gums strong and cures the bellyache."

The boastful claim for betel chewing reminded Arjun of Uncle's claim for smoking. It surprised Arjun to think of Uncle. Or rather, it surprised as well as dismayed him to think of Uncle only now. Could such a close relative, murdered so callously, have no hold on his daily thoughts? In recent weeks he had rarely thought of home or the attack on the caravan. Even worse, sometimes when he tried to remember Gauri's face it was a dark circle with features only vaguely drawn.

Rama continued to talk while he enjoyed the peppery

quid. He told the new kavadai that his own gaja had died a few years before in battle. Pulling down the top edge of his dhoti, Rama exposed a long, jagged scar from his right hip to his belly. "This is what I got in that battle. I could have another gaja of my own, but I prefer just to train them." He shrugged, his eyes suddenly misting. "No other gaja could take his place."

The next morning, while Arjun swept the hut, Skanda came in. Their master, Skanda said, had just been called for a conference at the war camp near Ellora, so today Skanda was in charge here. He made clear that he expected obedience from a troublesome Brahman. "I'm going to show you," he said, "the only true way of handling elephants."

He led Arjun to a storage hut where handlers kept their supplies. Skanda picked up a short pole with a curved, finger-long metal hook at the tip. This was the ankus, the chief means of controlling an elephant. He showed how to prod with it—a brutal stabbing motion. Afoot, you used the hook to grab loose folds of skin along the leg and urge gaja forward or backward. Mounted, you twisted the ankus around in the ear or close to the eye. "That gets their attention," he noted with a smile. Then he demonstrated the use of a valia kole. With this long pole you poked the animal in its joints. He found a short rod with a blunt, heavy end of metal. With this cherya kole you banged the animal on its skull or neck or trunk or backside. "A good place to hit him hard is on the ridge of the spine. Gaja doesn't like it. And another thing he doesn't like is this. You make a little slit in his skull with a knife. Then when he gets troublesome"—Skanda made a twisting motion with his hand—"You worry the wound just so." He had other suggestions too for having fun. For example, gaja liked to drink toddy, and if you gave him enough of it, the stupid, drunken beast would stagger around until he fell over like an axed tree. "Now you know what to do," he concluded, "when the old man lets you have your own gaja."

"When will that be?"

"When will that be?" Skanda repeated in a mocking tone. "Do you really care? All you care about is getting out of foot-soldiering, because Brahmans hate to walk." After reciting a long list of tasks he wanted the new kavadai to carry out, Skanda warned that he would make sure every one of them was done right.

A few days later Rama returned, which made Arjun's life much easier. With the master came some unexpected good news: Skanda, having completed his training, was being sent to the war camp near Ellora for further military training. "Remember what I told you," Skanda said to Arjun when leaving for his new assignment. "If you listen to that weak old man, you'll never be a good mahout."

Once the older kavadai was gone, Rama turned his full attention to the younger. He taught Arjun nearly twenty commands used by mahouts to control their elephants. A docile old tusker knelt on Rama's spoken order so that the mahout and his apprentice could climb up and sit on its back. Seated in front, Rama explained each signal of hand or foot or voice that gaja must obey. *Must* obey. Rama said, "Never let gaja get away with anything. If he knows a command, he must never refuse it. Never. Not once."

After putting the tusker through its paces, Rama took his new apprentice to the same supply hut. Just as Skanda had done, he demonstrated the use of the ankus and the other handling poles. Then he threw them disdainfully into a pile. "The main way of controlling gaja is through your toes. You nudge him at the base of the ear while calling out your command." When his apprentice seemed puzzled, Rama asked what was wrong. Arjun told him of Skanda's advocacy of pole jabbing and knife twisting. Rama was silent for a while. Then he said, "Skanda never did those things here. If he had, I would have thrown him out. He said those things to make you act like a fool. But I have seen mahouts do such things when they knew better. I have seen wounds kept open with knives and holes cut in ears. I have seen an ankus used to dig into a gaja's head. I have seen them hobbled with iron shackles that have inward-pointing spikes. I have seen mahouts strike a gaja on the ridge of the back, which can cripple a full-grown bull." Rama shook his head sadly. "Mean mahout, mean elephant. Lazy mahout, lazy elephant. Good mahout, good elephant. A good mahout keeps an ankus with him but rarely uses it. His toes, though, are calloused. You will learn something very special, Arjun."

"Has it to do with discipline?"

Rama nodded. "You must dominate the beast and become his master. Without his total respect, he'll trick you. You must always be the master. Yet if you do it through cruelty and suffering, gaja will never forget. And someday, without warning, he'll lift you in his trunk and dash you against a tree."

 7

ARJUN SOON LEARNED TO MOUNT an elephant without help. He scrambled up the side of an old tusker as it knelt with its forelegs stretched out ahead. There was a liquid, unsteady feel to the fatty skin that sometimes caused Arjun to lose purchase as he sought a foothold going up, so that he slid back down and had to start again, much to the amusement of onlooking mahouts. No wonder, he thought, you needed to be good at climbing trees.

Once up, he sat just behind the elephant's head with feet under its ears, toes tucked inside a rope that circled its neck. For many hours he practiced signaling commands with his hands and feet, tapping out emphatically what the elephant had to do: turn left, turn right, go forward fast, faster, slower, go backward, stop, kneel. He went on excursions with the tusker through neighboring woodland. What amazed him was how an elephant could judge the headroom a rider needed in the forest. Often the old gaja pulled down branches and creepers that would otherwise have knocked off Arjun's turban.

The young kavadai learned to use an ankus with discretion, applying just enough pressure on the hook to assert his authority. Arjun had an inherent sense of how far to go. Rama realized it too. "You'll be a good mahout. In your hand the hook isn't a weapon but a way of telling gaja what to do. You use the ankus on him as you might on yourself. That is very good."

Months went by. Sometimes at night he awakened with a start from a dream, having seen Gauri more vividly than he could imagine her when awake. His sister was singing one of her wordless songs, her eyes shining. She waved to him, then turned and disappeared into a thick forest. In another recurrent dream, always of long duration, he stood on a riverbank and watched Nataraja, knee-deep in the water, rocking back and forth, back and forth, back and forth.

Meanwhile the seasons were changing. The hot, dry months of April and May gave way to the monsoon rains of summer. Grasses and shrubs shot up as high as an elephant's belly, among them a legume whose pealike pods were relished by the grazing herd that trained little during this steamy, muddy time. Arjun worked with the old tusker as much as weather allowed, but when none of the herd went out for training sessions and the rains ceased briefly, he took hikes through the forest. He saw cuckoos ravenous in berry-laden bushes and butterflies darting among long-stemmed prickly lantanas. At dusk he went down to the river and watched fish owls hunting along the bank. It was out here, alone, that he created a new waking image of Gauri. Perhaps she didn't look as he envisioned, but in his memory she regained a recognizable face. The past and the present, separate in recent months, came together again and left him with enthusiasm for elephants and renewed desire to find his sister.

During the rainy season Rama spent much time in the hut with his apprentice. He described war in the vast region of the Deccan where Chalukyan rulers had struggled many years against rival kings. He continued to acquaint Arjun with the nuances of elephant life. He explained the migratory pattern of wild herds as they responded to changes in season. Soon after the rains ended, they descended from the highlands and followed the eastward movement of monsoon clouds. When grasses became dry and coarse from autumn winds blowing over them, the herd moved on, finally reaching the valleys rich in thorn scrubs and jackfruit. During the rainless months of winter, they sought moisture-bearing plants along low-lying rivers, where they shifted from grazing to browsing. At such times they stripped bark from trees;

still hungry, they tore roots from the ground. Toward the end of the blazing hot spring, they gathered in larger herds for a return to the highlands, where monsoon showers, just beginning, would cause fresh grass to sprout. This was how they lived, moving from east to west, then west to east, following the seasons as they had done from time beyond memory.

Arjun had little sense of where things were in the country, so Rama taught him. He drew a map on the damp earth. The western half of India was divided into north and south by the Narmada River. Below the river lay the Chalukyan Empire ruled by King Pulakeshin the Second, whom Rama had served proudly most of his life. Above the Narmada stretched the vast realm of the great warrior Harsha. "Last time I went to war camp," Rama told his apprentice while folding a quid, "they talked of nothing but Harsha. Spies said he dreams of conquest below the Narmada. If Harsha crosses it and invades us, we'll need young mahouts like you. And more elephants for a great war."

The vahinipati came to camp near the end of the rainy season to prepare for an expedition into the Dasarnaka Forest, which was famous for harboring wild elephants at this time of year. Forest tribes lived there and worshipped the warrior-goddess Durga, who they thought lived in this region because it was the most beautiful in the world. They existed by hunting and supplying elephants for the Chalukyan army.

Arjun, already acknowledged as a kavadai of promise, went along to complete his training. A band of forty men and a half-dozen elephants set out from the high country. When they left the training camp, it was still drizzling. As the expedition moved eastward and reached the verge of the Dasarnaka Forest, mists were clinging to shrubs and trees with the tenacity of stormclouds. A dozen tribesmen, dark and naked, came out of these mists so quietly and suddenly that members of the expedition, gasping in surprise, fumbled for their weapons. The vahinipati (this time he walked instead of rode) negotiated with the tribal chiefs for half the afternoon. It was done over many betel quids. The dark little men—squatting, not sitting, around a smoky fire—swallowed the bitter juice, unlike the vahinipati and his guards, who spit it out. Finally the tribesmen agreed to accept salt, cloth, and iron blades for their work.

The expedition set up camp. They waited for several hundred men from the tribe to build a corral for captured elephants. This keddah was made from sturdy logs, lashed together by rattan cord. It was large enough to hold fifty beasts or more. The keddah contained more than a dozen trees with their lower trunks stripped of branches so elephants could be tied to them. Except for a ramp of earth leading into the keddah from the entrance, a deep ditch surrounded the space inside. It was dug wide enough to discourage elephants from leaning against the bamboo walls and bowling them over. The tension on two ropes, each tied to a slender tree on opposite sides of the gateway, held the gate open. Then the tribesmen built outside platforms for men to stand on. Looking down from a platform into the enclosure, Arjun tried to imagine what Rama told him: Some wild elephants went crazy when first captured. It was often necessary to thrust lit torches at them or prod them with poles to keep them away from the gate.

"You have not yet seen their power," warned Rama.

It was true. Arjun's training had prepared him to appreciate their restraint and intelligence but not to fear them.

Nor did he fear them a week later when, with Rama and other members of the party, he went to look at a herd grazing in the neighborhood. He saw a mother with her calf. At the sound of a crow cawing, the fearful calf rushed between the mother's forelegs, turned, and peeked out from beneath her belly. An ancient female led the herd from patch to patch of grass, her shrunken frame and halting gait belying her authority. Where she went, so did the most powerful tuskers. A young gaja, scarcely taller than Arjun and with long reddish hairs on its shoulders, cavorted in the bushes until one glance from the old female brought him to a halt. The herd grazed serenely.

The next day, however, they gathered behind their leader and trotted forward, trying to escape from the loud noise. Forming a long arcing line, tribal beaters were banging pieces of metal and shouting to keep the elephants heading in the direction of the keddah. The louder the noise the faster they moved. Arjun, on the keddah platform, saw them approaching through the forest. He was reminded of something Rama had once told him. You couldn't get away from a charging elephant by zigzagging back and forth; elephants were faster than people and turned more quickly. The best way of escaping an angry elephant was to lead him to a hill, because gaja slowed cautiously while going down. But there were no hills here, only moist valleys and heavy thickets and dense woodland.

He felt the bamboo slats under him tremble, then rattle as the swaying old female guided the herd toward the outer lip of a bamboo funnel that narrowed to the keddah's gateway. Urged on by the tremendous din on both sides and behind her, she led forty other elephants between the wing walls into the stockade. Arjun watched a tribesman scurry up a ladder set against one of the slender trees that held the gate open. The man leaned forward with a knife and cut the rope, springing the gate shut.

The elephants were penned inside, churning around like fish in shallow water.

From the platform Arjun noticed a large tusker bang the coiled tip of its trunk against the ground while forcing a sharp blast of air through the nozzle. The sound this made was metallic, as if coins were being shaken vigorously in a sack.

Facing the tusker, other bulls did the same thing. A few of them kinked their tails and drew back their heads. Lifting their trunks as if preparing to strike like a snake, they shuffled a few moments, then rushed forward. But when they reached the ditch they halted and edged away, trumpeting. Involuntarily Arjun stepped back, although they couldn't possibly have reached him, and almost fell off the platform. Rama chortled. "Ah, you've seen their power!"

Several more times the bulls prepared to attack. Their hind legs danced from side to side. They held their ears out to the fullest extent, making them seem even larger, while they grunted and roared and made the sound of coins clinking. Finally they charged the gate again, but lit torches and sharp poles forced them back. In the chaos, one of the bulls shoved a half-grown male into the ditch. Snorting and squealing, he couldn't get out. He circled the ditch, then came to its end near the entrance ramp and huddled there fearfully. He reminded Arjun of the calf peering out from between its mother's legs.

The noise from elephants and tribal beaters (they had kept up the banging and screaming) continued for a long time. Then suddenly the old matriarch, who had been trotting around the edge of the ditch seeking escape, headed for the center of the stockade and halted under a tree. Letting her ears go limp against her skull, her trunk unfold and point to the ground, she stood there motionlessly. That seemed to be a signal for the beaters to cease making noise. They backed away from the enclosure.

Then the herd also grew silent.

"What happens now?" Arjun asked his master.

"They'll do what she does." And sure enough, even the most aggressive tusker calmed down. They started to move toward the center and closed ranks around her, their own trunks dangling like rope.

Rama said, "In a few days, when hunger weakens them, we'll cull out what we want, one by one, and let the others go."

Arjun was looking down at the trapped young male cowering in the ditch. "What happens to him?"

"Ah, well, he won't be able to get out by himself. And we'll have enough on our hands with those we keep."

"So he'll stay in the ditch?"

"Until we're done with our work."

"And then?"

"Getting him out would be difficult and take a great deal of time. We'll let them have him."

"What do you mean?"

Rama pointed at a group of tribesmen squatting nearby. "They'll kill him and have a great feast. When something like this happens, they always get the gaja. That has always been the way."

8

A FEW DAYS LATER, THE MAHOUTS began work in earnest. Their task was to sort out and individually noose the animals selected for the elephant corps. They entered the keddah mounted on the well-trained females brought from camp, whose purpose was to keep the captive gajas under control by flanking and maneuvering them. These females were called koomkies, and without them nothing could be done with wild elephants.

To subdue and train each captured beast the vahinipati assigned either a mahout or an experienced kavadai. The officer's corkscrew curls and ear loops of silver were no obstacle to his authority. Arjun was reminded of the matriarch who led the herd in spite of her advanced age. Real power was not always apparent.

Moreover, the major seemed to like making these assignments, shouting his orders from the enclosure platform. Arjun realized that handlers were assigned according to their ability, because those with the least skill got the first animals, who were smaller and weaker and more quickly rendered docile. Boxed in by a koomkie on either side, each gaja was slowly led from the herd. Dropping to the ground, the handler looped a rope around one of its hind legs and tied it to a tree; sometimes, with the aid of an assistant mounted on the other koomkie's back, he passed a rope around the elephant's body and secured that too. It took nearly all day, but by dusk a dozen members of the herd were shackled to trees in the enclosure.

"This is a good thing about gaja," Rama told his assistant as they returned to the forest camp at mealtime.

"When he knows he's truly captured, gaja makes the best of it. Quickly he sets about learning what is asked of him."

But the next day a crusty bull started to threaten another crew of mahouts. All half-dozen koomkies surged around him and finally led him to the gate and out of the keddah—he was too dangerous to keep. Then, under the shouted orders of the vahinipati, mahouts got their koomkies to guide the very old and the very young and the pregnant females and the tuskless males from the enclosure. Beyond it the released members of the herd headed for the forest, trotting away as fast as they could, squealing in their newfound freedom.

That left about thirty in the keddah. More than half of the elephants secured to trees overnight were ready to be led from the enclosure into "crushes," also prepared by the tribesmen. Built against the trunk of a large tree, a crush was a cage of timbers—four upright posts and three horizontal bars—just large enough to hold one elephant. Once an animal was led inside, other bars were inserted to hold it under the chest and groin so it could sleep.

Meanwhile, other beasts were culled from the herd still in the keddah and tied to trees available again. Arjun glanced at Rama, wondering if the vahinipati would finally select his master. But other mahouts and kavadais got the assignments. Rama didn't seem to care; after all, when his elephant died, he hadn't wanted another. That was not true of Arjun, however. Most of the other kavadais were given their own beasts to train with help from mahouts. Arjun envied them. He realized that aside from finding Gauri, nothing else mattered as much as this. All of his training coalesced into a yearning for his own elephant to ride and train and to be with, yes, to be with as he might be with friends back home, racing to the pond or into the fields, everyone yelling, everyone laughing, everyone happy to be there.

Two days later only a half-dozen elephants remained in the keddah. All the others were either in crushes or had already proved compliant enough for minimal tethering to trees. The half-grown male spent his time kneeling in the ditch. Tribesmen had fed him plenty of grass to plump him up for their feast.

This morning, as usual, the vahinipati came to survey the remaining beasts. Every one of them was a large, powerful tusker. Four mahouts, among them Rama, stood near the major and awaited his decision.

Five kavadais, including Arjun, stood farther away. They couldn't overhear what the officer was saying.

When the vahinipati finally walked off, Rama motioned for his assistant to follow him beyond earshot of the others. He turned, frowning, and said to Arjun, "You ride the smaller koomkie. I'll ride the other."

Arjun tried to match Rama's glum expression with his own, but he couldn't help smiling from excitement and relief. It seemed as though the master had finally accepted a gaja and would let him help train it. Soon they were entering the keddah on koomkies. Arjun suppressed a desire to call out eagerly, "Which one, Rama? Which one is ours!"

As they approached the remaining elephants, Rama pointed to the largest. Although he hadn't eaten for a week, the young bull was strong enough to raise its tusks high and glare balefully over its lifted trunk.

Rama halted and Arjun came up beside him. "He's about your age, boy," the master said. "Look at him. Forty of us left camp together. Twice that number wouldn't outweigh him. This is a fine young tusker. Just hope he's still young enough to obey females. Are you ready?"

"Yes, I'm ready."

"You know what to do?"

"I've watched carefully."

Rama nodded. "Yes, I know you have." He guided his koomkie in a circle around the tusker. From the opposite direction Arjun did the same. They came up on either side of the young bull, allowing the two koomkies to reach out with feathery trunks and lightly touch the arched spine and ears and skull of the anxious gaja. Arjun could hear him breathing heavily, but Rama's hope was answered: The tusker was quickly calmed by the females. At their handlers' command, they gently nudged him. In this way they got the powerful beast to shuffle forward a little, close to a stout tree.

Then Rama slid off his koomkie and adroitly slipped a long rope behind gaja's hind leg, knotted it, and made it fast to the tree trunk. He didn't try to get a rope around the body, but instead put another rope around the other hind leg and tied it just beneath the first, thus hobbling the bull. Fortunately, the koomkies had soothed him enough for Rama to do this without difficulty. Finished, he scrambled away and called for his koomkie to come over and kneel. Rama mounted again.

Arjun could see the sweat gleaming on his face.

Rama pointed to the hobbled bull. "He is yours, Arjun."

The boy was thunderstruck.

Rama smiled broadly. "Oh yes, I mean it. The vahini-pati agrees with me. We think you can handle this gaja. Tomorrow, if he's calm, we'll put him in a crush. Then you and you alone must give him water—about twenty bucketfuls. And grass—keep it coming." He added with a scowl of warning, "Be worthy of him, Arjun."

The next day they tried to move him, but the tusker was too agitated by being hobbled, so they waited another day, then another. He was noticeably weak then and followed submissively when the koomkies led him to a crush.

Be worthy of him, Arjun thought while lugging buckets of water from a nearby stream. Be worthy of him. Not only did Arjun bring grasses, but he located the legume with pea pods so beloved by elephants. And from prickly lantana plants he managed to pluck sweet-smelling orange blossoms for a special treat.

Feeding and watering the elephant exhausted him. That evening, Arjun sat half dozing in front of the fire. Rama studied him closely, then said, "Are you afraid of your big gaja?"

The question aroused Arjun. He turned to his master and looked into eyes that were critically narrowed. "He is very big, very powerful."

"You're afraid of him."

"Yes," Arjun admitted.

The master shook his head. "Elephants smell fear. You must not even think of fear around them. If you can't overcome your fear, you must give this up. Promise me. I don't want to be responsible for your death." He went on to speak of other things. A spoiled elephant was a cunning devil, deceptive and sudden in its wrath, so it was unwise to reward gaja too often and too soon. Anything demanded of gaja must be performed. If necessary, beat him, but only to convince—never merely to hurt. That meant persistent beating was more important than painful beating. Once begun, the beating must lead to only one conclusion: Gaja did what he was told. If a handler ever relented in his discipline, the beating did nothing except build up in the beast a terrible resentment, so that some day, when the handler least expected it, gaja would turn on him and gore him or toss him against a boulder.

"Make gaja obey every command," Rama said again. He was preparing himself a quid. "Finally, he must lie down on his side and give a great sigh." To illustrate what he meant, Rama sighed as loudly and deeply as possible. "It is gaja's way of surrendering himself to you." Rama tucked the folded leaf inside his gum. "Until this happens, consider him dangerous. After he has done this, you are his master and friend. Go then and sit beside him and let him sniff you with his trunk while you soothe him with words. Believe me, once this happens, he is your companion for life. All you need then is one thing: you must devote your life to him in return!"

What his master asked of Arjun—to feel no fear—was the hardest thing in the world. Arjun understood that seeming fearless was not enough. He must somehow be without fear. He had been around elephants long enough to believe in their deep perception of a man's nature. If he felt afraid, he could never hide it from the tusker. That night, lying awake, Arjun wondered if tomorrow he'd face the big young gaja without fear. But how did you wish away fear? Or did you simply tell yourself you didn't feel it and the feeling went away?

Toward morning, just before falling into a short but deep sleep, Arjun realized something. He suspected that Rama knew he must realize this on his own or never realize it at all. Fear couldn't be wished away, but maybe it could be replaced. While thinking of each command used with a gaja, Arjun realized suddenly that his fear had left him for that time. If tomorrow he thought only of how the training must be done, fear might never get in. Was it possible that by thinking one thing he could escape feeling another? There was no choice but to try. That assurance allowed him to sleep.

And that way of defeating fear proved successful the next day, and the next. Arjun surrendered himself to the work at hand, leaving no room for anything else. First, a heavy block of padded wood was lowered onto gaja's back, giving it a chance to feel an object there. After a day of this, Rama ordered his assistant to accompany the saddle. Arjun did not hesitate but climbed over the timbered side of the crush and straddled the padded block. The contact of his thighs against warm hide surprised him, and for an instant he felt panic. Then his eyes focused on the trunk, its end lifting and turning to smell what now was on the tusker's back. Arjun knew he must secure himself, then take charge. He sat forward on the beast's withers and slipped his feet under the neck rope. Pressing down with the toes of his left foot, he called out firmly, "Turn left!" The tusker swung its trunk around front and let it droop motionlessly as if intent on something. Arjun repeated the signal countless times, although gaja could not have known yet what it meant. At Rama's suggestion, Arjun began signaling a turn to the right. An entire morning was taken up this way.

When they quit to eat something, Rama touched the boy's shoulder. "It went well."

"Nothing happened," Arjun muttered wearily.

"Oh, yes, something happened. Gaja listened. He

knows who you are. He also knows you are telling him things." Rama studied the boy before continuing. "Your spirit must become one with his. If the two of you aren't close, terrible things can happen in battle. Of course, gaja will be afraid at first. They are all afraid at first—it's the noise and motion. But he must trust you enough not to panic. That's the test of greatness—his and yours too. In battle, no matter what happens, mahout and gaja must depend on each other."

Rama scooped up rice in his right hand. "This afternoon, give commands again and continue doing it the same way for the next few days. Get him used to the pressure and the sound. Then when you're sure he knows everything you say is meant for him, change from foot pressure to the ankus." When Arjun looked surprised, his master nodded. "Yes, the ankus. You must let him know there's sometimes pain in his life now. He'll learn to expect it if he doesn't listen and obey. When you introduce him to the ankus, when he feels the hook's pain for the first time, gaja might resist. I think this one will. Be prepared for it." Rama added thoughtfully, "If you feel like jumping, well, jump. It's not a disgrace."

Arjun didn't quite understand, but he knew better than to question his master. When Rama wanted him to do something without help, he must do it.

A few days later, mounted on the tusker, Arjun tapped its head with the curved portion of the ankus' hook and called out, "Stop!"

"Harder," ordered Rama, who was leaning over the top timber of the crush.

Arjun hit the tusker's head smartly and yelled, "Stop!"

"This time," Rama said, "give him the hook when

you give him the command."

So Arjun turned the ankus around and dug the hook in enough to draw a little blood when he shouted "Stop!"

The elephant shuddered. It felt to Arjun as if the entire earth was moving beneath him.

And then it happened. The tusker began shaking.

Gaja was bending each foreleg rapidly in succession and swaying from side to side. The rocking and shaking bounced Arjun violently around, yet he held on to the neck rope. One of the stout timbers of the crush came loose. Spectators were yelling, "Jump off! Jump off!" But Arjun held on, although under him the great body seemed to be expanding, joint and muscle and bulk, and it heaved like a boat in a storm. Arjun did not consider jumping. He felt that he could not let go, that he was tethered to this beast as much as it was tethered to the crush. He had no idea how long the thunderous shaking lasted, but finally the tusker slowed, the vast body seemed to shrink to a normal size, and gaja halted, its breath coming in thick gasps through the feebly waving trunk.

Looking up from the gray head for the first time since the shaking had begun, Arjun noticed his master smiling.

"That was good, boy," the mahout said, slapping the timber for emphasis. "You just shortened the time of training."

Later, at the evening fire, Rama glanced slyly at his assistant. "Is there something you want to tell me?"

After a long pause Arjun said, "I was afraid."

"Of course." Rama shrugged. "So was he. Too afraid to be aware of your fear, so your fear didn't matter. What he did is called the Great Shaking. Tuskers that age and younger do it sometimes. But he won't do it again, because you stayed on. Understand me? He won't feel the same fear again. If you had jumped off, he'd think his shaking meant something important, so he might try it again. To do that, he'd give in to fear until maybe it became a habit, and he'd be lost to us. But you used the ankus and stayed on." Rama laughed. "He thinks now there's nothing important to fear. There's only a little pain sometimes." He patted the boy's hand. "Tomorrow you'll start training him outside the crush."

 9

THE MOUNTED BOY WAS SOON teaching gaja a dozen commands. At night, after feeding and watering the tethered beast, Arjun sat nearby and sang. He sang religious songs because they were the only songs he had learned in the village. He sang of the gods Vishnu and Shiva and Ganesha. He sang of Indra and Karttikeya. He sang of devotion to the gods in a scratchy, uneven voice. If only Gauri were here to sing her wordless songs, Arjun thought, the young gaja would learn how sweet and gentle a human could be from the sounds she made. Gauri would not fear gaja, and nothing ever feared her. She never slapped at annoying flies the way everyone did in the wet season. Some people called her stupid for not even trying to wave them away. Arjun had grimly watched people roll their eyes when the mute girl walked through the village followed by a cloud of flies. People said, "The flies know they're safe around that one!" And snickered. But Arjun had never believed his sister was stupid. On the other hand, he had never believed that holy men in Kashi could help her talk, because Gauri didn't need help. She just didn't want to talk. That was his opinion, although even his parents scoffed at the idea that their daughter could talk if she only wanted to. Where was she now? Arjun felt she must still be alive. If she were dead, he would know. How? He didn't know how, but he would know.

The tusker did not like to back up. Whenever he got the signal to go backward, he hesitated as if unsure of the command. Arjun remembered his master's warning: Never let gaja get away with disobeying. So one day when gaja simply stood there and refused to go backward, Arjun sunk his hook into the fleshy skull depression between the ears and repeated his order. He repeated it again, digging the hook in until blood really flowed. He repeated the order again. He didn't twist the ankus' hook in the wound, as some handlers did, but held it firmly against the seeping blood. Again he repeated the order. He felt his patience might last forever, yet there were tears rolling down his cheeks. Arjun hated what he was doing, but not even Rama could have stopped him from doing it. In these crucial moments he understood that his destiny and that of the elephant depended on his own strength of will. Again he repeated the order, his voice high but not shrill and anxious. His command had the solidity of a rock. Go backward. Go backward.

Finally the tusker moved backward. He was given the order again. This time he moved backward immediately. Once more the order. Once more instant obedience. Arjun stuck the bloody ankus in his belt, then ordered gaja to kneel. The great beast knelt without hesitation. Dismounting, Arjun looked steadily at the soft brown eyes. He felt tears in his own, but his gaze never wavered.

Suddenly gaja moved. With the slowly unfolding

motion of a long wave, he slid over and onto his side. He opened his pink mouth so that Arjun could see the great, wet slab of tongue inside. And gaja made a sound. It reminded Arjun of his master mimicking the elephant sigh of surrender.

So the tusker was at last his.

Arjun stepped closer, knelt, then sat beside gaja's head, one hand on a tusk, the other on the wrinkled skin beneath the animal's right eye. The boy whispered, his lips against the leathery ear, "You are my friend. I have never had a friend like you. We'll live together and go into battle together. The gods have decided it."

Standing some distance away, Rama had seen this happen, and soon everyone in camp was coming up to Arjun and congratulating him.

That evening the master rolled two quids and handed one to his assistant. Waiting until Arjun tucked it inside his mouth (flinching from the peppery sensation), Rama said, "Healthy beasts don't get fat. So don't overfeed gaja just to please him. You must teach him to carry his head high with his trunk half rolled. This is how you do it." Rama described bamboo skewers with sharp ends rigged between chest and chin. This was harnessed to gaja during the day, until he learned the right way to carry his head. "You must now give him a name," Rama said casually and laughed at Arjun's look of confusion. "Of course you must. I can't. The vahinipati can't either. Only you, who know him so well, can name him."

Long into the night Arjun thought about it, but a suitable name did not come to mind. During the next day's training he kept muttering names, but none of them sounded right. After the evening meal he went out into the forest where gaja was tethered. Lately he had fallen into the habit of talking to gaja as if every word he spoke was understood.

"When I lived in the village," said Arjun, "I was a Brahman with a sacred thread, and my head was shaved except for a topknot. I was taught to read and write, although it didn't mean much to me. I wasn't interested in praying and reciting slokas. But now I wish I'd paid more attention, because I need to find a good name for you. One that will make you proud. The priest would know one, so would Father, and if Uncle were still alive I'm sure he'd think of a dozen." Walking over to the elephant, Arjun put out his hand for the long, curling trunk to reach down and feel his palm with the soft, liplike end.

At that moment Arjun found the name.

It seemed as if his need for knowledge had supplied him suddenly with enough memory to find what he was searching for. He remembered the priest reciting from the great book of war, the *Mahabharata*, and his mind filled with images of the battlefield at Kurukshetra as he had pictured it through the priest's droning words.

Gandiva. Ah, yes. Gandiva.

The name was on Arjun's lips even as he recalled the facts that went with it. Gandiva was the magical bow of the warrior Arjuna, given to him by the god Varuna. This bow of many colors came with two inexhaustible quivers and the power in itself of a thousand bows. At the war's end, Arjuna threw the greatest bow in the world into the sea, so in this fashion it was returned to its owner, King of the Sea.

As the namesake of the legendary archer, Arjun was going to be a warrior too. And his weapon? Gandiva!

When he told his master the name, Rama nodded in approval. "It's good to take a name from the book of war. Have I told you the name of my gaja? Airavata. I suppose as a good Brahman boy you know who that is."

Arjun did. Airavata was the white four-tusked elephant ridden by the god Indra, who wielded the thunderbolt and controlled the weather. Indra was also the father of the warrior Arjuna. It seemed to Arjun that there must be a hidden reason for the names of gods and warriors to be linked to him and Rama and their elephants. But this thought was soon dispelled by the master.

"You can call gaja anything, you can name him after a god or a great warrior or a glorious weapon, but it won't keep either of you from proving to be a coward or a fool." When the boy seemed crestfallen, Rama added, "You had better give Gandiva a noble look to match his noble name." He then showed Arjun how to oil an elephant's head daily with the thick juice of a special plant until it became a black and shiny crown, separate from the natural grey of the animal's skin. Then he taught Arjun how to decorate gaja's face with symmetrical patterns drawn in chalk.

But later that day, when Arjun was coming into camp, he overheard Rama talking to another mahout.

"Well, it's his choice," Rama was saying.

"It's an arrogant choice," declared the other mahout. "What is this boy? All of fifteen or sixteen? How much does he know about elephants? How dare he use such a fancy name! He acts like a Brahman," the mahout said in disgust.

"He acts like a man who takes pride in what he does. Who believes in the gaja he works with. And someday the name will prove right. They will both live up to it."

"How can you know such a thing?" the mahout asked with a sneer.

"I have seen the two of them together. Only one other mahout and his gaja have shown me the same promise."

"Ah, and their names?"

Rama, laughing, pointed to his own chest. "I am the mahout. The gaja was my Airavata. We were like that." He stood, arms akimbo. "Do you believe me?"

The other mahout nodded quickly. "Of course. I believe you."

One afternoon, after training, Rama waited for the boy to tether Gandiva. "Let's walk a while." The master took his assistant for a stroll through the forest. In a random way he began talking. The tribesmen would probably capture other elephants in their keddah for other units of the Chalukyan elephantry. Forests throughout the Deccan supplied animals for the army. Now that Harsha threatened from the north, perhaps four or five hundred elephants would ultimately arrive in the war camp for final training. Rama claimed that their own expedition had been lucky. They had found a herd near enough to the keddah for beaters to take only half a day getting the beasts inside. Sometimes it took a whole week to maneuver a herd into a keddah. Rama fell silent. Arjun waited.

Then, with a sigh, the master continued. Mahouts and their elephants would go to a special camp for training in warfare. This was near the main camp at Ellora.

Rama fell silent again as they reached a fast-moving stream in the forest. Arjun knew his master well enough to know that the purpose of all this talk had not yet been revealed.

"The whole army, before going on campaign, assembles at Ellora," he went on. "Our vahinipati will have one hundred elephants under his command. A sena will have two vahinis of elephants and two of infantry and cavalry. For battle the king will probably take two or maybe three senas. That means an army of thousands of men and horses and four to six hundred elephants. It's a sight to behold," he muttered, shaking his head.

"And you?" Arjun asked timidly.

"What do you mean?"

"Will you be there too?"

Rama seemed flustered. "Ah well, I'll return to the training camp at Paithan. I've had my war."

So this was what he had really wanted to say: They would now be parted.

Then Rama turned from the stream and motioned for Arjun to follow. "The vahinipati wants to see you. But first there's something else to do."

There was a blacksmith in the expedition, and so, in front of approving onlookers, he struck off Arjun's iron anklet.

The blacksmith and Rama toasted each other with a cup of strong palm toddy. Then the master glanced at his assistant, who was bent over, looking at the mark around his ankle left by the ringlet. "In the elephantry," Rama said, "we don't wear chains to prove loyalty."

Then with another motion he ordered Arjun to follow him to the vahinipati's tent. Here Rama stopped.

"Go in alone."

"What is this for?"

"Go in alone!"

The vahinipati was chewing a quid when Arjun pulled aside the tent flap and entered. Glaring, the officer looked the boy over. "I've never made anyone so young a mahout in my vahini. Don't prove me a fool."

A mahout? Arjun looked at two sergeants who sat along the edge of the tent, grinning.

"Repeat after me," the vahinipati ordered him. "I am a mahout loyal to King Pulakeshin of Chalukya."

Arjun repeated that, haltingly.

The officer continued. "I belong to my gaja."

"I belong to my gaja."

"I serve my king by living for my gaja."

"I serve my king by living for my gaja."

The vahinipati reached down and picked up an ankus lying beside him. Smiling, he offered it to Arjun. "This is yours now."

When the boy left the tent, he glanced wildly around for Rama, but the master wasn't going to share with him this moment of triumph. So the boy rushed into the forest where Gandiva was tethered and told him. Arjun stayed with him that night without returning to camp for the evening meal or for sleeping.

The next morning, when he returned, to his dismay Arjun discovered the master packed and ready to leave, along with half a dozen others who would be returning to Paithan.

Seeing his master, Arjun touched the new ankus strapped to his belt.

"You are proud of that," his master remarked. "Good. You earned it. Do you ever hope for a sacred thread and a shaven head?"

"I'm a mahout now. I think only of Gandiva . . ."

Hearing him hesitate, Rama said, "You think also of—?"

"My sister."

"You told me about her, didn't you? Wasn't she taken

by dacoits?" Studying the boy, he added, "There's nothing you can do about that. Don't waste your time on regrets. Do your duty. The book of the great war tells you. In that section called the *Bhagavad Gita*. Remember it, Brahman?" The master threw his head back and closed his eyes in memory. "The great Arjuna doesn't want to fight, because many of the foe are his relatives. But Lord Krishna convinces him he must fight anyway, even if he kills people loved by him. Why? Because he is a warrior and it is his duty." Rama opened his eyes and smiled faintly. "Of course, you learned that from priests eager to teach you. I learned it by sitting in the shadows and overhearing priests who never knew I was alive."

Arjun said nothing.

"Soon you'll be in a war camp with a hundred other mahouts and their gajas. Then a time will come when everyone assembles and marches out to defend the glory of King Pulakeshin. That's your destiny, Arjun. Think only of that. Your king, his glory, your destiny." Pausing, he glared at the boy. "Who are you?"

"Arjun Madva, handler of the great Gandiva."

Rama frowned and shook his head. "Well, he has yet to prove himself great. But thinking of him that way is a good start for a young mahout."

Making two quids, he handed one to Arjun. "As one mahout to another, keep your gaja strong and happy and obedient and steadfast. There is nothing else."

"I will miss you, Shri Mahout Rama."

The little man turned away, tucked the quid in, and spit a great red stream of betel juice.

PART TWO

◆ 1 O ◆

FOR THE THREE-WEEK JOURNEY to the war camp, the vahinipati rode an elephant. Arjun would grow accustomed to seeing officers ride this way: on a large padded saddle with rings to which a body girth was tightly secured. Neck and crupper ropes further stabilized the saddle. Day after day on the trail Arjun would look up and see the officer's ear loops of silver jiggling as the elephant swayed.

Except for a few advance guards, the company followed their officer on foot through rolling woodland interspersed with fallow fields. Nearly all the handlers walked on the left side of their gajas, just behind the ear. They had better control this way, since the animals swung their trunks and heads more easily to the right. Arjun stayed on the right side because Gandiva was "left-handed."

The vahinipati ordered frequent rests to keep the great beasts fit and happy. In spite of their size or perhaps because of it, elephants sometimes lacked endurance, and the vahinipati didn't want them to arrive at the war camp exhausted. Every third day the company halted for them to browse in the dehydrated leaves of winter. When the caravan passed through villages, people gave alms to the handlers in honor of Ganapati, the elephant-headed god known as the Remover of Obstacles.

Throughout the journey Arjun stayed to himself, having no friends among the mahouts and kavadais. He realized that some of the handlers were jealous of him for getting a promotion to mahout at such a young age. Until his master left, Arjun had never fully appreciated the respect given to Rama and, as a consequence, the power wielded by him. Many of the men on the expedition had treated Arjun well because they deferred to Rama.

Although polite to them, Arjun now matched their cool reserve with his own. Growing up in the world of Brahmans had prepared him to behave with haughty restraint. Not that he had ever liked it. Such aloofness had always oppressed someone so spirited. People in the village used to whisper about his lack of dignity. "That Arjun will never make a good Brahman. There's the wildness of an outcast in him." Now, however, he was able to use what he had learned as a boy in order to protect himself. Arjun understood that he couldn't win respect through silence and abject humility as he had done in the infantry barracks. What had been appropriate then would be wrong now. After all, he must assert himself for his gaja and display the authority expected of a mahout. So he called up into memory the solemn power of a Brahman countenance. He felt it in the taut muscles of his face, the cool stare of his eyes, the thin set of his mouth. Rejected as a newcomer whose quick rise had been championed by someone no longer around to help him, Arjun Madva became more of a Brahman than ever before.

But one night he left his blanket and crept out to see Gandiva. The elephant was still awake, quietly munching some leaves pulled from the upper branches of a small tree. Arjun stood nearby until the beast turned and fluttered the end of his trunk lightly over the boy's face and chest. Arjun put his head against the leathery skin. "There's no one but each other," he said tearfully. "I must tell you this, even if it sounds weak and complaining. I am not weak, I am not complaining, I am . . . lonely," he murmured. After a long silence, he added, "Or I would be lonely without you. Because of you, I'm not lonely." Arjun began humming. He wanted the sound to give Gandiva understanding of the solace that sometimes came from the human voice, that had always come from the voice of Gauri.

Rama had been right about the war camp for elephants. It was a tumultuous place with a vast tethering area and rows of barracks and many officers, some of whom wore earrings more ornate than those of the vahinipati.

Because there was so much for Arjun to do and learn, his sense of alienation faded. With dozens of other handlers and elephants, he and Gandiva spent their days mastering formations for the battlefield and commands for wheeling in unison with two hundred other teams. All handlers had to polish their martial skills with spears, bows, and swords, then adapt them for use from the moving platform of an elephant. Such daily tasks were overseen by training sergeants, each in charge of a dozen teams.

Arjun was assigned to Vasu, a heavyset mustachioed Chalukyan. From the moment of meeting this sergeant, the boy knew he was in trouble.

"I've heard about you," Vasu said gruffly. "Do you remember Skanda? Lazy if he wasn't watched? Another of Rama's favorites!"

Arjun nodded uneasily.

"Skanda trained here. He told me you'd probably come through this camp, and here you are." The sergeant grinned unpleasantly. "You're the Brahman boy who would rather ride than walk, is that right? Rama never had good judgment about people. About elephants, yes. I admit that. But not about people." With this pronouncement the sergeant tramped away.

Arjun was therefore not surprised during training when Vasu had a contemptuous shake of the head always ready for him, a sarcastic guffaw at any mistake he made. Vasu inspected Gandiva thoroughly after each daily bath at the local river, and searched until he found a single small crease of dirt on the vast body. When the other teams left the riverbank, Arjun had to keep Gandiva in the water and scrub until his arms ached.

Vasu made bitter references to "the stupidity and deceit of recruits these days." Such pronouncements always ended with him turning to stare at Arjun. After training ended for everyone else, the sergeant ordered him to jab countless times at empty air with a sword or a lance because "you don't know how to use a weapon."

The sergeant's treatment brought Arjun the sympathy of others at the camp. In their third week there, one of the trainees sat down beside him at the evening fire. Arjun recognized him as Hari, from a village somewhere in the Deccan. They had spoken only a few times.

After a long silence Hari said, "I think it's your elephant."

Arjun turned to look at him. Hari was about his own size but perhaps five or six years older. He had a long, thin, haggard face, yet in training sessions he often smiled. Arjun knew the others liked him. "Some people

think it's because Rama was your master," Hari contin-
ued. "He was a great warrior in his time, greater than
Vasu, and everyone knows it. That could be the reason.
But I think Vasu covets the gaja you brought to camp."
Hari grinned. "Oh, yes. Your gaja is the finest here, and
everyone knows it."

"Thank you," Arjun said warily.

"Most of us think Vasu will lose," Hari declared.

"Lose?"

"The battle you're in. Don't you know you're in a
battle with him? So far you're holding on. For one thing,
you have better control of your gaja than we do of ours.
For another, you're a fine archer."

"But not good with the lance." Actually, Arjun had
improved with the lance since infantry camp.

"Good enough so you shouldn't need practice after
everyone else is done."

Arjun glanced sideways at him. "You say most of you
think Vasu will lose. Don't you think he'll win?"

"Well, I admit he's won before. In every group that
comes through this camp, he picks someone to break. He
likes to do it, and he's good at it. And this time he's
picked you." Hari paused and gazed at the fire. "But we
don't think he'll win."

"Vasu will lose," said Arjun.

"Ha! Good! That's good!" Hari laughed and
smacked one hand against the other. Getting to his feet,
he said, "That's the way, Arjun. Come have some palm
toddy with me. I know where to get it."

Arjun shook his head. "I don't drink toddy, but thank
you. And thank you for saying good things about
Gandiva." Cocking his head and looking up at Hari, he
added, "And for not saying what people really think."

"Why would I do that?"

"To give me courage. People really think Vasu will break me."

"I don't."

Arjun studied him before saying, "I believe you." Then he said, "But others believe he'll break me."

With a shrug, Hari began walking away. Then the thin young man glanced over his shoulder and called out gaily, "And they'll be wrong!"

No one ever said that Vasu was a poor teacher. In Arjun's opinion, the sergeant's understanding of elephants seemed as thorough and profound as Rama's own. For this reason Arjun listened carefully to the sergeant, while also fearing and hating him.

The boy learned, for example, that an elephant will never roll over on its rider. Even though, on command, gaja will deliver with its trunk an ankus, a rope, or a banana to someone riding on its back, it will never pull him off or reach over to another elephant and pull that rider off.

Vasu knew strange things about elephants. If you measured the distance around gaja's front foot with a rope and then doubled the length, you would get the height of gaja at the shoulder. Arjun tried it with Gandiva; it proved true. For the first time he realized how immense the foot of an elephant really was.

He learned not only from Vasu but also from the elephants themselves. At first he had seen them as animals who submitted meekly to circumstance, just as he had submitted to it when the army bought him. But now that he knew elephants better, Arjun realized they were not that compliant. They learned, one way or another, to make the most of their lives. Whether living in captivity or in the wild, they managed to enjoy whatever was possible. Elephants didn't give up, even when they gave the appearance of it. They found ways to live each day fully.

Even so, they suffered from being in the army. The time came when a half-dozen elephants had their backs fitted with heavy coats of iron mail. Such confining armor frightened or annoyed all of them at first. And then long knives were lashed to their tusks. They shuffled, turned, stamped, and trumpeted as their handlers tried in vain to calm them. At last they halted and merely fretted and showed their discomfort by snorting—all except a young bull, who kept turning and stamping. He was finally subdued and stretched between trees by ropes tied around his fore and hind legs. The tusker would keep on the coat of mail and remain stretched until he wore it without complaint.

Arjun, Hari, and others had watched this happen. They were aware that soon their own gajas would be forced to wear armor.

Hari said, "Stretching won't be needed for your gaja, Arjun. When you tell him to wear the iron coat, he'll do it." Hari sighed. "I know mine will have to be stretched."

Hari was right on both counts, but Vasu came around anyway and glowered at Arjun as he rode armored Gandiva.

"No trouble?" bellowed the sergeant.

Arjun shook his head.

"What did you do to that gaja? Tell him to wear it for your sake?" Vasu asked sarcastically.

"I told him to wear it for his own sake. That way he wouldn't be stretched."

"And you think he understood you?"

Arjun shrugged. "At least he wore the armor."

On impulse the sergeant strode over and banged on the left side of the iron coat with his ankus. The brutal clanging surprised Gandiva enough to shift and sway and thump a foreleg hard on the ground.

"Ah!" cried Vasu. Looking up at Arjun, he waved the ankus. "See that? See how wrong you are? Look at him resist!" The sergeant shook the ankus at Arjun again. "Keep that gaja in the coat of iron all afternoon. March him until sunset up and down this field."

"But—" Arjun began. "It's too hot!" It was May, the hottest month of the hottest part of the year.

"Then maybe he'll learn."

"Maybe he'll get sick—"

"Are you telling me what's right? Are you disobeying a command?" The sergeant was smacking the curved part of the ankus hook against his palm.

"Walking all day in that iron with the sun high and the heat terrible, he might die."

"Do you know more about elephants than I do, boy?"

"I know this elephant," said Arjun evenly. Then he ordered Gandiva to kneel. A dozen other mahouts watched in silent awe and confusion. Arjun was not sure what he was doing either. But he felt the need to go on.

Having dismounted, he stood facing the sergeant, who was holding the ankus chest-high. Arjun was slightly taller but lighter. I will have to fight this man, Arjun told himself. So much sweat got in his eyes that he had to rub it away with his forearm. But he stood there, feet wide, in a stance of readiness. He would not draw his own ankus until attacked.

Vasu kept glancing up nervously at the animal, who

was eyeing him.

And then the boy understood. If Arjun were hit or even threatened by the sergeant, Gandiva would surely attack. Vasu feared the powerful trunk that could lift and whirl and dash him to the ground.

Lowering the ankus, Vasu chuckled awkwardly. "You will regret this, boy."

Arjun did not reply. He took hold of Gandiva's tether, and, without another glance at Vasu, turned and led the elephant away.

Later, Arjun stood outside the vahinipati's hut, waiting to be heard. He had been summoned there by a guard.

When he entered, Arjun noticed the sergeant sitting cross-legged to the vahinipati's right. The officer was chewing betel and drinking toddy.

"What have you to say for yourself?" the officer asked brusquely.

Arjun explained his refusal to walk his elephant in the hot sun in a coat of mail. "I was afraid for him," Arjun ended.

"Afraid for him? Like a mother for its child?" asked the vahinipati, raising his eyebrows.

"Shri Vahinipati, when you made me a mahout, I repeated the words you said. I have never forgotten them: 'I serve my king by living for my gaja.' And so that is what I do."

For a few moments the officer chewed his quid thoughtfully. "Yes, I see. I believe you do." Turning to the sergeant, he said, "What do you think of that, Vasu? Have you and I forgotten our own vows to do the same? No more punishment that threatens the well-being of a gaja." Turning back to Arjun, he said, "As for you, don't be impertinent. Do as you are told. As long"—he paused and glanced at the sergeant—"as it doesn't hurt your gaja. After all, what good is a dead animal to the army?" He faced the sergeant again. "No more of that, Vasu. No more foolish and wasteful punishments. Do you hear?"

"Yes, I hear, Shri Vahinipati."

"Go, both of you, get out," the officer said in a voice of annoyance. "Only one thing matters to us. Getting ready for Harsha when he sneaks across the Narmada with his thieves. Never forget that, Vasu. Or be prepared to serve your king on foot."

Outside the tent, gripping the boy's arm, Vasu halted.

"Hear me now. I admit you won this battle. And so you'll have no more trouble from me during the rest of training. Everyone will know you humiliated me. You'll gain respect and I'll lose it. It will be common knowledge: A mere boy made a fool of the warrior Vasu." The sergeant released Arjun's arm. "But a time will come when you least expect it, when you think life is good, when you relax and bask in good fortune and believe you are strong." Vasu began smiling. "And at that time you will die. But just before dying, you will see the man who killed you." The muscular sergeant fisted his hand and thumped his chest. "You will see me."

 I I

THE HUMILIATION FOR VASU, the triumph for Arjun, and the tension between them did not last long, because the boy was sent to another camp, near the village of Ajanta. Only fifty teams were there, having been assigned from larger war camps. The mahouts were strangers to one another, so Arjun was readily accepted for what he was: a young mahout of promise, who had the rare gift of controlling his gaja by the mere nudge of a toe at the base of either ear.

Soon he became the friend of a somewhat older mahout from the northern Chalukyan capital of Nasik. Karna had a raspy, shrill voice, yet he himself seemed to enjoy listening to it because it was always in use. Exceedingly thin, Karna would sit as straight as an arrow, weaving the fingers of his bony hands together and just as quickly unweaving them, his eyes half closed. Having assumed this portentous attitude, he would then describe all sorts of things to the village boy. Karna had a keen memory for details. By using it extravagantly, he gave the younger mahout a vivid sense of tumultuous life in a big city. Unweaving his fingers for a moment, he ticked off on them the special inhabitants of Nasik: snake charmers, wandering musicians, craftsmen who made conch-shell bangles, stall vendors offering garlands, scented powders, and sandalwood for sale. He talked of the dangers of life there—thugs after dark and housebreakers with rope ladders. A man accused of crime had his hand thrust into a pot containing a cobra. If he lived, he was set free. Karna had known such a lucky man, his own brother.

Rolling his eyes, Karna spoke of beautiful women praying in the temples. They were bedecked with hanging ropes of pearls and wore eye salve of the blackest powder and anklets with tinkling bells. Seen almost daily in Nasik were high officials of the court, often accompanied by long-robed priests and astrologers carrying staffs topped with half-moons of burnished copper and by guards banging drums to clear the crowded street. With his own eyes he had witnessed the comings and goings of the Chief of the King's Harem and the Officer of the Royal Household and the Commissary General.

Pleased with Arjun's look of wonder, Karna continued. "I have also seen the Lion's Seat—throne of King Pulakeshin. Forty men carry the Lion's Seat through Nasik streets to celebrate feast days. It's gold and studded with gems, and the four feet of it are shaped like a lion's. Once I saw the king himself sitting in it. I tell you, he has the look of a ruler. Eyes that burn, thick arms, a chest broad enough for two men." Proud of his knowledge and experience, Karna added with a satisfied smile, "Of course, Arjun, you haven't seen much."

"Not yet," the boy confessed.

"Stay in this army, you'll see the world. Do you know why you'll see the world?" When Arjun said nothing, Karna entwined his fingers emphatically. "Because our king will conquer it!" Having made such a pronouncement, Karna pursed his lips, narrowed his eyes, separated his hands, and placed them on his knees like a Brahman teacher. "Now then. Let me find out, boy, if you understand what you're looking at. What have you noticed about the gajas brought here?"

Arjun considered the question for a few moments. "Every one of them is big and strong, very big and strong."

Karna nodded. "Bigger, stronger, faster than others. The finest in the Deccan. Well, what do you make of it? Only fifty of them. Brought here from other camps. Well, Arjun? Tell me."

The boy frowned uncertainly.

"Then let me explain. The officers have something in mind."

"What do you mean?"

Karna shook his head. "It's not my place to know exactly what they have in mind. But I think we've been chosen for something special."

A week later, Karna's speculation was confirmed by the visit to camp of the gajadhyaksa, superintendent of elephants. This official assembled the mahouts and told them what they already knew: Elephants were important in battle. A stout, handsomely robed, elderly man, the gajadhyaksa then lectured the fifty handlers on elephant virtues that they most likely appreciated as much or more than he did. "Gaja should breathe vigorously and trumpet loudly," he declared. "He must have large pores in his skin and long, thick ears and heavy legs and good color. Only that sort of superior beast is now here. Along with you, the best mahouts in the army. You have been selected for something new. You will form the first elephant vanguard." He paused to let this declaration have its effect. "When our king meets the invader, the elephant vanguard will lead him!"

Later, at the evening campfire, Arjun noticed that Karna was seated alone beyond the flickering light. Arjun went over and crouched beside his friend, who continued to gaze sulkily into the night air. When Arjun asked what was wrong, Karna turned to grimace at him.

"You know nothing, Arjun, absolutely nothing. There has always been a vanguard force of archers. They always go first. They shoot a few volleys, then retreat to safety. Until now, the elephantry has come behind them. Do you understand me, Arjun? Until now the archers have softened up the enemy with their arrows. Only then do the elephants go forward." He paused for emphasis.

"Now we are the vanguard."

"That means we're special."

Karna shook his head. "It means," he said, "fifty elephants will charge Harsha's front line without arrows preparing the way. It means," he concluded grimly, "we'll soon be entering the next life."

"But why would the generals want to sacrifice us?"

"You don't understand, do you? Harsha has always bragged about his elephant corps. So our king wants to prove he too has powerful elephants and brave men. We'll be sacrificed to the king's vanity and pride."

Arjun had never heard anyone speak critically of the king. Karna showed the blunt candor of a Kshatriya, although he surely wasn't one of them. Arjun admired his friend's outspokenness while hoping it didn't get him into trouble.

During the rainy season, officers assigned to the new force strived hard to get it into fighting shape. Bowmen and lancers, trained elsewhere, were brought in and placed with individual teams. Beside its mahout, each elephant carried two bowmen and two lancers in a howdah, a large wooden box lashed with heavy rope to the animal's back. Much time was spent in accustoming elephants to a full-out charge while carrying so much weight. What amazed Arjun was the speed at which they could traverse a field. The thick circular slabs of their feet seemed almost detached from their wobbly legs, creating a chaotic-looking, ungainly trot. Yet the considerable distance they covered so rapidly was proof of their quickness and power.

A camupati, usually in charge of an army's complement of two hundred elephants, arrived in camp to lead the vanguard of fifty. The turbaned colonel wore quilted trousers, patterned with red and blue stripes, and a white tunic embroidered on both shoulders with a golden wild boar—the Chalukyan coat of arms. The sound made by the camupati preceded his appearance; a dozen copper rings on his arms and legs were filled with rattling pebbles. Karna learned that he was the king's cousin, a reckless warrior always eager to prove himself in battle.

"He is bad for us," Karna noted with a disapproving shake of his head. "Such a man will lead us to destruction. We are doomed. Fate has played us a trick."

Arjun went away thinking about Karna's grim prediction and sense of hopelessness. What would his master say? Ah, that was easy. Rama would say, "You are not responsible for what your commander does. You are responsible only for yourself. You cannot tell fate what to do. You cannot question what has no answer. You can only do one thing with confidence—your duty. Do it and you will be at peace." In accepting his master's imagined counsel, Arjun began to feel a deep sense of calm. Never again would he listen seriously to Karna's pessimism. Complaint and grumbling had nothing to do with soldiering, with duty, with honor, or with peace of mind.

Even so, their friendship continued. Arjun tolerated his friend's need to feel superior, because the talkative mahout from Nasik was also good-natured. If Karna predicted doom, he also told entertaining stories and shared anything good that came his way.

One morning when heavy rain prevented training, Karna suggested a visit to the hilly ravines near Ajanta. For hundreds of years Buddhist temples had been carved into the side of a horseshoe-shaped cliff there. It wasn't far away, only an hour's walk from camp. Such an excursion would break the monotony of raindrops beating down on the thatched roof of their barracks.

So the two friends slogged out to the Ajanta caves. They climbed a granite stairway that led up the cliff from a whitewater stream below. Karna had come here previously because he was a Buddhist. Until now Arjun had never met a Buddhist—there hadn't been any in his Hindu village. The local priest had called Buddhists misguided and foolish. Even so, in the magnificent reign of King Ashoka, centuries earlier, devotion to the Buddha had been far more popular than devotion to Shiva and Vishnu. Today only a few people in the Deccan still called themselves Buddhists. The village priest used to claim that in some parts of the land Buddhism was prohibited, its temples burned, its followers executed.

Arjun said nothing about that but maintained a respectful silence as Karna, ever talkative, expounded on the life of a Buddhist monk. For his only possessions a monk had one begging bowl, one water pot, three pieces of patternless cloth, a needle, some thread, and a staff. He ate one meal daily. This came before noon and consisted of scraps placed in his begging bowl. He could not labor for profit or take food that came from the loss of any life.

Arjun wondered if such harsh discipline accounted for the faith's present lack of popularity. Karna seemed to think so. After confessing that he rarely lived up to the Buddha's precepts, Karna charged that few devotees ever did. Waving his hand upward as they navigated the slippery rocks, Karna said, "And yet temples are still dug from the cliff and people still pray in them." He glanced at Arjun and muttered bitterly, "Your Shiva and Vishnu and the rest of your gods can try, but they'll never stop our devotion to the Buddha."

Arjun shrugged. It was not a discussion that interested him. "Maybe they don't try" was all he had to say. When Karna glowered at him, he added, "Maybe they think devotion to the Buddha is no different from devotion to themselves."

If Karna considered that possibility, he didn't admit it but lapsed into uncharacteristic silence. They arrived soon at the first cave. It had been hollowed into the shape of a spacious hall with rows of pillars. Arjun could not imagine how much rock had been clawed from the cliffside to make this temple, but in his mind's eye he saw an endless line of bearers carrying stone-filled baskets on their heads.

A wizened man in the saffron robe of a monk sat at the entrance. He gave them flares that they lit at a little fire inside. Holding their torches, they walked into the rock-cut interior to stare at walls and ceiling covered with paintings. In the back was a man-sized granite image of a seated Buddha. Two people were prostrating themselves in front of it. Another sat with hands steepled, lips moving soundlessly.

Then the visiting mahouts turned to look at an old man in a loincloth who, by torchlight, was painting on a wall. Quietly they squatted and watched. Growing impatient after a while, Karna suggested that they leave. Arjun agreed, but only after extracting a promise from his friend to return the next day.

They came back the next three days and watched the artist at work.

First he covered a section of wall with cow dung mixed with chopped straw. Then, after smoothing and leveling it, he coated the surface with fine white clay. To this ground he applied cinnabar red and lamp black and burnt brick and various tints taken from local minerals. The oval face of a man began to appear, his olive skin opalescent, his dark brows arched like drawn bows, his full lips as red as chilis. As if from the depths of the sea, his shoulders materialized, then his arms. Clouds and flowers and birds, thus far briefly sketched, came into view around the emerging prince.

"I'm tired of watching," Karna grumbled. "Aren't you?"

Arjun shook his head.

"Why not?" Karna demanded. "We do nothing but sit in a gloomy cave and watch him mix colors with a knife and then brush them on the wall so carefully and slowly, ah! so very carefully and so very slowly that I nearly fall asleep. If you were a religious boy I might understand, but you're not even a Buddhist. Why do you like to watch?"

"I don't know," Arjun said truthfully. After a pause he added, "There's nothing but a blank wall. Then a face appears and other things. What was not there before is now there. And what is there is not like anything else. It seems as if the world's been changed."

Karna shook his head disdainfully. "Well, don't expect me to come back."

"All right, I'll come alone," said Arjun. He would have done so but for a break in the rains. Work in the camp commenced again. Soon other officers were coming for inspections, and rumors of war multiplied, and preparations for departure began in earnest. Arjun never again saw the caves of Ajanta.

I 2

AN IMPERIAL ORDER ARRIVED.

Within a day the elephant vanguard left camp and headed for an assembly area not many days' travel away. As they rode in single file toward their destination, Arjun from his high vantage point had a sweeping view of the Deccan's landscape: green fields, gentle hills, and lazy streams beneath a depthless expanse of blue sky. There was always someone sitting by the roadside in the shade of a tree, motionless, as if awaiting destiny. Storage pots lined the walls of villages. A round black pot sat in front of a small hut with a tiny doorway. Arjun dreamt of that pot on the first night of their journey. He dreamt of filling it at a well, again, again, and again. He was alone in the village, filling a pot with water.

After returning the next night, this dream of isolation never entered his sleep again, perhaps because the elephant vanguard had reached camp, a hectic and boisterous place where three entire senas were being mobilized for combat. Assembled there already were more than five hundred elephants, four thousand horses, and fifty thousand foot soldiers. The area teemed with shouting and neighing and trumpeting and the squeal of turning wheels and the clang of metal. There was little space for privacy here, no space for dreams to occupy.

Arjun learned from Karna that a nearby range of hills was honeycombed with temples devoted to Buddha and Shiva. There wasn't time, however, to visit them. Each day new units arrived to find a place for bivouacking. Foot soldiers set up their tents in the middle of camp, while cavalrymen corralled their horses on a plain to the west and mahouts hobbled their elephants in woodland to the east.

The king and his courtiers were still to come, but vast stables in the midst of camp foretold his eventual arrival. The smoke of resin kept mosquitoes away from animals belonging to the court. Roosters, ducks, and monkeys were introduced into the stables; they ate insects that otherwise would burrow into the flesh of royal horse and elephant. Peacocks strutted in the stable yard to frighten away snakes. Meanwhile, a phalanx of blacksmiths added to the dust and grime by burning heaps of wood for charcoal.

Daily arrivals had turned the camp into a village, then a town, and now a city, so that it began to resemble the tumultuous Nasik of Karna's account. Women journeyed out from the capital to set up tents on the outskirts of camp. A quarrelsome rabble of vendors also appeared, ready to sell anything to the bored troops. Farmers streamed into the neighborhood, bringing carts loaded with rice and lentils for sale to the commissariat.

Meanwhile, outfitters worked hard to finish equipping the army for a full-scale campaign. Along with repairing broadaxes, lances, and swords, they forged nets and plates of iron for both man and beast. Other armorers fashioned shields and helmets for noblemen, incising the metal surface with images of the Chalukyan boar.

Generals continued to plan strategy under the supreme command of the Mahasenapati. Also in camp—his arrival acknowledged by kettledrums—was the bhatashvapati, lord of the army. According to Karna, this warrior belonged to the royal family and wielded more power than anyone aside from the king.

Although horsemen despised the elephantry, a few of them treated Arjun with good-natured civility. They invited him to their encampment, where he watched them train. A cavalryman carried a whip, rode bareback, and chiefly controlled his mount by pulling the reins attached to ivory prongs fitted into a piece of stitched rawhide circling the horse's mouth. The cavalrymen wore breastplates and yellow turbans, and most of them were good enough with the bow that they could hit a target two hundred paces away at a full gallop. They taught Arjun a few things about horses. Bad ones had long teeth, eye sockets too large for their heads, an absence of firm whorls of hair on their flanks. Good horses were narrow-necked and tight-mouthed and crazy-eyed. The cavalrymen joked with the young mahout, urging him to get reassigned to a horse. After all, horses were easier to control than elephants, less easily frightened, and less likely to run amok when confused or angry.

One of the cavalrymen had nothing good to say about either horses or elephants. He was a weathered fellow, bowlegged and irascible, who predicted that the day would come when animals weren't used in warfare. Even though his companions scoffed, he held steadfastly to his opinion. The only reason to have a chariot drawn by horses, he maintained, was so the king could sleep in it the night before battle, weapons beside him, as Chalukyan kings had done since time began.

This cavalryman was, like Karna, critical of his superiors and even made fun of the ashvadhyaksa, superintendent of horses, "who seats a horse worse than any man I have ever seen. If he falls off his mount in battle, I won't be surprised." The cavalryman also reminded Arjun of the infantry sergeant who had once told him to forget animals and become an archer.

That very sergeant now appeared in camp, waving up at Arjun from a line of passing infantry. "You, boy! Remember me? You should have stayed with the archers. Did you think you'd be above everyone else, looking down?" Glancing over his shoulder, he called out, to the amusement of his comrades, "I hear they've got something special waiting for you elephant people in the vanguard. Soon you'll be lying on the ground looking up!"

Later that day, while scrubbing Gandiva's hide with a bunch of coarse leaves, Arjun noticed his old vahinipati striding toward him. The officer acknowledged Arjun's respectful bow with a nod so vigorous that it made his ringlets bounce. "The colonel gave me a report on you," the vahinipati said. He waited for that to sink in. "The truth is, Arjun, you have not shamed me." The vahinipati smiled faintly. "May the gods be with you when the charge begins."

The very next day, while leading Gandiva down to the riverbank for a drink, the boy met his old friend Hari from war camp. After they embraced and talked a while, Hari became suddenly grave. He stared thoughtfully at elephants wading in the shallow river. Their trunks were tossing streams of water over their glistening backs. "When I heard you were in the vanguard," he said without looking at Arjun, "I was sorry."

"Don't be sorry."

"I don't want to lose such a good friend." Hari turned with a wan smile. "Oh, you'll have your share of glory, if that's what you want."

"I don't ask for it."

"Maybe you'll get it anyway. Unless the vanguard panics and runs."

"Do you expect that?"

"Some do. The whole army is betting. The enemy will break the vanguard. The vanguard will break the enemy. Of course, the cavalry is against you, but then they hate elephants."

"And you, Hari? How do you bet?"

"On you." Hari laughed, tears in his eyes. "Of course. What else? On you, Arjun. On you!"

To the boy it seemed as if the whole world was congregating here, because later that day he noticed Skanda grinning at him from a crowd of soldiers gathered around a field kitchen.

The tall mahout was eating rice from a banana leaf. "So here we have Rama's pride and glory!" he called out, gesturing for Arjun to come over.

After a moment's hesitation, the boy did—out of curiosity about his master. "Where is Rama? Is he here?"

"Rama's still in Paithan. Sick," claimed the older mahout, scooping up rice in his fingers. "They say he won't see another rainy season."

Arjun's face must have shown his distress, because Skanda laughed. "*You* look like the one who's sick. Well, I don't blame you. I'd be sick too if they put me in the vanguard. Nothing but a wall of spears facing you, boy. Nothing but a hail of arrows." Skanda swept his fingers across the banana leaf. "But it's a shame to lose such a fine gaja," he said, shoving the last few grains of rice into his mouth. "I saw you on him yesterday. He's a good one."

A week later, with the arrival of the king and his retinue, the vast array was ready to depart for the north and a confrontation with Harsha's army from the land of Vardhana.

Arjun was up before daylight, tending to Gandiva. He

painted a tilaki mark with red kumkum powder on the elephant's forehead. Many of the mahouts did this. For some, it was a symbol of the third eye that opens with enlightenment. For others, the crimson circle stood for the god within. For Arjun, the red dot made his gaja even more fierce-looking. While applying the powder, he leaned close to Gandiva and whispered, "I have learned much from you. Now I hope you teach me courage when we face the enemy."

He fed and watered Gandiva before eating his own morning meal. As far as the eye could see, the countryside was dotted with cooking fires. They created the look of ground mist, their smoke gathering in blue streams that slanted away and drifted into the gardens of outlying villages.

Before sunlight reached the treetops, a loud call for departure was sounded by a multitude of kettledrums struck with mallets, soon joined by the shrill blare of horns and conch shells. Along the length and breadth of the huge encampment there was a ponderous awakening, as men, horses, and elephants got ready to leave.

Camp sweepers dug out tent poles, and others rolled up the tent hides for storage in leather bags. Kitchen helpers gathered up cooking utensils and shoved them into sacks for loading in bullock carts. Donkeys, tied together in a long single line, carried foodstuffs for the commissariat. Infantry units fell into loosely defined squadrons and headed out at the command of their marshaling officers. Horses of the officers were fitted with harnesses hung with bells; whistles used for signaling were tied to the bridles. Footmen led the horses ridden by harem women; servants trotted alongside the animals' flanks to fan the women with fly whisks and hold long-stemmed umbrellas over their heads. Neighborhood onlookers lined the way northward to watch the noisy procession wind slowly from sight, leaving in its wake an enveloping cloud of dust.

Aside from cavalry outriders, the first segment of the great force was made up of field kitchens drawn by oxen. Mangy dogs, barking and snapping at their legs, scampered away yelping when rocks were thrown at them.

The main army was led by a captain called the nayaka; he was selected for this post because of experience in former campaigns. Four horses abreast pulled his chariot. Later, when nearing a place of possible encounter with the foe, he would put the army into the makara—crocodile—formation to avoid surprise attack. At the outset, however, the army followed a simple plan: Two columns of infantry were flanked by cavalry and elephantry, and a baggage train brought up the rear. The king, his harem, and his generals rode midway in the line of march. In the royal chariot drawn by a team of six dapple-gray stallions, the tall, somber king stood next to the driver. He wore a boarskin mantle with peacock feathers trailing from the shoulders. His hair was long, plaited into a thick strand that reached the small of his back.

Having a good view from his perch on Gandiva, Arjun could see loops of gold dangling from the royal ears. They reminded him of his first look at the vahinipati who had selected him for the elephantry and changed his life.

The legions of Chalukya headed due north, straight for the Narmada River, where Harsha would probably cross into their territory. Because the expedition could travel no farther than ten miles a day, it was two weeks before

Chalukyan outriders saw the serpentine Narmada glittering among hills.

It took only another day to establish Harsha's whereabouts. Scouts located his main force just south of Ujjain, a week's march away. The invader had taken and looted the old city.

"Ah, I have always wanted to see Ujjain," Karna told Arjun when they heard where Harsha was. "The great poet Kalidasa wrote about Ujjain. He said it was a town fallen from heaven to bring heaven to earth. He said its palaces were like mountains and its houses like palaces. The great Chandragupta ruled from there, and so did Ashoka. They left gardens and ponds unmatched in the world. Why should a brute like Harsha enjoy such beauty? Why shouldn't Ujjain belong to our king?" For a moment Karna seemed to forget that his own life must be risked for his king to possess the famous old town.

The next morning the Chalukyan army assembled on the south bank of the Narmada. The crossing took two days. To ford the Narmada, which at this time of year was placid and fairly shallow, many elephants brought planks down to the riverbank and laid them in place to build a temporary bridge. The vanguard didn't take part in this operation. The camupati kept his precious vanguard elephants on the south bank, where they could watch others labor. Arjun noticed someone waving at him from one of the working elephants. Squinting, he saw that it was Vasu, grinning and waving as if they were old friends. Directing his gaja to go nearer, the sergeant finally halted within shouting distance and raised his ankus high.

"If you live, boy," he called out, "remember my promise! When you least expect it!" He turned the gaja and went back to work on the bridge.

After reaching the river's north bank, Pulakeshin's army skirted the little town of Mandlesir and set forth in the makara order of march: ranks of light infantry marching ahead; files of heavy infantry surrounding the king, his harem, and his generals in the center; elephants, including the vanguard, coming next; the sluggish baggage train bringing up the rear; and columns of horses patrolling the wings.

Scouts rode in frequently with updated reports on Harsha's movement. He was heading in a leisurely way for the town of Mandlesir. Suddenly Pulakeshin broke off his march northward and circled to the west. That night there was grumbling among some of the younger mahouts, who liked to boast of their eagerness to fight. "Have we come all this way to run from the enemy?" But with a wink Karna assured them of the king's good sense. "None of the senapatis, not even the mahasenapati, is more cunning than he is. With him leading us, we might have a chance." He added with sudden gloom, "Our only chance."

The next day they headed north a few miles, then curved eastward and turned south to approach Mandlesir again. Scouts reported that the enemy was within striking distance. Harsha's army, considerably larger than Pulakeshin's, had pitched camp in front of the river town. They were in no hurry to ford the river, but ate and danced and foraged in the countryside.

So by letting Harsha reach the river unopposed, Pulakeshin had blocked his opponent from a potential escape into the surrounding hills. Harsha's back was to the Narmada, whereas Pulakeshin could retreat if necessary.

That night the Chalukyans drank toddy and sang

merry songs. Clearly their king had given them an advantage in the coming battle. But Arjun took no comfort from it. In the evening's final sunlight he had seen a papery flash of wings just above his head. Was the flight of that bird an omen? Would his soul fly away tomorrow? Just like that? Like a bird? A sudden motion—and gone? Might he then find Gauri? Would their souls meet again?

On the eve of battle every elephant team stayed close together. One of the archers on the Gandiva team must have seen something in the young mahout's face, because he scooted over and sat beside Arjun. "In the old days before battle," he began, "a little elephant was shaped out of earth from an anthill—the anthill being sacred to Lord Shiva. Then a priest dedicated the little statue to Shiva on a mountaintop or in a field with only one tree. This was supposed to numb the senses of the enemy."

When Arjun said nothing, the old man continued. "We common soldiers drink here, but over there, in the royal tents, they're saying fancy prayers to their armor and swords. It's what the highborn do. They'll purify the umbrellas held over the king's wives and purify the drums and honor any other fool thing they can think of. But listen, young mahout, to what I'm saying. I have been twenty years in the army, so I know. And it's something you must know." He touched his lips as if telling a secret. "Have you ever watched a mouse get caught by a cat?"

Arjun shook his head.

"The mouse squirms to get free, it wiggles like a worm, it fights and tussles, and then suddenly lets go. It goes limp, just like that, although it's still alive. It surrenders to death as if it were no more difficult than falling asleep. That's what a man must do in battle, when he feels himself dying. He must give in like the mouse and everything will be fine." He patted Arjun's knee. "If it comes to that, young mahout, relax and let it happen. Then you go with dignity."

Later that night, in his bedroll under the stars, Arjun heard his comrades around him, their coughing and snoring and outcry from nightmares. He had never talked much to the members of his team, because they formed a unit apart from him and Gandiva. Yet the old archer had put into his mind the idea of a mouse dying, of the wise and simple way a mouse died.

He heard a voice nearby—Karna was calling softly to him. "Are you awake? I am. I can't sleep. I'm thinking of tomorrow. Not that I'm afraid. No, not at all, because the king will see to it we win, even if his generals make mistakes. I fear our camupati will be much too reckless. But what would the Buddha think of such killing? When we shouldn't eat living things, how can we kill them? These questions bother me, Arjun. But I'm not afraid, no, not at all. Never think so." He rolled over and soon he was breathing heavily. Karna was asleep.

But Arjun couldn't sleep for thinking of the mouse. It occurred to him that a mouse was the vehicle of Ganapati, the elephant-headed god. Shiva had his bull to ride and Vishnu his bird and Varuna his crocodile, and for other gods and goddesses there were the swan, the buffalo, the deer, and the goat, but none was stranger than the mouse who carried Ganapati, the potbellied god, the fattest of them all. Ganapati was also was the Remover of Obstacles, a scribe, and a thinker. No wonder such a god chose for his mount the wise little mouse.

What if tomorrow a wound left him dying? Arjun asked himself. If it came to that, he'd struggle like the captured mouse, but in the last moments he'd give up his life without a murmur, respectful of fate.

In the morning, when officers came around, they laughed and joked with one another and seemed almost eager to die in battle. After all, a true Kshatriya felt it was a disgrace to die peacefully in bed.

At infantry camp Arjun had listened to soldiers discuss in their own way what it meant to die on the battlefield. Such an honorable death released a warrior's ancestors from past moral debts and enabled them to proceed toward God. According to the *Vamana Purana*, claimed a soldier who could read, a hero dying in battle was escorted directly to heaven by celestial nymphs.

Arjun kept thinking of the mouse while he and his team of soldiers lashed the howdah to Gandiva's back. He was still thinking of it when the rattling of pebbles in copper armlets heralded the arrival of the swaggering camupati. The officer assembled the elephant vanguard for some final prayers, which were chanted by a Brahman priest. Arjun settled for a few moments into the memory of his own village priest and his Brahman family—father, uncle, cousins, men who wore their hair in topknots and displayed the sacred cotton thread of their class.

He watched now as a Brahman ceremony was conducted. Camphor was burned, ashes dispensed among the worshippers, water sprinkled on their heads, and an offering of flowers made at a makeshift altar. Stiltedly the priest announced he was going to intone slokas 9 to 18, chapter 269 of the sacred text of the *Agni Purana*, devoted to the worship of the elephant: "O the great powerful! You are the holy carriage of Vishnu! You are gigantic and possess speed like the wind. Indefatigable, ferocious. Killer of the enemies of the gods. Let Indra be on your back to protect you from harm." Then to Shiva the priest raised his hands in supplication: "O Great God Daskhinamurti O Nilakantha O Mahakala O Bhairava! You are always victorious! You destroy the enemy! Hear our prayers O Shiva O Shiva O Lord O Shiva!"

Nearby a war drum was being ritually bathed and worshipped with loud chanting and prayer. None of this had an effect on Arjun. He was thinking only of two things: Rama's steadfast belief in the truth of duty, and the wisdom of a caught mouse.

Elsewhere, war elephants were being draped with coats of mail and their tusks fitted with long swords. No such armor and weapons would be used by elephants in the vanguard, because for them the speed of attack must prevail over safety and power. The same principle held for the mahouts and soldiers in the howdahs too, for unlike those in the regular elephantry they could not wear heavy mail. The camupati insisted that they use only the quilted cotton and leather vests of light infantry for protection. "You will not weigh down the gajas by wearing masses of iron. You will give a lean appearance in the charge. You will not look like motionless rock statues!" he had told them. Many of the mahouts were now drinking toddy and giving it to their gajas from buckets. The elephants sucked up the heady liquor with their trunks, blew it into their mouths, and snorted loudly. Some of the mahouts were close to reeling. Officers admonished them to let the toddy be.

Marking Gandiva's forehead with a tilaki dot, Arjun turned to Karna, who was lifting a goat bladder filled with toddy to his mouth. "Good luck, my friend."

"Good luck, my friend," Karna repeated with a smile, then drank. With a grimace he added, "We'll need it today."

 **I 3**

A FEW HOURS LATER, emerging suddenly from a ravine, the Chalukyan army marched across the rocky plain that fronted the town of Mandlesir. Harsha's own scouts had already reported to him, so his forces were deploying into a defensive alignment before the Deccan rival appeared.

The Chalukyan formation had been given the name "vajra"—thunderbolt—by the bhatashvapati, lord of the army. This was to celebrate the innovation of an elephant vanguard. Behind the vanguard, alone and on foot—such a show of bravery was traditional—came the nayaka, who held the Chalukyan standard up high, rippling in a light breeze. When the elephant charge began, he would give this flag to a bearer, draw his sword, mount a chariot, and lead the main body's attack. Behind this solitary officer stood two ranks of archers and behind them two ranks of elephants shining in armor, their soldier-filled howdahs rolling like ships in an ocean swell. Next came an array of heavy infantry, many thousands, effectively surrounding the center where the king would remain throughout the battle. Pulakeshin the Second must be protected at all costs, so only half the heavy infantry was available for attack, the other half acting as his bodyguard. In such warfare, if a side lost its king, it lost the battle and must retire immediately or dishonor the king's name. Bringing up the rear was light infantry, composed mostly of recruits and mercenaries. On the wings, flanking the main force, were roving squadrons of cavalry.

As the vajra moved into position, Arjun looked to either side of the front rank. Between one elephant and the next, spaced about fifty feet apart, waited a score of horsemen. Acting as a decoy, they would initiate the charge by galloping full speed toward the enemy line. At the last moment they planned to swerve away and let the elephants attack alone.

The young mahout noticed that Gandiva was already carrying his head high, his ears held straight out, stiffly, evincing his awareness of combat to come. Elephants could see best to the sides; their vision forward was unreliable unless they carried their heads low. During a charge, with heads high, they couldn't scan at a low angle. That meant they could not clearly see the foe until moments before reaching the enemy line. Such poor eyesight would surely help them concentrate during the charge. They wouldn't see the lances, eight feet long, raised up to skewer them as they hurtled forward. But surely Gandiva and his comrades had already smelled their counterparts over there—elephants brought from the Kalinga forest, perhaps a thousand strong.

From behind him Arjun heard the musicians banging drums, both large and small, and clanging cymbals together, and blowing conch shells and horns. Turning for a last glance over his shoulder, he saw banners flapping at the head of each infantry unit. From the king's chariot flew the white boar emblem. Seeing the royal pennant gave him a surge of pride, and for an instant he imagined Rama there beside him. He exchanged smiles with the old veteran archer.

Yet Arjun's tongue was so dry he might have walked all day through a desert. Under his thighs he felt the great animal's warm hide pulsing, as if Gandiva's heart was already pumping blood fiercely in the excitement of a charge. Arjun leaned forward and caressed the leathery skin while he looked across the plain at the troops of Vardhana. All along the front line were bamboo long-bows almost as tall as the archers who held them. He also had glimpses of the infantry ranked behind them. It was too far away to see their eyes, but not so far that he couldn't see their weapons and armor: iron-pointed pikes, tapered wooden maces, three-pronged lances, two-handed slashing swords, leather and plate vests, padded helmets, cane shields.

Abruptly, from the midst of bristling troops, appeared a single elephant that wore a ceremonial headdress with eye holes and long colorful tassels. On its back rode a tall figure resplendent in a white robe, on his head a chaplet of white flowers.

Arjun didn't have to be told that this was King Harsha or that the elephant was Darpashata, known far and wide as the royal favorite. He judged Darpashata to be a fine animal, but no finer than Gandiva.

Back and forth the king rode in front of his troops, whipping up their spirits by waving his sword in the clear morning air. Then, without warning, he turned and headed Darpashata toward the Chalukyan lines.

Within shouting distance, King Harsha stopped and made a funnel of his hands to bellow out a taunt: "If I don't clear the earth of you, I should hurl my sinful self into flames fed by rivers of hot oil!" Trotting back to his own lines, Harsha reentered them like a man vanishing into a thick forest, then took his regal place among the bodyguards. Getting off Darpashata, he sat in a splendid chariot under an umbrella adorned with rubies and sapphires. Every man in both armies knew its name: Abhoga. This renowned umbrella had shaded the king on many expeditions of conquest throughout the north.

Because of his restricted position with the river at his back, Harsha had to sacrifice any hope of attacking and rely solely on defense. With this constraint in mind, he had decided on a stolid old formation, the suci. It consisted of a front rank of archers, then alternating rows of elephantry and infantry, and finally horsemen in the rear. It was more cautious than the Chalukyan generals might expect after hearing Harsha's arrogant taunt.

Arjun was glad his own king did not make a show of exhorting the troops. It meant that King Pulakeshin put his trust in them, quietly, confidently. When a rapid roll of the kettledrums began, signaling the charge, Arjun yelled with all his might in a frenzy of pent-up emotion, part anticipation and part fury and part joy because something beyond imagining was about to happen.

From his chariot a few paces in front of the elephant vanguard, the camupati, its leader, waved his sword several times. The cavalry surged ahead, followed by elephants worked into a trot by their mahouts.

The charge had begun.

The distance between Arjun and the first rank of archers was not much longer than many of the practice fields where he had trained, yet it seemed as if each step Gandiva took didn't take them closer to the enemy. Arjun felt that the plain was unrolling away from him as fast as they traversed it, that Gandiva would never get them from here to there. He had the odd impulse to turn and question the old veteran archer in the howdah just behind him—Is this fear I am feeling? But then he saw something ahead that froze him to the swaying back of the elephant. The rank of archers had taken one step forward, then reached into the quivers fastened to their right hips.

Although his sight jittered from the springy ride, Arjun watched in horror as the bowmen did what he himself had done many times: They lowered their heads while fitting arrow to bowstring, then raised their heads while drawing the bow and aiming upward to loose the first volley.

Bending forward, Arjun stretched out against the elephant's neck, just behind the jutting brows of the massive head. He awaited a humming sound; it came a second later. Behind him someone cried out, but Arjun didn't turn. Instead he raised up and looked forward. Archers were lowering their heads again, so again he splayed out against Gandiva. Another sighing noise came from overhead, and with his face bouncing against the elephant he saw with one unsteady eye a throng of arrows speeding so close overhead that he might have reached up and touched them. The spearhead force of Chalukyan cavalry was returning from its sham charge, galloping back between the elephants. Arjun noticed the driverless horses of the camupati's chariot aimlessly turning—the brave colonel and his driver, far ahead, must have been killed.

Arjun took another look forward. The enemy archers were getting close enough for him to see their eyes, staring wildly. They lowered their heads again, but many heads were erratically bobbing. The sight of elephants bearing down on them was causing the bowmen to lose their discipline.

Rama had always claimed that elephants smell fear. They must have smelled it now, because high, frenzied trumpeting began among the charging elephants. A bloodlust trumpeting. Arjun shouted happily when he saw the line of frightened bowmen suddenly crumble and scatter. Overhead came another shower of arrows, this time traveling from his own lines. Without turning to confirm it, he knew that Chalukyan archers, having shot a volley, were running thirty paces ahead. They'd halt there, draw their bows, fire again, and go forward another thirty paces.

Arjun had reached the enemy's foremost rank. He felt a jolt, another, another, before realizing that Gandiva had either trampled bowmen underfoot or kicked them aside. All around him was the sound of metal disks whirling through the air, of bows twanging, of rocks from slings whistling, and the terrible sound of men crying out in pain. Arjun went blindly on, hearing behind him the oncoming charge of the main elephantry. He felt Gandiva surge one way, then another, tossing his trunk and sluing his feet from side to side as he bludgeoned anyone in his path. Glancing around, Arjun was appalled to see many of the vanguard elephants going down from arrow and lance wounds. But not Gandiva! he thought, nudging the great beast forward with his toes. And not some of the others in the vanguard. By their headlong charge, they had broken through the first line of defense. Ahead was a rank of infantry, which flowed away from the advancing elephants like waves from the shore. Yet arrows were flying from its midst and lances were thrust backward by fleeing men. Arjun saw one of the enemy halt, leap sideways, and swipe at a passing elephant with a long, sickle-like weapon. With a swinging motion like that of cutting wheat, he struck the hind leg, hamstringing the beast so that it crumpled with a high-pitched scream of anguish. Arjun knew this elephant and the mahout who toppled over its head to the ground. An enemy soldier pierced the mahout's chest with a lance.

As Gandiva plunged into the midst of the enemy, Arjun saw what he had been expecting all along: Harsha's famed elephant corps, which had been sandwiched between infantry ranks. What he had not expected was their hesitation and apparent confusion. The sudden reckless charge of their foe had unnerved them as they waited in a stationary position. Many of them, panicking, raised their tails like wart hogs, turned precipitously around, and lumbered off toward the town of Mandlesir and the Narmada River.

Straight ahead of him Arjun saw the gaudily decorated favorite of Harsha in the act of escaping. Darpashata's mahout was desperately jabbing an ankus into its neck, trying to escape the Chalukyan onslaught. But Gandiva reached the royal beast before it could maneuver out of the way. Arjun heard the ripping entry of Gandiva's tusk into Darpashata's left rear leg, the wounded animal's squeal of pain, the sucking sound when a foot of ivory was withdrawn from bone and gristle.

A gasp of horror went up from Harsha's men as they saw their king's elephant crippled. Trumpeting in victory, Gandiva raised his trunk high, even as a trio of arrows struck it. Arjun felt a sharp pain in his right thigh. Looking down, he saw the feathered shaft of an arrow sticking from his leg. For a moment he felt weak enough to faint; then, gripping the neck rope, he held on as Gandiva bolted forward into a melee of men and elephants. Arjun knew he must keep going in spite of the pain, just like a mouse caught in the jaws of a cat. In front of his misted eyes passed images of men fighting. Bearded men wearing necklaces of beads were wielding swords with both hands; other men with blackened faces and blood-red sashes around their stomachs were leaping up and down, howling, waving clubs; officers in gold turbans were whirling broadaxes; troops encased in iron coats of detachable plates from their neck to their knees were so weighed down that they waddled like ducks and fell prey to lighter-armored Chalukyans.

As Gandiva turned rapidly to swing his trunk at lancers, Arjun held on, going in and out of consciousness as he saw other things flash before his eyes: odd-looking rods with four or five projecting forks, iron mallets, slings, nooses of thick rope, long hooked poles not unlike ankuses.

Arjun glanced at the arrow in his leg. The feathered shaft looked strangely like a new appendage, something that had grown into his body, something that would always be there. The idea of this permanent and terrible invasion was even worse than the pain.

Leaning forward, gripping the neck rope, he rested against the hot body of his elephant. For a few moments, he closed his eyes as if to shut out the combatants swirling below, but his ears were filled with the sound of signaling whistles, war whoops from the various gulmas trying to stay together in some semblance of order, and drums banged and conch shells blown—a wild cacophony in addition to the worst of sounds: the pervasive grunting and screaming of men fighting and dying. He opened his eyes just in time to see an elephant charging from the side. With a sharp nudge he brought Gandiva around so that tusk smacked against tusk without damage. From the attacker's howdah a lance was thrust forward, which Arjun deflected with the hook of his ankus. The two elephants surged past each other, losing contact. Gandiva shuffled forward with Arjun hanging on. Looking down, he noticed arrows protruding from the great beast's plunging right leg. None of them were deep enough to mortally wound or even disable Gandiva, but they seemed to infuriate him like a swarm of bees.

Arjun felt his consciousness fading, just as Gandiva reached the edge of the battlefield. Looking back at the howdah for the first time, Arjun saw, to his dismay, the old veteran propped up against its side, an arrow shaft protruding from his forehead, his open eyes glazed and staring as emptily as those of a dead mouse. The other soldiers were gone, having either jumped off in fear or fallen off wounded. By now the whole battlefield resembled the jittery chaos of frantic ants. It was worse than anything he had ever imagined. Arjun held back tears as a new wave of weakness surged through him.

Exhausted, he could do no more. Nudging the elephant, Arjun turned Gandiva toward the Chalukyan lines.

 **14**

A LARGE NUMBER OF HARSHA'S panicky elephants plowed through Mandlesir, bowling over flimsy huts and shops. Others circled the town and headed straight for the river.

Reaching it, some stood belly-deep, refusing their mahouts' command to go on, while others, wading into mid-channel, sank beneath the surface and rolled and shook until their mahouts and howdah-soldiers fell into the water. Weighed down by armor, many of the men drowned. Still other elephants bolted across the plain, where Pulakeshin's cavalry hunted them at leisure, one by one, slaughtering them with arrows from a safe distance.

Luckily for Harsha, his rear-guard horsemen roared up the flanks and caught the advancing Chalukyans in a pincer movement that temporarily blunted their attack.

This enabled his infantry to regroup. They formed the mandala defense, a series of tight concentric circles facing outward.

Even though the Chalukyans had plainly won the day and stood a good chance of annihilating the invader, King Pulakeshin decided to order a withdrawal. It was a decision that followed a basic principle of warfare. Desperate men facing destruction fight harder than before, which can mean heavy casualties for the victors or even negate a victory altogether. The possibility of such a reversal increases when the defeated army is the larger, as it was in this battle.

And so, quite prudently, the Chalukyan troops broke contact with the enemy and pulled back across the plain.

That night the two armies camped close enough for the screams of each army's wounded to be heard by the other side. Few slept that night. Arjun didn't; he lay twisting in pain, although the arrow, having missed bone, had been removed without complication.

Wandering among the wounded, Hari finally found him. Arjun learned that the camupati had indeed been killed during the initial charge, and later, so had the vahinipati.

Lying there, his bandaged leg throbbing, Arjun remembered the first time he saw the vahinipati—the long earrings, the corkscrew curls. But he didn't have time to reflect on the admired officer's death before Hari told him of another one.

"Your skinny friend," Hari began haltingly. "I met him once with you in camp. He seemed like a fine fellow, if gloomy . . ."

Arjun tried to sit up, but the pain kept him down. "Karna," he murmured.

"Yes, that's the one. Karna. Well, he was run through. Not much suffering, I think. I saw him on the ground. The lance was still in him—went right through him. No, Arjun, I'm sure he didn't suffer much." In a sudden but calculated change of mood, Hari added enthusiastically, "Your gaja is great. I went to see him for you. They removed at least fifteen arrows from him, yet tonight he ate his fodder. He behaved as if nothing more had happened today than working with you on a training field."

"I want to see him."

Hari patted his friend's shoulder. "When you get better. All those arrows in him did less damage than the one in you."

"He's truly all right?" Arjun had fainted soon after reaching the Chalukyan lines. He remembered ordering Gandiva to kneel and feeling gaja respond under him, then . . . nothing more.

"He's fine," Hari assured his friend. "But let me tell you this. It's a gift from the gods that any of the vanguard lived. I couldn't imagine such a charge before seeing it. Now having seen it, I still can't imagine it. Of your fifty, only twelve gajas survived and seven mahouts. Fifty against thousands! But you did it, Arjun. Your vanguard broke their line. And of all the heroes today, none was greater than your gaja!"

Later in the evening an officer came to Arjun's side. It was the nayaka, whose past bravery had earned him the right to lead the main attack today. His arm was in a sling, but he had insisted on seeing "the young mahout." Kneeling beside Arjun, he said quietly, "You acted like a true-born Kshatriya."

Arjun didn't say he was a Brahman—higher than a Kshatriya in the minds of many people. What did it matter?

"Your gaja, mahout, is a great one," continued the nayaka. "He crippled Darpashata. The Joy of Harsha's Heart had to be destroyed."

Arjun said nothing about that; he loved elephants too much to enjoy their suffering, even if they belonged to the enemy. In the polite and solemn manner of a Brahman—it must have surprised the nayaka—the boy thanked him for commending Gandiva, who had tried not to embarrass the elephant corps by carrying the name of a magical bow.

As he lay awake awake that night, Arjun searched his memory for a verse from the *Bhagavad Gita*, the religious poem so often quoted by the village priest. Arjun finally recalled it:

He is not born, nor does he ever die;
Nor, having come to be,
will he ever more come not to be.
Unborn, eternal, everlasting, this ancient one
Is not slain when the body is slain.

The "ancient one," according to the priest, was Atman, the immortal soul, the indestructible "that-which-is." So tonight, where was the "ancient one" that had resided in the tall, thin body of Karna? Where were all the ancient ones who had left their mangled bodies on the field of battle today? That verse from the *Gita* had been spoken by Krishna to reassure the warrior Arjuna that anyone he killed in battle was not truly killed. Looking beyond the physical self, you must find the Other, the immortal self that emanates from God. So the priest had explained. But for Arjun, locked into horrific memories of the day, such an explanation was only words. Misleading words. And so was the idea of lila, of divine play, of the world created without premeditation by the joyful Shiva.

Lila? Had the battle been nothing but play, sport, cosmic fun?

In his pain and exhaustion that night, in his grieving for the dead and sympathy for the dying, Arjun would have believed anything about the world, anything at all, before believing it was created out of joyful play.

The next morning Pulakeshin ordered his army to march. There was no need to stay here longer. Scouts had confirmed the extent of his victory. Perhaps more than half of Harsha's elephant corps, five or six hundred, were killed or wounded or missing. Survivors had wandered across the river and no doubt were rambling helter-skelter through woodland and fields. Armed villagers would probably kill the wounded and weaker ones for food. The infantry had sustained major losses, at least ten thousand, maybe more. The cavalry alone seemed to be truly in one piece, though its casualties also numbered in the thousands.

A spy would later describe how Harsha's astrologers, who had encouraged the expedition and predicted total victory, had been executed publicly for incompetence. A long time would pass before Harsha recovered his military might, let alone his desire for conquest.

Pulakeshin's army marched westward around Mandlesir and crossed the Narmada farther downstream, avoiding contact with the enemy. Scouts would report that Harsha seemed content to hunker down while his troops nursed their wounds and prepared for the long journey home to Vardhana.

Wounded Chalukyans rode in bullock carts, except for officers, who lay in howdahs carried by elephants. Out of respect for the few surviving vanguard mahouts, Arjun was also put in a howdah. He worried about Gandiva, who shuffled behind, the arrow wounds ugly and beginning to fester. But Arjun was unable to walk more than a few steps and could do nothing to help his friend and comrade.

Propped against a side of the howdah, Arjun stared up at the clouds overhead. From the motion of the elephant beneath him, the clouds swayed like white sails on a choppy sea. Hours of slow marching lay ahead. The gray clouds were as lumpy as clods of mud thrown against the sky, but instead of rain they brought only wind that buffeted the howdah in which Arjun sat. His thoughts drifted. They funneled at last into images of home: a lane, a pond, an old buffalo, the bamboo fan cherished by his father, the face of his mother intent in prayer. Then a question entered his mind that had not been there recently, that had not been there before the battle: Where was his sister, where was Gauri? The question faded like sunlight. Then he recalled the tiger in the canebrake, the assault on the caravan.

Images of recent violence began assaulting him, images so recent that each detail had the feel of something happening now. He relived moments on the battlefield. They overwhelmed him by their ferocity and chaos, until the chaos dominated his thoughts, until he felt amazed by the memory of such confusion and tumult and disorder. Training camp had not prepared him for it. The main idea there had been to organize men so they acted together. But on the battlefield in front of Mandlesir, each man had separated from his companions and fought or died on his own, until the battlefield appeared to be a writhing mass of disconnected arms, legs, and grimacing faces. How they regrouped into a semblance of order was still a mystery to him.

Another passage from the *Gita*—the exact words escaped him, but not their meaning—dealt with both the killed and the killers. The killer thought he had killed the dead man; the dead man thought he had been killed; neither understood that no one had killed and no one had been killed. Could this be true? What did it really mean? Arjun had never asked the priest, who probably would have told him such questions were not for boys. But now he wondered with the intensity of someone who had experienced war. No one kills and no one is killed. But Karna lay dead and someone had killed him. Hadn't that happened? The Gita said no.

If the great poem told the truth, then everything that happened on the battlefield was hardly more than a dream. Killer and killed could smile at each other because no harm had actually been done.

Karna and the old veteran and the others in the howdah and the vahinipati and the camupati and the thousands of dead, both friend and foe, and the hamstrung elephants too and the disemboweled horses, every living thing that had stood that day on the plain of Mandlesir and suffered and died, all of them, every single one, were the same now as they had been before the battle.

Could that, finally, be what lila meant? That such a battle occurred only in the playful mind of God?

If so, it would take away the sting of horror. But it would also take away the reason for doing anything, since nothing finally mattered, since nothing happened to anyone but God. It was too difficult to understand. Arjun regretted his lack of attention when the village priest had explained such things. Perhaps if he had listened, he could make more sense now of life and death. But it was also possible that these things still mystified the priest.

Arjun lay back and watched the clouds pass by. He accepted each one without questioning why it was there one moment and gone the next. A cloud appeared, drifted beyond view. Another came along, soon to be replaced by another. They moved endlessly, silently, calmly. Arjun let the passing of clouds happen, one moment after another, until the moments lulled him to sleep. He slept even while the elephant beneath him lumbered heavily into the Narmada and started to wade across, with the big tusker Gandiva, wounded but still strong, plodding behind.

As he slept, Arjun dreamed of a battle in which all of the combatants were children. Most of them were younger than he had been when he left the village a couple of years before. The thin, vulnerable bodies clashed, the small voices cried out in pain, and the smooth little faces twisted into grimaces of fury just as the bearded older ones had done on the battlefield of Mandlesir. Then suddenly, as if ending a game, they threw down their weapons and raced for a pond, where they splashed one another and laughed and mounted awaiting buffaloes and headed into the nearby woodland to pick berries.

Like a great beast that licks its wounds in a familiar cane-brake, Pulakeshin's army returned to the old marshaling area below the Narmada and set up camp there for several weeks. Weapons were repaired while the wounded recuperated. As young and strong as Arjun was, it took him less time to regain his health than it did other men comparably wounded. His intense need to help Gandiva also hastened his recovery. As soon as he could walk,

Arjun waved off the groom assigned to tend the big tusker. "I'll take care of him," Arjun declared, then led Gandiva down to the nearby river, where he packed warm mud into the suppurating wounds. Rama had once taught him to do this. The master had said, "I learned how to tend wounded elephants by watching them tend themselves. They make for water and slap mud on their wounds. It dries and keeps insects away and sucks out the yellowness." Within a week the bull elephant was better.

Within two weeks Arjun was up on Gandiva's back, wincing from residual pain and soreness yet eager to practice his handling skills again. Gandiva's reputation made it impossible for Arjun to work him without drawing a group of admiring spectators.

Nevertheless, one onlooker had not come out of admiration. Vasu stood quietly among the others until Arjun saw him. Then he began waving both hands, calling out, "Remember, hero! We have yet to meet! Remember! One of these days!"

That evening, while Arjun sat near a fire where mahouts had gathered to drink toddy, a mahout from another unit came to visit him. It was Skanda.

He began with an apology. In the past, Skanda claimed, he had failed to understand certain things. "First," he said, "I didn't know you were such a good handler. Second, that you were brave. Third, that you had truly earned the good will of my master. To atone for my mistake, I've sent word by someone going down to Rama's camp. He'll tell our master how well you did in battle, you and your gaja. Let us be friends."

It was a request that Arjun heartily accepted, although the next day he heard some news that made him question the sincerity of the older mahout. Apparently, the generals had decided to retire the elephant vanguard. Although it had worked against Harsha, this method of attack might prove disastrous a second time, especially if an enemy had time to devise a suitable defense against it. That meant a return to the regular elephant corps for the vanguard survivors—for all except Gandiva and his mahout. They were reassigned to guard the harem and the court.

So was it possible that Skanda's change of heart was no change at all? Did he simply want a friend close to power?

Arjun was rarely suspicious and mistrustful. Yet until now he had never seen a good side to Skanda. He meant to view this friendship cautiously. Meanwhile, there was the sudden change in his military role to think about.

There wasn't even time, however, to think about that. It was rumored and almost immediately confirmed that the king, who was greatly pleased with his triumph over the invader, had decided to undertake his own campaign of conquest. The Chalukyans were going to march all the way to the east coast, more than five hundred miles away, "to ensure the cooperation and good will of people in the Andhra country."

During this long march eastward, Arjun and Gandiva would travel with the harem and the court, less to defend them than to satisfy their curiosity. They all knew about the elephant who had destroyed Harsha's favorite, and they wanted to know more about the boy-ish mahout who controlled that massive bulk with the mere nudge of a toe.

 **15**

WITH A LITTLE HELP FROM other mahouts and kavadais, Arjun had always taken care of Gandiva's bathing and feeding, but now he had a groom and two fodderers assigned personally to him. His sole remaining duties were to ride Gandiva and to make sure that his royal elephant was properly attired.

Properly attired—Gandiva must look regal every day. So from the parikarmin, the king's ceremonial marshal, Arjun learned how to dress Gandiva for appearances before royalty.

Wide swaths of vermilion paste had to be smeared on the great bull's forehead. White conch shells were hung from his ears, gold plates fitted to his tusks, bronze anklets with tinkling bells attached to his rear legs. These trappings were required during a military campaign; for the palaces in Nasik and Badami, the ceremonial paraphernalia would be even more complicated. To appear in a royal courtyard, Gandiva must have his mouth covered with a veil of red cloth and his back overlaid with a caparison of reddish leather on which a golden saddle sat. Lashed to the pommel was a white umbrella of imperial authority, with precious jewels dangling from its edges. In addition, the royal elephant had a variety of colored silk scarves draped over his neck and rump. Drummers would rhythmically sound out each ponderous step he took.

So much ritual reminded Arjun of village festivals, when the priest spent endless hours fussing over such things as the powdered markings drawn on forehead and arms, the stitching of borders on special robes, the exact length of tassels on flywhisks, and the setting of flowers and fruit in precise patterns on the altar. As Uncle used to say, "It's enough to drive the gods themselves crazy."

But complex ritual might not be Arjun's most difficult problem.

That might be the chief steward. This emaciated old minister ran the king's household, which included the royal elephants. When Arjun was summoned to his tent in camp, the chief steward stared at the boy a long time before muttering, "Young, very young, too young." He had a low, breathy voice, as if the act of talking was an effort. "But they say you're brave. Not that it matters. What matters is your elephant killing Harsha's elephant, isn't that true? That's why you're here. People want to see who you are."

Arjun said nothing.

"Our sovereign majesty keeps only three elephants. The old one can't go on a long campaign. Two have been with the court many years. Their mahouts know what's demanded of them. And now there is you." Sighing, he squinted from watery eyes at Arjun.

Arjun said nothing.

"Youth won't get you far. Oh, at the moment the court is curious. But when the novelty wears off and they see you're nothing but a mere boy . . ." The chief steward waved his hand dismissively. "At any rate, for the present here you are. Here we are together." The old official regarded Arjun keenly, as if scrutiny alone could explain why such a creature held any interest for the court, even for a while. "Do as you're told. Do well and your life will be good. Someday you can go back to your village, buy some land, plant vegetables. Do you understand?"

Unsure of the chief steward's meaning, Arjun kept silent.

"Lower your gaze when the king's women speak to you. Never discuss them with those brutish mahouts you live with. Many of the women will give you gold baubles. Keep these treasures, don't buy toddy with them. Do well, show discretion, be humble, wash frequently, and you'll have rewards. Keep what you get. Do you understand? You'll walk away rich." Pausing, he waited for a reaction. "But you're not doing well at the outset, are you? So far you haven't spoken a word. Can you talk?"

For a reply Arjun merely stared at the official. The question seared his memory, for he had often heard people ask his sister, "Can you talk?" Cocking their heads and looking her up and down, they would say the words very slowly—"Can . . . you . . .talk?"—as if doubtful she could understand. Gauri had met their curious stares with her own, and said nothing. Arjun was now refusing to answer the same question. Perhaps Gauri had also deliberately refused. In a similar mood of defiance, had she decided not to satisfy their curiosity?

Awaiting his reply and receiving none, the chief steward asked again, this time in a rising tone of irritation, "Are you incapable of talking? They didn't tell me you were dumb. Can it be you're dumb? Are you dumb, boy?"

Returning to the present, Arjun was alarmed by his own impudence. Not even a general would defy the chief Steward. "No, Excellency, I am not dumb. I am . . . just not sure of myself in your noble presence. I will do what I'm told."

The old man blinked angrily. "Then answer when I ask."

"Yes, Excellency."

Continuing to study the boy, he said, "Now tell me the truth. Were you brave?"

"When Gandiva charged, I went with him."

"Were you afraid?"

"I think so."

"You think so?"

"When it seemed like we would never get across the field, I knew I didn't want to get across it. I wanted the field to go on forever. So I must have been afraid. But then we were at their lines." He paused.

"Yes?"

"After that, I was in the midst of everything."

"By 'everything' you mean the battle?"

"Yes, the battle."

"Did you look for Darpashata and send your elephant against him?"

"No, Excellency. My gaja attacked on his own. I did nothing."

The chief steward pursed his lips thoughtfully. "Some people would say such brazen truthfulness is bravery."

Arjun did not comment. He might have said that bravery in his Brahman household had been a lesser virtue than honesty.

"So it was not your idea?"

"No, Excellency."

"And you're telling me it was the elephant's idea?"

"Gandiva wished to prove his greatness."

"That is your opinion?"

"Yes."

The chief steward was unaccustomed to brevity from those he questioned. He expected people to say more than necessary in their explanations to him. Impatiently he continued, "Well, boy, go on. There must be more to it."

"Once I was in the midst of everything, I had only to go forward."

"Go forward?"

"Yes, go forward. Move toward the enemy's heart. That was my duty."

The chief steward scoffed. "It can't be so simple. You raced an elephant into enemy lines and humiliated a great warrior-king and you say it was your duty?"

"My master, Shri Mahout Rama, said duty is everything." He added thoughtfully, "What else could I have done on the battlefield?"

"You might have turned from the thick of it and tried to save yourself. You wouldn't have been the first soldier who did."

"And lost everything. Including his life."

The chief steward smiled faintly. "That's a reasonable answer. You're young but capable of defending yourself. By that I mean defending yourself with words. It's something I rather respect. Since apparently we're being truthful, I'll tell you a little secret. If I had to choose between bravery and survival, I'd choose survival. Perhaps, mahout, you've managed to choose both today. At any rate, you've survived this talk with me. Not everyone does. Be pleased with your victory. And do as you are told."

January, a cool, dry month, was ideal for long marches. Flushed with recent victory, the Chalukyans set out in mid-January for a campaign of conquest in the east.

Although he scarcely had time to acquaint himself with court procedures, Arjun was placed in the center of the march, behind the generals and the king but just ahead of the harem. Some of the time these royal women rode horses. Tall parasols were held over their heads by bearers trotting alongside. But at other times of the day, when the heat increased or they felt exhausted by so much traveling, the women retired to ox-drawn carts that had arched roofing and curtains. The wagons looked like huts swaying in the wind.

Here, in the secured royal center, Arjun saw a different kind of march from what he was accustomed to. Carriers of betel supplies had little banners tied to their backs. Sheaves of javelins belonging to courtiers were stowed in carved wooden cases and carried with ceremonial dignity by turbaned porters. Ornately patterned buttermilk pots were protected with wet cloth seals. All sorts of baskets accompanied this regal procession. They contained firetrays, pots, spits, saucepans, drinking vessels of bronze. Pillows of samuruka leather, the softest deer pelts, surrounded the inside of royal wagons. During the march, all kinds of sweets were dispensed to the traveling women. Servants handed them bamboo tubes loaded with mango sap and black aloe oil and roasted bits of meat. They drank ambrosial possets composed of spiced herbs, milk, concentrated butter, and rice. They ordered servants to feed their horses and oxen special tidbits.

To alleviate the pungent smell of so many animals, the king's women held little bags of musk to their noses and bunches of cloves and clusters of nutmeg. They compared the size and carving of their rings of hippopotamus ivory, and played dice within their curtained wagons. Their squeals of delight and laughter drifted into the dustclouds raised by foot soldiers and horses and elephants.

Although he traveled in front of the harem contingent, Arjun had glimpses of the veiled women. They wore bodices overlaid with dewdrop pearls, their foreheads had a pale orange hue from saffron paste, and their jewelry clinked with each movement they made.

After the first few days Arjun felt a sense of relief. The chief steward was wrong: Nobody in the court was interested in him or in Gandiva, so they could go about their duties in peace. Every night they bivouacked with other elephants and mahouts far beyond the royal circle. Arjun hadn't forgotten the chief steward's warning, so when mahouts began questioning him about the harem women, he declared without hesitation, "I will say nothing about them. Nothing. Ever."

That silenced the mahouts while strengthening their respect for him. One of them even drew him aside and said, "Good work, boy. Keep silent. If you don't make a mistake, someday the king himself will recognize you."

Behind the harem rode courtiers and noblemen, many of them relatives of the king—in-laws and distant cousins. A few of them started to come alongside Arjun and chat for a while. Where was he from? How long had he been a mahout? Had it been easy to train his gaja?

His answers were courteous, his manner so dignified that curiosity increased among the courtiers. Finally, word got to Queen Sutanuka, chief of the king's wives, that the young mahout conducted himself unusually well.

Whenever the march halted, royal elephants and horses were taken beyond the resting women and allowed to graze along the road. But during one such halt, a servant girl ran up to Arjun while he was leading Gandiva into nearby woods.

"Her Majesty Queen Sutanuka," the girl said, "wishes to see you."

When Arjun hesitated, she added impatiently, "Get off that elephant and let a groom take him. You come with me."

Arjun was rushed to a royal wagon with the curtains pulled back so he could see the queen half reclining on pillows. Noticing Arjun, she patted her veil to make sure it was secure. A kneeling servant girl ran the ivory teeth of a rekha comb through the royal hair. Queen Sutanuka wore a loose-fitting gown of bright blue, fastened at the waist with a jeweled belt from which loops and tassels hung. A woman in her thirties, she had large eyes accentuated by black kohl. On her brow were painted circles and triangles in red lac dye. Her many rings, bangles, anklets, and necklaces glittered in the glow of a candle that dimly lit the wagon's interior. Her large, dark, intensely brilliant eyes, staring above the veil, reflected the golden light.

She began by putting Arjun at ease, praising him and his gaja for bravery. "My son is a few years younger than you," she said, her words slightly puffing out the veil's surface. "I pray to Lord Shiva he proves as brave. You are surely a Brahman," she stated casually, as if it were an undeniable and obvious fact. "Perhaps that's why you named your elephant Gandiva—you have knowledge of the *Mahabharata*. How well you named him! A magical bow. You aimed him on the battleground, and his tusk, like an arrow, went straight to the mark. Now tell me your history."

When Arjun began, the queen interrupted him by saying, "Don't look down like a slave. Look at me."

Arjun spoke at length and more openly than he had to the chief steward, because the woman listened intently, without interruption, while the servant dressed her hair.

When at last he stopped talking, Queen Sutanuka drew aside her veil for him to see her smile—a rare gesture of trust and approval from a Chalukyan queen. "I should like to hear your sister sing." The veil dropped as she added, "You must have faith she's still alive. Yes, don't frown so. It's quite possible. If you serve our king well, you'll be known far and wide. And because of your reputation, so will your story and your sister. People will search for her in the hope of pleasing you and earning a reward. I hear you do your job out of respect for duty. That's a good reason. But think, Arjun. For you there's another reason to succeed at what you do. Even a better one." Sighing, the queen turned her head so the servant girl could finish piling her hair into a kind of halo, holding it in place with golden combs. "You already have friends, young mahout. Consider me one of them."

The queen's words were like those treasures promised by the Chief Steward. Arjun took them into the afternoon march, kept and cherished them. They gave him hope and purpose. He had already dedicated himself to a life of honorable duty as Rama would have wished of his apprentice, as his father and poor uncle and whole family would have expected of a Brahman boy. But now, because of the queen's wise counsel, he viewed his military success as a possible way of finding Gauri. That afternoon, often, he ran his hand lovingly across the bristly hairs on the top of Gandiva's head.

 16

SOMETHING HAPPENED, a month out of camp, that was of

no interest to the court and of scarcely more to the troops. But everyone in the elephant corps was keenly interested.

The mahout called Skanda had been killed. By his own gaja.

He had been tethering it to a tree after completion of the day's march. Without warning the beast turned its massive head, curled its trunk around Skanda's waist, lifted him high, flung him to the ground, and then crushed the bleeding man with a hammerlike blow of his huge right foot.

The mahouts, Arjun among them, were sitting around the evening fire discussing what had happened.

One said, "It shows you can't trust the beasts. His turned on him without warning."

Another said, "It shows the treachery of fate. This could have happened to any of us."

And another: "I agree. Fate is most treacherous to mahouts. It comes out of nowhere."

Another: "Did anyone here know this Skanda?"

"I did," said Arjun. They turned expectantly to him. He would not mention his last meeting with Skanda, who had questioned him mercilessly about the court. Do they give you baubles? If so, let me sell them for you. What do they give you? Anything else? I can sell anything. Do the women confide in you? Can you learn their secrets? If so, we can threaten to tell unless they pay. Together we'll become rich.

After such an onslaught, Arjun had avoided talking to Skanda again. But to the listening mahouts he said merely, "Before I came along, Skanda was my master's kavadai. He was a good handler when he trained with my master."

Someone spoke from the shadows. "But when Skanda left your master, he stopped being good." A mahout walked into the firelight. "I saw him plunge an ankus into his gaja's skull and twist it."

"When did this happen?" someone asked.

"Months ago. But at the time I told myself, 'The gaja won't forget. He'll keep the anger burning in his heart.'"

That night, unable to sleep, Arjun recalled the look of Skanda: the lazy way he leaned against things, his sneering smile and observant eyes. Rama had always said if you mistreat gaja, someday without warning he'll kill you.

Without warning he'll kill you. Arjun was not thinking of elephants now. He was thinking of Vasu's threat.

Now and then, during the march, he caught sight of the vengeful man. A sense of dread swept through Arjun each time, as if he had abruptly recalled a bad dream. Sometimes Arjun saw the powerfully built sergeant in a passing contingent of the elephant corps. At other times he felt someone staring at him; turning quickly, he'd see the mustachioed Vasu in the distance. They never exchanged a greeting or even the faintest sign of recognition. Vasu seemed withdrawn and thoughtful. Should Arjun fear him? Or consider his threats empty? Was Vasu a spiteful bully or a proud warrior?

There was another problem that tested Arjun's ability to sleep. If the queen was right—and he felt she was—his reputation as a warrior must become greater. Not that he wanted it for his own sake. In truth, Gandiva was the hero. Admiring glances cast Arjun's way only made him uncomfortable. But his desire to find Gauri created in him an ambition to be recognized wherever the army went. According to the queen, someone might come with news about his sister and claim a reward.

Yet the queen's suggestion was probably less useful than it had at first seemed. After all, chances of finding

Gauri must surely be remote. The dacoits could have taken her anywhere, sold her to anyone. And she might be dead.

On the other hand, what choice did he have? The queen had convinced him: Let fame be the agent of your search. He imagined people running up to him along the road, palms out, yelling breathlessly, "I have seen a mute girl with a beautiful voice! For a reward I can lead you to her!" He must become known, this time deliberately.

So he went to the chief steward with a request. After listening, the old man shook his head in disgust. "There are six hundred elephants in this army, only three of which have the luxury of staying in the protected royal circle during battle. Yet you come to me requesting a return to the elephant corps, where you can fight and die. Are you mad? Do you want me to find you interesting because I always find mad people interesting? Go back to work and stop trying my patience."

So Arjun did.

The army continued its eastward progress until arriving in Kalinga country, ruled by the Ganga dynasty. These Andhran people were known for hot tempers and quick tongues, yet in an initial skirmish with Pulakeshin's forces they turned and ran. During that battle Arjun remained in the protected royal center, feeling Gandiva's body vibrate under him, a sign of frustration in an elephant. A few days later, on the verge of a forest, another clash took place and once again the Kalingan troops fled.

The next day the despairing Ganga king sent an emissary to plead for peace by acknowledging the suzerainty of Chalukya over the land of Ganga. In exchange he asked humbly for continued control of its resources. Pulakeshin agreed. His chief interest was to establish dominance and obtain vassals. He asked only that the Ganga kingdom

send yearly tribute to the capital of Nasik—specifically elephants, because the vast forests of Kalinga were famous
for them—along with a royal prince who must kneel at
the Lion Throne and declare loyalty to Chalukya.

Such ease of conquest inspired Pulakeshin to seek
more. Heading down the coast, his expeditionary force
was next aimed at Ganga's southern neighbors, the
Vishnukundins, a far more powerful people of the region.
The splendid court lived in luxury at their provincial capital of Pishtapura, fifty miles north of the Godavari River
near the coast, or at their southern capital of Vengi, only
a few miles from the shore of Lake Kolleru. Palukeshin's
generals warned him that the Vishnukundins could prove
to be formidable adversaries. Conflict between two such
powers would gain the attention of people far and wide.

The more Arjun heard of the impending war, the
more anxious he became. All of India would know of it
and learn, through song, of the exploits of heroes.
Perhaps another such chance to make a name for himself
would never occur. Stuck in safety among dignitaries,
he'd be forgotten. No one would seek him out and
declare, "I've seen your sister!"

Going again to the chief steward would accomplish
nothing, so Arjun, fretful and troubled, went to see the
queen. He knew this was a dangerous thing to do. No
one ever approached Her Majesty without first making a
request—no one except the king himself. But Arjun was
made reckless by frustration. During a break in the
march, he strode up to the queen's curtained wagon and
called out loudly, "Please, Your Majesty, I'm aware of my
impudence and I beg your pardon, but hear me, Majesty,
please, please hear me!"

The last word was hardly out of his mouth before

three guards had Arjun on the ground, arms pinned back, a dagger at his throat.

The curtain parted slightly. In a voice of imperial authority the queen ordered them to release the boy. "Let him come forward."

Arjun got up and took a few tentative steps toward the wagon.

"Closer, closer, mahout," she ordered. "What brings you here so desperately?"

"I asked the chief steward to let me fight with the elephant corps."

"I see. To strengthen your claim as a warrior."

"As you suggested, Majesty. But he said no."

The queen shook her head, reminding Arjun of the Chief Steward's similar response, though she seemed to do it more from sorrow than from disgust. "Why risk your own life for someone who might be dead?" she asked. "I was wrong to suggest it."

"Please, Your Majesty—"

"I was wrong, Arjun. But say what you came to say."

"You told me great warriors become known."

"I'm afraid I did."

"How do they become known?"

"Bards write songs about them. Those songs go into villages along the army's path, then into distant villages and towns and great cities. People want to know who conquers them or who might conquer them. Nothing captures attention like conquest." With a sigh she added, "There are more songs about warriors than about love."

"Then I'll become such a warrior."

The queen was thoughtfully silent. Then she said, "It's clear you won't be dissuaded. And I share the responsibility for it. What do you want of me, Arjun?"

"I must fight in every battle. I mustn't be safe in the center. I must be out front and make a name."

"Ah, young Arjun . . ." the queen began sadly, then paused. When she spoke again, her words were crisp from resignation. "Perhaps it is fate. If so, there's nothing to be done. Your determination is quite as strong as fate, I can see that. So I'll have you returned to the elephant corps. And I'll do something else. I'll have the royal bards compose songs about you and your sister. Wherever the Chalukyans pass, your message will be left behind. In every village and town. And every wandering singer will carry it to places unknown. All of India will come to know of Arjun and his sister."

Arjun remained with the royal center on the march, but Queen Sutanuka saw to it that he was returned to the elephantry before reaching the Vishnukundin kingdom. It was a large and powerful state, its boundaries covering an area north of the Godavari River and south of the Krishna. To the west it was a tableland flanked by a low range of mountains. To the east, where the Chalukyans marched, it was a hot and humid countryside of great fertility that sloped gently to the sea.

Their first encounter with the enemy took place at the northern capital of Pishtapura. It was a durga, a fortress town, commanded by Prince Manchanna Bhattaraka. In front were earthwork ramparts for the protection of the fort's sun-baked brick walls. At each end of the durga stood a square tower with roofed balconies for archers. The only entrance to Pishtapura was a wooden gate wide enough for three chariots to drive through abreast.

Pulakeshin's generals agreed that the only way to take Pishtapura was by siege. Usually this meant enervating a citadel and waiting for starvation. Because the Vishnukundins had ample warning of the Chalukyan approach, however, their fortress larder was doubtless well stocked. To starve them out would take many months. The durga must be stormed.

To prepare for such an assault took several weeks. Horsehair ropes and winches for a catapult had been brought along in the supply carts, but the war engine's framework needed to be cut from trees in a nearby forest. One end of a long shaft of timber was secured by a gear system to the framework. The other end was attached to a winch by a strong cord. A stone heavy enough for three men to lift would then be placed in a spoonlike cavity hollowed out of the shaft. Winding the cord tight would draw the shaft back. Release would come by freeing the cord from the winch. The power for springing the shaft forward would come from a pent-up thrust of ropes twisted around the end secured by gears. Propelled into the air, the stone missile would arc over the durga's walls and disrupt the defense inside.

The Chalukyan engineers also built a battering ram from a huge log. Its head, encased in iron, was designed for hammering the main gate. Sixty men, moving in unison, would hold on to thongs inserted into drilled holes along its sides. It was suspended by chains from the overhead beams of a "Tortoise," a wooden structure built to protect the ramming party from the arrows and stones that would be hurled from the besieged durga's walls. Covered with damp clay and green hides to prevent firebrands from catching in the wooden roof, the Tortoise would be a mobile fortress as it moved forward on spoked wheels.

When Arjun heard that four elephants would push

and pull the Tortoise into place against the gate, then serve as battering rams themselves, he saw this as a chance for glory. Without hesitating he went to the nayaka who had led the army at the battle of Mandlesir.

"Of course I remember you," said the nayaka.

"And my gaja?"

"Of course."

"He is strong and fearless. We would be privileged to do siege work."

"You're determined to be a great warrior."

"Yes, Shri Nayaka, I am. We would be privileged to pull the Tortoise."

Smiling, the nayaka gave his approval. "Then such a privilege you shall have."

 17

FOR MORE THAN A WEEK the Chalukyan archers laid down a barrage of fire against the bulwarks of the fort, and horsemen sought in vain for any noticeable weakness in the defense.

The mahasenapati, in consultation with other generals, recommended to the king that the time had come for a frontal assault, the initial and vital part of which was to breach the gate.

Gandiva was fitted with an iron headpiece shaped like a V, so the point would face the gate they were to storm. Bands of cork and iron covered his entire back to protect him from arrows. Arjun carried a broad shield. Because his commands came from toe nudging, he could hold the shield over his head with both hands. The other three mahouts, needing an ankus to establish control, would have to hold their shields with one hand only.

The four elephants—one pair pulling and one pair pushing—were harnessed by thick hawsers to the Tortoise. Sixty men crouched inside it. Gandiva, one of the pulling elephants, trumpeted loudly as the housed battering ram groaned into motion. A contingent of archers trotted ahead of it, halting at intervals to send a covering fire at the protective earthworks. Defenders did not hold their positions long but retreated from the ramparts and ran through the open gate, which then clanged shut.

As the Tortoise lumbered forward, its wheels squeaking and grating, Arjun could see on the parapets and in the tower balconies a line of archers, their bows half drawn in anticipation of the coming attack. They crouched out of sight when missiles from the catapult sailed over them, then reappeared, bows half drawn.

He waited until they drew the bowstrings taut, then raised his shield over his head. The waddling Tortoise had almost arrived at the entrance to the durga. A succession of thuds against his shield, like the sound of thick hail, told Arjun that the first volley had been loosed. An arrow was sticking between plates of the coat of mail covering Gandiva's neck. Arjun halted him at the gate, turned, and released the shackle that secured Gandiva's neck rope to the Tortoise hawser. Now that they were free of the battering ram, with another nudge he aimed Gandiva at the gate. The impact of the powerful beast's pointed headpiece against the wooden planking almost unseated Arjun. Glancing to his right, he saw that the rammers had already got the stout log into swaying motion. Then it smashed against the gate, buckling a section with the first blow, cracking timbers with the second.

"Forward!" Arjun yelled, urging Gandiva with a rapid nudge of his toes. The pointed iron headpiece struck the gate again, and this time, the battering ram having already weakened the center section, the elephant pushed it in, his body beneath Arjun's legs hot and vibrating. The entire gate suddenly split, fractured in every direction, and within moments scattered into splintery fragments. Arjun felt himself going forward into an open space, his head just evading a spearlike particle of gate still clinging to the frame, his lowered shield looking like the back of a porcupine. His ears were filled with shouts of triumph, the sound coming from behind, as Chalukyan infantry surged forward to enter Pishtapura. He too was shouting. What he felt was now familiar: tension in his throat, his mouth dry, his eyes blurring from the thrill of battle, and beneath him Gandiva seeming to swell and shake as if the whole earth were moving, the upheaval catastrophic, the cause of it beyond knowing.

Fortress and town were soon captured. Many defenders escaped, among them Prince Manchanna Bhattaraka. Chalukyan troops first looted the provincial palace and then torched the market area, killing many of the troops but allowing the populace to flee with whatever belongings they could carry—a military custom of the time.

One of the four siege elephants had received numerous spear thrusts in the belly and died before nightfall. A portion of gate had crashed down on the second elephant, breaking his spine. Gandiva and the fourth elephant had each suffered at least half a dozen arrow wounds, but none serious. Two of the four mahouts had been killed, a third had lost an eye. Only Arjun emerged unscathed. He didn't know why this was so. He refused to entertain the idea that the gods favored him. That had been a childhood fantasy, and after his encounter with the tiger in the cane rushes, he wondered if divine intervention had saved his life. But war had taught him otherwise. He recognized his vulnerability; he bore an ugly blue scar on his leg to confirm it.

This time the young mahout's exploits won him an audience with the king. While yells of victory and screams of anguish still echoed among the smoking ruins of the raised fortress, King Pulakeshin sat in his tent with a view of fallen Pishtapura. Eating a slice of mango, he motioned for Arjun to approach.

Since his assignment to the royal center, the mahout had often seen the king, but never, until now, this close. A shiver of dread went through him as he met the steady gaze of those wide-set, heavy-lidded eyes, at once skeptical and demanding.

"I have noticed you," the king said in a voice that sounded ominous even when the words were not. "You ride a splendid beast. I believe he brought down Darpashata. Is that right?"

"It is, Your Majesty."

"And without any prompting from you."

The chief steward must have told him, Arjun thought. His mouth felt dry as if he were going into battle. "That is true, Your Majesty."

"Today, did he push against the gate without prompting?"

Arjun smiled. "No, Your Majesty."

"I understand your master was Rama. The greatest of mahouts." Taking another slice of mango and staring at it thoughtfully before popping it into his mouth, the king said, "You seem to be following in his path. When I first heard of you, after the battle of Mandlesir, I decided not to see you. Is that surprising? I guessed the truth," he said with the matter-of-fact confidence of someone never contradicted. "The elephant, not his young mahout, decided to attack Harsha's favorite. But today, it was you, not the elephant, who made the decision. Today you were no longer a boy. And today you have earned a reward. What do you want, mahout? Ask and you shall have it." The king motioned to a courtier who held up a leather bag of gold. "This? Or a horse? Or a jewel-handled sword?"

"Thank you, Majesty, but serving you is the best reward."

The king smiled faintly at the graceful compliment, then asked Arjun what he would like for the *second*-best reward.

"In that case, Majesty, I would like a white robe with a large boar woven in gold on the breast. A broad belt of black with tassels of many colors hanging from it. And a bright red turban."

After grimacing, the king chuckled and looked around at his courtiers to see if they were laughing too. "Come, boy. Do you want the enemy to single you out?"

"I do, Majesty."

The king shrugged, as if unable or unwilling to fathom such a vainglorious attitude. "I keep my word. If that's what you want, that's what you'll have. Go to the parikarmin. He'll make this *dazzling costume*"—the king emphasized the words ironically—"to your specifications."

The marshal of ceremony did as the king requested—had a white robe, a black belt with brightly colored tassels, and a red turban made for the young mahout. When some courtiers saw him in this costume, they snickered at its gaudiness. Others grumbled that the young elephant handler was trying to outshine them. Nor did the troops like it. Many hooted at Arjun when he rode by, whistling and calling him "pretty thing."

Even Hari was upset by this change in his friend. He came to Arjun's campfire one night shortly after the royal mahout had been seen in the pretentious clothes.

"People say you've become puffed up and foolish," Hari declared gloomily.

"What do you think?" asked Arjun.

Hari waited a moment before blurting out, "I think they're right. I think you've forgotten who you are. I think your master would be ashamed."

That last remark hurt Arjun, but nothing could shake his determination. If Gauri was alive, this must surely be the way to find her.

By royal order, Arjun was reassigned to march in the king's party, along with the bhatashvapati and the mahasenapati and other generals and the superintendent of horses, the superintendent of elephants, and the chief steward himself.

The old mahout who ordinarily took this position on the march was outraged that he must now ride with the harem. "I began with the women many years ago," he complained to other veteran mahouts, "and now I'm going back to them. I have served my king well. Why am I demoted? What have I done to deserve this insult? Why should a boy take my place? So vain and stupid a boy too. He'll wear the colors of a dozen birds into battle!"

Pulakeshin crossed the Godavari River and attacked the capital of Vengi, which lay near the northern shore of

Lake Kolleru. Madhavavarman the Third fled to an island fortress in the middle of the lake, too old to defend his country against such a conqueror.

At the battle of Kolleru Lake, Gandiva disabled a half dozen large tuskers and, with Arjun's constant urging, cut a swath through the infantry. At least three arrows were deflected by Arjun's chain vest, worn under his robe. Another grazed his left arm. A club hurled at him nearly dislodged him from Gandiva's back and left an ugly, fist-sized bruise on his right thigh. But everyone who saw him agreed that the young mahout had fought with demonic fury.

Within a few days, while the victorious army was resting, a song about Arjun's exploits had been composed and was being sung. Soon afterward, carried from camp by soldiers on liberty into the countryside, the song was heard in vanquished Vengi and neighboring towns and villages.

But in spite of his success, Arjun felt near to despair.

Hari had been killed. Shot through the neck with an arrow.

Attending a mass cremation, Arjun watched his friend's ashes mingle with those of many other dead. He wept for the loss of such a loyal friend. During Vasu's harassment of him in training camp, Hari had encouraged him to stand fast. How often had he had seen Hari's haggard face break into a smile!

Arjun wept too for his own failure as a friend. Instead of letting Hari think he'd become a glory seeker, Arjun should have told him the real reason for the changes in him. By confiding, he could have put his friend at ease. He had withheld too much of himself, too many of his thoughts and feelings. Perhaps fear had made him wary—the fear of ridicule. Hari might have scoffed at him for hoping to find Gauri by risking his life. Refusing to recognize this fear in himself, Arjun had simply deprived his friend of the truth. Given the chance, Hari would have understood and honored their friendship.

Now, with him gone, Arjun was friendless.

Except for Gandiva.

Ah, the great gaja was always with him. That certainty raised Arjun's spirits. Patting the bristly head, Arjun leaned forward to say, "You and I, old friend, we're still together. It will always be so."

One morning the army staggered into motion like an animal sluggish from sleep, its destination the land of the Pallavas, which the king had marked next for conquest. Crawling slowly down the coast like a huge centipede, it passed farmers who plowed their fields with apparent indifference to war and conquest. Yet among the thatched huts on either side of the road there just might be a girl who couldn't speak. And her wordless songs might reach Arjun through someone who had heard them. "I know who you are." In Arjun's imagination someone was trotting alongside Gandiva, looking up. "I know where your sister is, too. I can take you to her."

 18

AFTER CROSSING THE KRISHNA RIVER, they continued to the town of Nellore on the edge of the country ruled by the Pallavas. They crossed into it, a land called Tondaimandalam or Dramila or Tamil Nadu, after the language spoken there. Bounded on the north by the

Penner River, on the south by the Ponnaiyur, on the west by the Eastern Ghat mountain range, and on the east by the Bay of Bengal, the Tamil kingdom had for its capital a renowned city named Kanchi. Ka stood for the god Brahma and anci meant worship, so that Kanchi was the place where Brahma came to worship. Religious pilgrims called it one of the Seven Holy Cities.

Arjun's uncle, who had traveled widely to sell his goods, always spoke of Kanchi in awe. It was, like Kashi, a city so sacred that a man dying there found instant salvation. But Uncle had never gone there. After all, Tamil cottons and silks were quite as good as those he had to sell, and anyway, he couldn't speak Tamil, and besides that, those dark, slim, bright-eyed little people were dangerous, of unstable temper, and easily took offense. To initiate the building of a temple, they sacrificed a child and buried it under the first-laid beam. They worshipped terrifying village goddesses, each of which was more difficult to please than the last. To placate such a demanding and angry goddess, a priest would often stroll through the village with the entrails of a lamb wrapped around his neck, its liver hanging out of his mouth. Hearing such stories, young Arjun had decided against ever going to Tamil land.

Now he was going there to fight against a great king, Mahendravarman, whose liking of war was matched by his liking of music and poetry. All of that made him a worthy opponent for King Pulakeshin, just as Harsha had been. Arjun felt that he was living at the center of the world, that nothing had ever been or would ever be as important as what was happening now: the struggle of titans for supremacy over the gods' favored land.

Every evening for a week there were bright red sunsets. They were supposed to be harbingers of battle, but no battles took place. Not even a scouting party of Tamils was seen. The marchers saw only dry, scrubby countryside dotted with grotesque formations of granite and at intervals thick clumps of forest. When a surge of bloody sunset broke against palm trees, the resting army sometimes heard jackals barking, monkeys screeching.

The Chalukyans, those people from the interior, began to have glimpses of the sparkling bay, an endless expanse of water. Seeing the ocean had been Arjun's fondest boyhood dream, but now the sight of it meant nothing to him. It was merely a place where naval battles took place. The once observant boy was now a warrior whose eyes had a steady forward gaze into imagined battles. They saw little else.

The expeditionary force took frequent rests, often halting for two or three days. At those times archery contests and drinking bouts took place among the officers. Everyone played at dice. From villages the troops bought rams and had them fight each other. They also paired off the little quail called lavaka, who invariably fought to the death. Otherwise the soldiers wrestled among themselves. And the betting went on. There was talk that the king, reportedly bored with the long campaign, was going to have two elephants fight. This proved to be a baseless and silly rumor. To lose an elephant in sport during a campaign of conquest would surely offend the gods, who expected reason, not frivolity, from men who led others into battle.

Snake charmers came along with cobras in baskets; hawkers of sandalwood and cheap jewelry showed up wherever the army camped. One day a roving band of musicians and dancers appeared at the roadside. No one threatened or harmed them. At that time such artists traveled the length and breadth of India, during war and peace, flood and famine, bringing dance and story and song into the lives of both commoner and courtier.

Eager for diversion, King Pulakeshin invited the roving troupe to entertain the court that evening within the circle of royal tents. In the pasture at the center, the musicians played drums and the stringed yal and the flute, while young women danced by torchlight.

The next day Arjun heard that the wandering minstrels had sung a song about a young man who became a driver of elephants and a renowned warrior and searched the world for his lost sister.

For Arjun the minstrels confirmed how widespread his martial reputation had become. Surely now he was a hero great enough to command attention anywhere. He began to think of himself as the true successor of his namesake, Arjuna, the Pandava warrior in the *Mahabharata*. To make such a comparison in public would be much too daring, too self-important. He could share it only with Gandiva. Against an ear as broad as three banana leaves laid side by side, the boy said, "Together, old friend, we've turned the heads of the gods. We're known far and wide. My toe nudging your ear is a wonder of the world."

As the army moved farther into Tamil country, rumors surfaced concerning the warlike nature of the Chalukyans' adversaries. Soldiers familiar with this land were sought for information. It was said that Tamil mothers rejoiced when their sons died in battle, because the gods took them instantly to Virasvarga, the heaven of warriors. If a nobleman died in bed, his corpse was thrust through by a sword to fool the gods into thinking he had died in battle. Mantras praising his courage and prowess were chanted to secure him a place in Virasvarga. The Tamils carved "hero stones" with inscriptions that detailed the exploits of great warriors. When Arjun heard of this, he thought of such a stone engraved with his name and that of Gandiva.

It was also said that Pallavan kings enjoyed nothing more than heaping insults on defeated foes. The crown of a vanquished king was melted down to furnish gold for anklets of harem women. If he possessed a guardian tree—common among royalty—it was cut down and converted into a war drum for the victor. And the conquered land was brutally laid waste. Not even rice paddies were spared by these unrelenting Tamils. They were known for throwing dozens of poisonous snakes into enemy camps. This last possibility led to the posting of more sentries at night.

But there had been similar rumors about the Vishnukundins, and surely they hadn't lived up to their reputation for savagery and pugnaciousness. As for Arjun, he didn't mind if the rumors about the Tamils were true. In fact, he hoped they were. Rama would have said, "The fiercer your opponent, the better you fight."

Although the sunsets did not bring a major clash, they were followed by quick skirmishes designed by the Pallavas to slow down the Chalukyan advance. Sallies of Tamil cavalrymen against the flanks and rear became common. Finally a pitched battle occurred on barren ground between the blue ocean and the green hills. Perhaps five thousand Pallavan troops took part, but clearly Mahendravarman was not yet ready for a full-scale confrontation. A few days later another force met the advancing Chalukyans for a brief but fierce encounter. The Tamils were testing Pulakeshin's tactics and determination.

Because of these probing assaults, the Chalukyans were also getting familiar with their opponents. The Tamils were quite small and dark-complected, with thin black mustaches and earrings that looped down to their shoulders. They carried wooden shields painted red and at least two daggers at their waists. Their chief weapon was a long, three-pronged spear that they wielded with great dexterity. Before charging, their infantry did a frenzied dance—violently pumped their bent arms and repeatedly leapt high in the air, grimacing and showing their brilliantly white teeth. To shade the officers from sunlight glare, Tamil servants held umbrellas of peacock feathers over their heads, even during an engagement. Others carried flags on which were painted the Bull That Gives Victory, symbol of the Tamil worship of Lord Shiva, who rode the bull, just as Ganapati rode the mouse and Brahma the goose and Indra the elephant.

In every fight Arjun distinguished himself by hurling Gandiva into the thickest part of the melee. As his reputation grew, Arjun's behavior changed, until Hari might not have recognized his old friend

Arjun's need for recognition so overwhelmed him that he lost sight of why he felt such a need. The desire for glory had become a goal in itself. When Arjun did think of his sister, a terrible sadness came over him, as if in his heart he knew she was dead. But mostly his mind was alive with images of battle and delight in his own prowess. He considered himself worthy of the songs glorifying his exploits. And perhaps he really was divinely protected.

After all, he wore bright colors into battle, making himself a sure target, yet he survived. Others went down, but he survived. And in each encounter, displaying bravery —reckless bravery—he made a name for himself. And with each triumph he got nearer to his goal of being a great, no, of being the greatest warrior.

Now that the advancing army was harassed almost daily, various elements of it were moved to new positions in the line of march as a defense against ambush. One afternoon the harem wagons were moved past the elephantry. A curtained wagon in which the queen often traveled came alongside Gandiva. The curtain drew open, so Arjun could see the glint of a golden eardrop inlaid with sparkling gems. On a pale forehead hung a loop of gold studded with emeralds, the emblem of Mahadevi Sutanuka, chief queen of the Chalukyas. Her eyes met his. He expected her to pull the veil aside and let him see her smile. At least she'd wave—even slightly. But nothing happened. It was as if she were looking at a stranger. Why would she ignore yet stare at him? Did she disapprove of what he was doing? Did she think him a fool to risk his life so boldly? That couldn't be, Arjun decided. Now that he was great, perhaps she no longer needed to help him or even be friendly. No matter. He was keenly aware of the upward glances of admiring foot soldiers, the sidelong looks of envy from cavalrymen.

He began to think of himself and of Gandiva as existing apart from others, walled within an invisible circle of their own making. After evening meals, he would leave the convivial mahouts and go straight to the elephant-tethering area. Leading Gandiva away from the others, Arjun would talk to him a while, then curl up and sleep close to the huge round feet. No other mahout would do such a thing. A sleeping elephant might roll over on him. Or if a gaja slept standing up and suddenly awakened and wished to lie down for a while—gajas did this often—it might forget its handler was underfoot, and so crush him.

Arjun's sense of being indestructible led to a new attitude toward Vasu, his old tormenter from training camp. Whenever they saw each other, Arjun stared until the rugged sergeant averted his eyes and turned away. After the second skirmish, Arjun noticed that Vasu wore a bandage around his left arm. Wounded or not, though, he was no longer a threat. Proof was in the submissive way he averted his eyes.

After a number of skirmishes with Pallavan forces, the nayaka approached Arjun. "You've done very well, mahout, but good fortune is always in short supply. Especially for a soldier. Let me suggest a change. Take off the red turban and colored belt and white robe the next time we go into battle. Wear just a loincloth and a coat of mail."

"Aside from what I wear, do you think the enemy knows about me?"

The nayaka thought before answering. "It is possible. Does that please you?"

"Yes."

"Enough to risk your life for?"

"Yes."

The nayaka shrugged. "Then do as you please."

It was May—in Tamil country the hottest and driest month of the year, the forerunner of monsoon. Soon the rainy season would begin. Clouds were already rolling in, obscuring the sky much of the time. There were no blood-red sunsets to predict battle. Even so, a battle occurred, a great one, the Battle of Pullalura, a few miles north of the capital city of Kanchi.

The morning was humid, close, and so hot that many of the troops were bathed in sweat before the priests had blessed the boar flags and war drums. King Pulakeshin was sweating too, though he had ritually washed before dressing for battle. He wore a coronal ornament, a circlet of silver whose ends were shaped like the interlocking jaws of two crocodiles. For that reason this crown was called the Makaramukha. In full regalia, he chanted a prayer to Trivikrama, God of Power, held up his sword, took sixty-four steps toward the east, bowed to the sun, and mounted his war chariot. Music played then. Meanwhile, the priests were blessing the royal umbrella with its handle of gold and fringe of dangling pearls. Then they chanted prayers for the Brhatketu, a twelve-foot-high standard with a five-foot-long boar painted on its banner.

A spy had brought word that Prince Narasimha would lead the Pallavas. Although his father was renowned on the battlefield and still officially in charge, Narasimha was the greater warrior.

"Let Prince Narasimha prepare to learn something," Arjun said to Gandiva as they awaited the signal to advance. "Today he'll learn of us, old friend." Patting the smooth, knobby skull affectionately and glancing down at the beast's girlishly long eyelashes, he murmured, "Once again, the brother of my soul, once again we go together . . ."

The Battle of Pullalura was hotly contested, the outcome in doubt for the entire morning. But then the Chalukyan cavalry rolled up the left flank while the elephant corps broke through the main Tamil line of heavy infantry. This forced Prince Narasimha to begin an orderly retreat toward the city of Kanchi.

Although the battle was not yet won, clearly the tide had turned in favor of Pulakeshin. His exhilarated troops began shouting and whooping as they surged forward.

Arjun was yelling too, nudging Gandiva to follow the main flow of action. Looking for an opponent to engage, he headed for a retreating elephant and had almost reached it when a motion to his right caused him to turn slightly and notice another elephant, a Chalukyan, coming alongside. In a final moment of extreme surprise, Arjun saw the grinning, triumphant face of Vasu and the iron shaft of an ankus swinging toward him through the air.

Arjun felt the impact, nothing more.

Unseated by Vasu's terrific blow, he fell to the ground, Gandiva's rear left leg just missing his head.

It took the elephant only a few moments to realize his handler was no longer mounted. Halting, with his trunk lifted backward in a frantic search for Arjun, he trumpeted so loudly that swordsmen paused in their thrusting and parrying. Then, turning with that speed and agility so remarkable in elephants, Gandiva began rushing in panic toward his own lines.

Seeing one of their own beginning to run back, other Chalukyan elephants ignored the efforts of their mahouts to keep them going forward. Trumpeting too, they turned and scurried after him, knocking over their own troops, mowing down anything in their way.

A few were brought under control, but most were panicky, especially the riderless Gandiva, whose trumpeting turned into squeals of confusion and loss and panic. Captains had no recourse but to order their troops to bring him down. A full line of archers released their arrows at the wild elephant heading toward them. He took on the appearance of a gigantic porcupine as arrows found their mark between plates of armor. Slowing, he staggered and his knees buckled and his great bulk keeled over like a sinking ship.

When he went down, some gajas hesitated and finally shuffled to a halt. Others, still dangerously agitated and made more so by Gandiva's death, had to be killed or disabled to protect the troops from their own elephants.

This unexpected turn of events brought the Chalukyan advance to a standstill. After quick consultation with his staff, the king ordered a general withdrawal, allowing the Tamils to gain their city gate without disastrous losses. Tired of campaigning, Pulakeshin would think better of laying down a siege. His exhausted army, its last energy sapped by the stampeding elephants, pulled back out of visual range of Kanchi. In the morning the king would begin the long trek homeward.

As stragglers headed for the temporary encampment, the clouds parted and the sun appeared not long before setting. A hue of deep crimson suffused the sky. Passing by a fallen elephant, an old soldier recognized this gaja as the one ridden by that boy he had once taught to wield a sword in infantry camp. Gandiva lay in a river of his own blood, his trunk in feeble motion like an ebbing wave, his kind-looking eyes glazing over, but his great heart still pumping, forcing him to feel the agony of at least fifty arrows in his body.

The old veteran knew almost nothing about elephants, but from years of warfare he knew all about pain. Wounded himself, he limped over to the suffering animal. Managing to lift his spear for one more thrust this day, he drove it down into soft tissue between blocks of bone in the beast's skull. And so Gandiva was at last set free.

PART THREE

◆ 19 ◆

THE ANKUS SWUNG BY VASU had left Arjun's nose and cheek so bloody that when Tamil soldiers searched the battlefield for survivors, they considered him dead until they heard him moan. They might have finished him anyway but for the way he was dressed; they thought that perhaps the tasseled belt and white robe with the boar emblem stood for Chalukyan nobility. So he was spared the fate of many wounded. Dumped into a wagon with other prisoners, Arjun was hauled away to the city of Kanchi.

When Arjun opened his eyes, the first thing he saw was a dirty blanket dangling in tatters from a beam. He heard coughing, groaning. His face seemed to expand and shrink rhythmically, in a wavelike motion that nauseated him. The nearest sound he heard was coming from himself: deep gasps of pain, one after another after another. Then it was dark.

Then it was light, then dark.

Then light again and dark. A bowl shoved roughly into his half-closed hand. He never moved. Bowl gone. Light and then dark. Then light again. Another bowl.

This time he managed to grip the edge, lift and bring it to his lips. Moving the muscles of his face caused intense, stabbing pain, but he managed to eat some of the rice gruel. What didn't spill he swallowed in spite of pain, and then the light faded, and it was dark. When the light came again, he raised himself enough to see bodies lying in a hut. A few men were sitting up. Someone walked over, bent down. A bowl. He gripped it and ate. The hut was hot and humid, then dark. The dark became light. He ate. The pattern of light and gruel and darkness continued endlessly. But he was sitting up now, listening to other prisoners speculate grimly on their fate. A rain shower, presaging the monsoon, beat a steady tattoo against the thatched roof for a while, then ceased. Arjun realized that his turban was gone. The torn white robe was mud-caked, streaked with dried blood. Crawling to the open doorway, he looked down at the still surface of a puddle left by the shower. Would Rama recognize him? Would Gauri? Would his own mother?

Someone did. Propped against a wall, a prisoner called out, "You! Yes, *you!*" he said, pointing at Arjun. "Where's your elephant? Can't protect you now, can he?"

But in this hut no one had the energy or heart for squabbling. The gentle sequence of light following darkness gave their spirits comfort, their bodies time to mend. Voices speaking replaced the sound of groaning. Someone guffawed. Another told a joke that drew laughter. A few of them, understanding Tamil, exchanged quips with guards who brought tubers and uncooked cereal along with gruel for their daily meal. As their health improved, some of the prisoners were removed from the hut and never returned.

Arjun was able to touch with his fingertips the pitted

and scabbing lacerations across his face. Although his nose was still a great swollen lump, he could breathe through it.

When he had recuperated sufficiently, Arjun was brought for questioning to an officer who spoke languages of the Deccan. The dark little man was seated on the porch of a building. A guard shoved Arjun down into a kneeling position of servility. His gaze lowered, the prisoner waited.

Finally the officer spoke. "Who are you?"

Arjun looked up at the narrow thoughtful face. "A mahout, Shri."

"A mahout? Come, if you belong to the royal family, we'll send an emissary to Vatapi for a ransom. You'll go home."

"Royal family?" Arjun smiled faintly. "No, Shri. I'm only a mahout."

"Yes? Well, then, why this . . . ?" He gestured at the robe with its gold emblem that Arjun still wore.

"I wanted to be known on the battlefield."

Such a peculiar remark caused the officer to study him even more closely. Was he lying or a bit crazy? At any rate, if the prisoner was a nobleman, a request for ransom seemed in order. But the Chalukyans had sensibly gone home, and the Tamil treasury was quite full, and to send an emissary on such a doubtful mission could prove irksome, fruitless, even demeaning. So out of expediency he accepted the prisoner's claim to be a simple mahout and raised his hand to have the strange young man taken away.

When the guard reached down to grab his arm, Arjun clasped his hands in supplication. "Please, Shri! Hear me!"

"Well, what is it?"

"My gaja—If you can find out . . . if anyone knows . . . if only . . ."

"What are you talking about?" the officer asked impatiently.

"If anyone knows what happened to my gaja—"

"As for that, it is common knowledge." He studied the prisoner again before going on. "Your beast, mahout, must have needed you. When you fell, he went mad and did great damage to your own troops. That's to your benefit," he said with a wry smile. "Because your beast proved helpful to us, he saved your life." The officer chuckled. "Nobleman or not, you'll live because of what he did." After a pause, he added in a low voice, "How strange you look. Is it because he died?" The officer pursed his lips judgmentally. "It's not like your brother died. Ah, well, mahouts are known to be strange. Your own bowmen loosed a few hundred arrows at the beast before enough of them got between armor to bring him down. I saw it with my own eyes."

"Dead," Arjun muttered.

"Oh yes, I think so. Quite dead. Not even such a tusker can take that many arrows and live."

Since his capture Arjun had lived with pain, but now he began living with grief too. And disbelief. The more he considered Gandiva's death, the more he felt it was impossible. How could such a noble animal be brought down? It was a question he took back to the prison hut. As night replaced day, he thought of it continually until disbelief turned to acceptance.

How had such a noble animal been brought down?

With arrows.

That was the plain truth. With arrows.

He had deluded himself into thinking of his life with

Gandiva as divinely protected. Now his foolish pride and sense of special destiny leaked out of him like blood from a wound. Rama would have said—Arjun never finished the thought. For the first time in memory he rejected his master's influence. Gandiva, his only friend, had been killed by arrows. Rama's words could not change that. Nor could they recover his sacred thread or improve his face. A new and surely awful life lay before him. Neither Rama nor anyone else could help him now.

Removed from the hut a few days later, Arjun was manacled as he had been when sold to the Chalukyan army. This time, however, it was not with a thin iron anklet but with a heavy chain fastened between leg shackles. He was hobbled like a wild elephant, then sent to a fenced-in encampment, where fifty or more slaves ate and slept inside lean-tos made of bamboo stanchions and banana-leaf roofs.

Each day the slaves were led to the site of a palace being constructed for Prince Narasimha. They hauled timber beams from wagons into a dense forest of scaffolding and ladders. Arjun had glimpses of a garden being laid out in a courtyard. Once, pausing for a moment in a doorway, he watched a man painting a wall in an already finished room. The full-length painting was of Parvati, the consort of Lord Shiva, dancing beside a pool.

Rama had not abandoned him. Arjun understood that after a while. His master's words returned like wise old friends. "Do your duty. No one can ask more of you, not even you." So Arjun worked quietly and humbly, thereby gaining the respect of his companions.

During the marches between slave camp and building site, Arjun saw his first great city. It was Kanchi. A brick wall defended its perimeter. Four gorpuras or gates were locked at night and made fast with colossal iron bars. Inside the city were many ponds and gardens and white-washed residences of sun-dried brick with covered galleries, raised terraces, and courtyards.

The city poor lived in barrel-roofed huts of waddle and thatch with palm-leaf roofs. The chain gang shuffled down narrow lanes past the shops of mat makers and basket weavers and coppersmiths and ivory dealers. Arjun had always wanted to walk through the bustling streets of a great city. He had never dreamed it would happen under these circumstances.

Tamil men glared at the passing slaves. Women stopped at their buying to glance curiously at them. These were dark women of luxurious beauty. He admired the way they tied their hair back in a bun, with a single lock curled under one ear. They wore bright silk scarves and striped linen robes that reached halfway down their thighs. Bronze anklets were curved to the shape of their feet. Each day Arjun waded through the floral scent of their many perfumes.

The great city also contained a multitude of dogs: mangy, ravenous, fierce, defiant. Rarely did they pay attention to humans, showing indifference to everything but their own survival as they roamed the city, underfoot and unwanted, with suppurating wounds in patches of bare skin from continual fighting. They were scavengers who mastered one another through a savage logic of dominance and submission. They curled up into tight little balls and slept on the sodden ashes of old cooking fires. Then they struggled up, shook, prowled, and fought again. "They have hearts of hell," Arjun heard someone mutter. A Kanchi dog established supremacy by never letting go of its opponent's neck until the vanquished animal rolled over, exposing its belly. Even this display of surrender was not always enough. The whimsical victor just might hold on, moving its jaws for a more deadly purchase. A howl of pain could bring a dozen more dogs on the run. Sometimes they leapt in and destroyed the conquered dog. Sometimes they merely sniffed and trotted away. Arjun feared and hated these dogs. They began slinking through his dreams, hunting him down, their small yellow eyes blazing.

The monsoon swept into Kanchi with full seasonal fury. The lean-tos had leaky roofs, so the slaves never got dry. Sores proliferated, clothing rotted, and insects drove some of them close to madness. Rats and bandicoots attacked the sick, who couldn't go out on work detail. Crows insolently snatched food from the hands of men too exhausted to defend themselves.

Arjun dealt with the daily torment by learning the Tamil language. He'd known both Kannada and Telagu at home, and in the army had learned some Maratha. He applied himself to the task, which the guards liked because they took pride in their complex language.

One day a slave from Andhra—taken prisoner a few years before during war with the Vishnukundins—caught a bandicoot who had come into a lean-to searching for grain. About the size of a hare, with long hind legs, it had a pale gray coat and a white belly. "Tamils hate them," the slave told Arjun, who shared this shed with him. "Bandicoots kill chickens and burrow under huts and come up through the floor and bite chunks out of babies. They're very good roasted."

Arjun and the Andhran hid the bandicoot under a

piece of cloth for two days until some wood they'd found in the yard dried out. They promised a hind leg to a guard in exchange for permission to build a fire. While the skinned animal was roasting, Arjun noticed someone watching intently from outside the lean-to, indifferent to a pelting rain. The man was tiny, hardly bigger than a child, with the brightest eyes Arjun had ever seen. While the bandicoot was cooking, the squatting man kept his eyes fixed trancelike on it and never moved.

Arjun's companion noticed too. "What are you staring at?" he asked roughly.

"Forgive me," said the little man. "I've eaten nothing but rancid gruel and uncooked cereal for a year."

"Then have some of this," Arjun offered on impulse.

"May I enter?" the little man asked.

Arjun's companion shrugged. "If he wants to give away his food, that's fine with me. Just stay away from mine."

The little man crept inside the lean-to, bobbing his head gratefully. "Thank you," he said to Arjun. "They have broken your face, haven't they? You once had a narrower nose, but now it is wider, isn't it? Don't fret. Someday it will bring you distinction. People will respect you more for a broader nose; it lends authority and the charm of age. They will say, 'Listen to him. Notice his important nose and the substantial scar on his cheek. Now there's a man of consequence, who has seen something of the world.' Ah, but this is a fine-looking animal!" He pointed to the bandicoot, which was starting to brown.

The three men watched it cook. A few others approached the lean-to, studied the situation, and went away. Whenever rats or bandicoots were caught in a lean-to, they belonged only to the catchers. There might have been as many as half a dozen men in this lean-to, but recently one had died, another lay curled up in a corner too sick to eat, and two others had been shipped to the quarries.

The little man regarded Arjun a long time before speaking. Abruptly, he said, "I am Manoja, the Mind Born, named after Kama, the God of Love, and believe me, I have followed that path faithfully with every woman who could stand me since I was your age." He paused, then said, "Younger."

"I used to weave the rope for making charpoys," he continued. "They said a bed made from rope woven by me never wore out, and I believe it." He twisted his hand rapidly. "This is the way it's done. No other way succeeds as well. I was taught weaving by a one-armed woman who used one hand and her teeth to make the finest rope in the world."

Later, when they had finished the bandicoot, whose roasted flesh had a loamy taste as if so much tunneling beneath huts had left the animal with dirt in its muscle and fat, the man called Manoja did not leave. Cleaning his teeth with a piece of stick, he behaved like a guest obligated to entertain his host with stories.

Manoja had been a housebreaker. He wore a black mask and carried a dagger, a digging scoop, a whistle to sound the alarm for companions, tongs for lifting, a candle and wick, and a rope. "And I carry with me a clever mind," he added with a wink.

"I'm not Tamil either. I come from the west coast, but I have learned to like these crazy people. Ah, they love language. For example, you think the name of this city is Kanchi. But out there in the streets people call it all sorts of things. I've heard them scold someone for calling this place Kanchi. I've heard it called,with absolute conviction, Praylaya Sindhu and Shivapuram and Vindupuram and Mumurtivasam and Brahmapuram and Kamapitham"—he took another rapid breath before continuing —"and Kamakkottam and Tapomayam and Sakalashuddhi and Kannikappu and Tundirapuram and Dandakapuram and Satyavratakshetra."

Out of breath, he grinned at Arjun, then added, "That's the Tamil for you—a language lover, long-winded and proud of his wits and ready to cry over a sweet little poem at a moment's notice. King Mahendravarman himself is a writer of plays. A notable one called *Mattavilasa* describes a drunken priest, his wife, an unscrupulous monk, and a lunatic." He cackled a few times, then said, "Poverty is the sister of contempt. Someone once wrote that. I, who can read, have seen those words somewhere. They are very good, very real."

The next day he came back. Squatting, he fixed Arjun with those brilliant eyes and began talking as if in the midst of a conversation. "It is definitely true that a Brahman is worse than a Kshatriya. The Kshatriya may kill you with a sword thrust, but those greedy Brahmans work you to death. Believe me, I know. I served a Brahman once in the capacity of a sweeper. When he wasn't praying, he was beating his servants."

And the next day he came to the lean-to and squatted outside until Arjun asked him in. He began without prelude: "I have always been tempted by munnir, the triple water loved by these Tamils. A mixture of milk from unripe coconut and the juice of sugar cane and the fieriest of foreign liquors well seasoned by burial in bamboo barrels." He smacked his lips. "It tastes even better than roast pork from a pig who's been kept from sows a long time."

One evening he appeared to be brooding. "You know nothing of what happens in this city of Kanchi. Some call it the dwelling place of gods, others the lair of demons. Worshippers of Lord Shiva flock here. Some are called maskarins, because they carry a bamboo cane. They're also called Pashupatas, because they worship the divine herdsman. Others go about with their naked bodies smeared with ashes and a garland of skulls tied around their waist. They drink blood and wine and cow urine out of them. That's the Kapalikas. All of these crazy people believe in suffering horribly for their sins, so they live on air and burn holes in their feet and stare at the sun until blind." He spit emphatically. "Instead of denying themselves life, they should embrace it." Manoja grinned. "Like I do."

He would come up to Arjun without warning, grip the boy's arm, and speak with the meditative quietness of someone talking to himself. "Strange things happen. And when they do, they mean more than you can imagine. For example, a fat, reddish-colored woman suddenly appears. Imps come along with more than four limbs. Horses cry and elephants won't take food. Bees hover around the fringes of royal umbrellas. Conches won't sound when blown. Black snakes crawl into the bedchambers of kings. Swords leap out of their sheaths. Wagons, setting out on a journey, turn back home of their own accord. Birds fly only in a curve to the left. Crows never stop cawing, even when a rainbow appears in the dead of night. When jackals cackle, fire comes from their mouths. When a harem woman holds up a mirror, she sees no face. Flags don't wave in the wind. When the sun comes out, the earth becomes cold. I tell you, boy, I have seen many of these things and heard of the rest. This world is strange." He shook his head in slow wonderment.

The world was also strange to Arjun. He dreamt every night of the dead coming alive on battlefields. They all had the faces of children. Panting bands of hungry dogs roamed among them. I was truly mad, Arjun thought, when I went into battle. I lived on the other side where death is everything. Now I dream of dead children and terrible dogs.

 2 0

HAVING TRAVELED OVER the ocean a great distance, southwest monsoon winds sucked up a vast quantity of moisture and dumped it as rain across India. Then mild steady winds out of the northeast curved down the Bay of Bengal and turned westward to cool and dry the water-soaked land. The process continued until sunny days heated the earth again and the parched soil awaited a new rainy season.

Heat-heavy winds blew across Kanchi, across the shriveled gardens and sweltering temples and dusty markets, as one pattern of weather moved sluggishly toward the next. Slave gangs labored to construct public buildings in celebration of the Pallavan king, whose Chalukyan rival, though undefeated, had wearily gone home.

Prince Narasimha's palace, the one that Arjun worked on, was nearly completed. The former mahout shared the old lean-to with Manoja; other occupants had all died of disease.

Arjun looked upon the housebreaker as a charming, unreliable older brother. Manoja lacked Gandiva's comforting presence and Rama's stern wisdom and Hari's heartfelt loyalty (once when the drum sounded to come get the communal gruel, Manoja scrambled for it, forgetting to rouse his napping friend), but he was close to Arjun anyway—as close as the other three had been. Manoja made his young companion feel that anything was possible; it merely needed encouragement to come out of hiding.

When not working, they spent hours together in the lean-to. Each came to know almost everything about the other.

"What was it like," asked Manoja, "living with an elephant? What was the best of it?"

"Traveling across rivers," said Arjun. "Or riding through the bush with trees sweeping past. Gandiva would brush away branches aimed at my head. He did it with his trunk, just at the right moment, without ever having seen me on his back."

"And the worst of it?"

"There was no worst. But it wasn't always easy. You needed to keep insects away from his ears and dig thorns out of his skin and collect fodder for him. Feeding an elephant, that's the most work. He needs so much to eat and he'll eat anything, but almost everything gives him a bad stomach."

Manoja grimaced. "I'd never get used to something that big so close to me. I'd rather be a spy."

He regaled Arjun with accounts of his service as a spy in many courts. Because of his knowledge of Deccan languages, he had often spied for the Tamils—so he claimed. A spy had to be tough, daring, without greed, and a judge of character. Ascetics and astrologers made good agents. With a wink he said, "So do women. And they're the best poisoners, the quickest thinkers, the most fearless."

It mattered little to Arjun that Manoja might have picked up such information from real spies. The tiny man loved life and was eager for more of it, no matter how much suffering it had already caused him—and that had probably been a great deal. Manoja's stubborn optimism, when transferred to Arjun, became courage to endure and hope for the future.

So during wet weather and dry, they shared the little shelter and ate the rancid gruel and managed to survive. Then one day Arjun returned from work to find Manoja curled up in a ball, shivering like a sick dog. When Arjun rushed to get him a bowl of water, the tiny man pushed it away. "My time has come. I want it to happen fast. Don't help me. Be my friend and stay away."

"I won't stay away."

The sick man, groaning and shaking, muttered, "At least don't help me."

Arjun sat beside him through the night and wiped his feverish brow with a wet rag when Manoja became too weak to protest. The next morning Arjun pleaded to remain behind with his friend, but the slave-gang officer said no. That night when he returned, Arjun found his friend dying. His stifled sobs must have been heard, because Manoja looked up and declared, "You haven't found it yet."

Overjoyed to hear his friend speak, Arjun said, "What haven't I found that we can find together when you're well again?"

"You haven't found it yet. Where you should be." After a pause, Manoja added, "You won't end here." The sick man seemed to lapse into unconsciousness, then suddenly opened his eyes. "You got this far. It would be too strange if you got no farther. Life is strange, but not that strange."

So much speaking tired him out, and he slept. Toward morning he gripped Arjun's hand and whispered, "I believe in you, whoever you are."

What did he mean? Arjun wondered, but the question would never be answered. Shortly after saying those words, Manoja fell into a coma and died.

Day followed day followed day, a monotonous and steady beat of time like the sound of the monsoon rains that were beginning again. When they prevented work on the palace, Arjun lay inside the lean-to and watched gecko lizards scoot across the thatched roofing. Sometimes they looked back from their large, round, brilliantly cold eyes. When the rains let up, he shuffled along with other slaves to the palace site. That was all. He said little to anyone. Cheerfulness had gone out of his life and with it life's possibilities.

One day the tedium was broken when Arjun heard a new slave singing in the camp. To the rhythm of two bamboo sticks knocked together, the Tamil slave sang of a Chalukyan mahout and his lost sister. Keenly aware of the song's origin and touched by its sadness (the mahout never finds his sister), Arjun understood that the song had taken on an independent existence, like another person, a stranger. It had grown away from his own life, and although the words told his story, they belonged not to him but to the singer and to any other singer who sang them. Arjun wondered if this was also true of a man's reputation, if it could be attached to someone who had never earned it or be removed from someone who had. He began to think that the truth didn't travel far. Close to you, the truth was truth. Farther off, it changed shape into something else.

You were who you were, no more, no less. The idea grew in Arjun's mind until he found comfort in it. All his life he had depended on others, even when he didn't admit it: in the village, in the army, in this slave camp. Now he felt as if everything added to him by other people had fallen away like leaves from a branch. Left was Arjun with the twisted face, a young man breathing at this moment, here and now.

And what of Gauri? A terrible doubt came over him when she came to mind. Perhaps Gauri had never been real. After all, he couldn't recall her face. Had she really lived? Of course. But possibly not as he remembered. Had he truly known his sister? Perhaps not—well, no, he really hadn't. The truth was he'd never tried to look beyond her silence and seek the truth of her. He began to think of Gauri in a new way. She was a shadowy presence in a childhood memory, recalled like a sunset of exceptional beauty. The real Gauri had been hidden from him. And by acknowledging that truth, Arjun accepted another: He had never tried to know her. Moreover, he'd used her loss as a means of ordering his own life, of making it better and nobler. Thinking of her now was like glancing over his shoulder at a figure receding in the distant mists.

Change did come, unexpected and considerable. Manoja might have said, "See what I mean? The world is very strange. Just when you think nothing will happen again, you're whirled around and stood on your head and become someone new."

A half-dozen slaves were selected for work outside Kanchi. The other five, Tamil criminals, were happy because nothing was worse than the Kanchi slave camp.

To stay here was a death sentence. They wanted to leave even though it meant being branded. There was more freedom where they were going and therefore more chance of escape, so they had to be plainly identified. As a prisoner of war, Arjun deserved the worst of labor camps, yet they chose him because in spite of harsh conditions he was still strong, a consequence of youth and his previous military life.

The shackles were removed from his ankles, revealing bluish scars like animal tracks. Held by two soldiers, he was branded with a smoking-hot iron. He heard the sizzle, smelled the odor of burning flesh, and nearly passed out from the pain. Once the burn healed, Arjun would carry the outline of a seated lion, big as a fist, on the biceps of his right arm. King Mahendravarman of the Pallava dynasty had chosen the seated lion for his personal emblem. Arjun now belonged to him.

"There you are, Chalukyan," said the brander with a grin, "you're ready for the quarry."

King Mahendravarman chose to build his cave temples not from soft, fine-grained sandstone, as done in the Deccan, but from the hard, close-grained granite of Tamil hillsides. To outdo his Deccan rivals, he had his carvers dig into the hardest of rock, which required more labor, the invention of new cutting skills, and a longer time to complete. For a temple at Mandagapattu, he had an inscription incised into the archway, which stated that this brickless, timberless abode for the gods had been made by Mahendravarman—adding to it the other royal names of Vichitrachitta (myriad-minded) and Chattakari (temple builder) and Mathavilas (addicted to joy).

Such a cave temple, called a vimana, usually consisted

of a pillared verandah with sculptured panels cut into the sides and a shrine set into the rear wall. The shrine was guarded by reliefs of dvarapalas, who were guards facing front and often resting on massive clubs entwined by snakes. The shrine cell was empty except for a portrait of the god worshipped there, painted in rich color on lime plaster. Mahendravarman and his son Narasimha were having hillsides scooped out throughout the kingdom as a testament to their devotion and evidence of their power and magnificence.

It was at one of these sites just west of Kanchi that Arjun and the other slaves arrived by wagon. Set among ridges of granite, the building area was called a quarry, even though what was valuable was not removed from there. The valuable part was the dark empty space within the rectangular opening on the gray cliffside, where a cave was being carved from one of the most unyielding substances on earth. Studying the cliff, Arjun remembered his first look at Ajanta, when he imagined the porters carrying rock from a cave. Now he would be doing it himself.

The new arrivals were barracked with other porters in a cluster of small huts within a wooden enclosure. Here the slaves were well fed and cared for, unlike those in Kanchi. They were treated better because along with hauling debris down the hill, some of them helped to rough-cut the cave with point tools and mallets, a job requiring both accuracy and strength.

During his first weeks, Arjun did nothing but haul basketfuls of rubble and stone chips down the hill to a dumping ground. Fifty men, half of them holding chisels and half of them swinging mallets, some on scaffolds and some kneeling, were hollowing out a verandah about fifteen feet long from the granite surface. Along the right verandah wall, a dozen silpins, master carvers distinguished by tall white turbans, worked on a bas-relief panel depicting Shiva, his wife, Parvati, and their son, Skanda. Arjun scuttled from place to place, gathering debris and putting it in a large woven basket to be carried by a sling on his back. He did his work silently, patiently, with the focus of someone fully engaged in it.

One day, when Arjun had just finished pouring a load of rocks into the dump, the work-crew chief came along. He was a bony man with a sharp chin and beady eyes. "Have you ever done bull pointing?"

When Arjun shook his head, the chief grimaced. "Well then, what have you done?"

"Handled a war elephant."

The chief looked him over thoughtfully. "First you'll learn to hold a chisel for bull pointing. Come along."

What Arjun actually learned first was the difficulty of doing anything to granite. You didn't really carve granite, you bruised and mauled it. Instead of carving across the surface, slicing off slivers of stone, you broke it down by pounding directly, crushing the surface until it disintegrated. The act of one man holding a heavy chisel against the granite surface and another man hitting it with a large mallet was called bull pointing. Once the approximate space was shaped by such rough cutting, a silpin stepped in with a short-handled iron hammer and a chunky flat-tipped chisel about the width of two fingers; with these he began the fine work of sculpting the rock into images and designs.

The work-crew chief handed Arjun a chisel while holding a mallet himself. "Grip your chisel lightly. You won't stop the force of the mallet blow by gripping it hard. All you'll do is get terrible blisters. Hold it lightly but firmly. If you don't, if you start thinking about something else and let your hand wobble, you could end up with bones broken in every finger. It happens all the time," he said with a shrug, motioning downward with the mallet as if smashing a hand. "Then you're no good to us anymore and we send you back to Kanchi."

So Arjun took up the chisel and became a bull pointer.

The cave-working slaves had special privileges. They were free to roam the surrounding hillsides and bathe in the local river. On the other hand, they weren't allowed in neighboring villages. Caught there, they'd be executed immediately. At sunset they lined up for curfew, called out their names, and were counted. Because of Tamil military camps nearby, the slaves never tried to escape but accepted plentiful food and a touch of freedom as their full measure of good fortune.

Arjun began to sense his own good fortune as days passed into weeks and he acquired the skill of bull pointing. He held the chisel at the precise angles ordered by the work-gang chief; holding the tool firmly but lightly, he let his whole arm absorb the ringing power of a swung mallet. The rhythmic work, the steady clang of hammers, the pervasive clouds of hot dust, united into a sustained harmony of daily life that replaced his old memories of battle and death.

After long hours of labor, he lay in his hut and watched the sunlight dancing between cracks in the roof. The earth beneath him seemed to creak like a dry board. He heard monkeys skipping in the banyans and among the floppy leaves of slim teaks. Sometimes he took a stroll into a nearby woods where cashew trees settled like nesting hens, their branches flounced out on the ground to form green tents. He walked by a pond with dry banks of cracked mud but with still enough depth for local buffaloes to sink down in to their necks and keep cool. They reminded him of home.

Clouds lay on the horizon like a pile of white stones. A small, orderly field of blood-red chilis covered a square of brown earth. Standing on a boulder near the top of a hill, he could see across the Tamil countryside: wood-apple groves and tamarinds and nim trees and thick stands of bamboo and long stretches of kusa grass with skinny, pointed stalks.

Without intent or effort Arjun Madva had regained the keenly observant eyes of his childhood. With them he looked at everything in wonder, freshly, as if for the first time. Manoja would have said, "You see? The world is very strange."

 2 I

HIS ABILITY TO ENJOY the look of the world around him also helped Arjun to see the work in front of him. As the hammering went on, he watched the intricate, light-catching planes of stone emerge from flat, blank surfaces. A cave temple wasn't built from the ground up but scooped out by a downward plunge of chisels. This action emphasized the immense weight and density of solid rock. Every time he entered the cave, Arjun surrendered to the permanence and security of the cool gray mass. It gave him a sense of belonging here. He'd not felt so much at home since leaving the village many seasons ago.

His bull-pointing teammate was an old Tamil criminal who, for a lifetime, had alternated between carving rock and stealing goods. The teammates worked well together, in almost total silence. Unlike some chisel-holders, Arjun never watched nervously as the big mallet swung over his head. He kept his eyes and mind on the position of the pointed tool and let the sure-handed Tamil take care of the blow.

They were assigned to rough-cut one of four pillars that would stand midway between the verandah's entrance and the rear shrine. It was a massive column, square at the base and top, octagonal in the midsection. Later, a master silpin would decorate it with low-relief sculptures of lotus flowers, lions, and elephants. Only the best teams rough-cut a pillar, because there was little room for error. Even the impassive old Tamil smiled proudly. Then by touching Arjun's hand—the one holding the chisel—he acknowledged his young partner's ability to learn and to trust.

The silpin made sure that they maintained the original surface as much as possible while gouging out the columnar shape. After releasing the pillar's essential bulk from surrounding rock, they worked on refining its geometric form. The silpin came around more often to inspect their progress. Finally he stayed with them, instructing Arjun how to set the chisel at the correct angle for the Tamil's blow. When they had finished the lower portion, he squatted beside the pillar and with limestone chalk drew on it the outline of an elephant about the size of a man's chest. Using a small mallet and a point tool as slim as a man's finger, he began chipping away stone. Now and then he employed a tooth chisel to correct the line. Glancing up at Arjun, he snapped, "Well, what is wrong?"

"Nothing, master."

"Then why are you looking that way? What are you looking at?"

"The gaja," Arjun admitted sheepishly, his eyes on the drawing.

Shrugging his heavily muscled shoulders in a gesture of indifference, the silpin hesitated, then turned to study it. "There's nothing wrong with this drawing. What's wrong?"

"It's not your fault, master."

The sculptor glared at him, then again at the chalk. "What do you mean, *my fault?*"

"Only a handler would know."

"Handler? Know what?" When Arjun said nothing, he shouted, "*Know what?* Come here and show me!"

Arjun shuffled forward and touched the stone. "A handler would know exactly how the back is shaped. Gaja's spine should be higher here, not here where you have it."

"What do you know about elephants?"

"I was a mahout."

"You?" sneered the silpin, but he turned once more and regarded the elephant's back, which had not yet been marked by the chisel. With chalk he reworked that part of the drawing, then asked, without looking at Arjun, "Is this it?"

"Yes, master."

In the following days Arjun watched the silpin create an image in stone, smooth it with files, and polish it with abrasives. Intently his eyes followed the chisel's contact with granite, at times as gentle as a wind touching grass, and at other times as bleakly precise as a sword thrust. He recalled watching a princely face take shape on the plaster of an Ajanta wall. He had realized then that the world could be changed by something a human painter, not a god, had created. What the Tamil sculptor carved now was the shallow-relief form of an elephant. It was an elephant but not an elephant. It existed first in the silpin's mind, then in the viewer's eyes, and it would never grow old and die but remain in this hillside for the age of a god. It had a lively appearance, so much so that its legs and trunk seemed poised on the brink of movement. It lived in its own way.

One afternoon during break time, while Arjun was admiring the finished relief, up came the silpin unobserved and stood beside him. "Notice," the sculptor said, "I cut the features to follow the rock's grain. Because of it, the rear of the elephant comes farther out than the front. Not the way a mahout sees an elephant. But this elephant stands out better from the background than if I carved it the way you'd see a real one. Of course, with soft sandstone you can cut almost any way you wish, so you don't have to worry about the grain. Sandstone won't chip or break into lumps the way granite does."

He grinned triumphantly at Arjun. "You people from the Deccan work in sandstone. You do it the easy way. It's like slicing through animal fat. But this Tamil rock—" He struck the granite pillar with his fist—"won't crumble until the gods themselves fall apart."

Arjun wondered if the silpin disliked him for finding fault with the chalk drawing. He had an answer soon enough.

The silpin called him away from work one afternoon and led the way down the hillside path, beyond the debris dump, to the bank of a nearby river.

"I've been watching you," the muscular stone carver

said. "Do you know what I see? Someone who looks."
He opened his gnarled hands, palms up, and stared at
them. "These aren't worth much and neither is a strong
back unless a man first uses his eyes. That's the secret."
He studied Arjun a long time before saying more. "You
can stay as you are, on a bull-pointing team, or you can
wear one of these someday." He touched his tall white
silpin's turban. "You can become my apprentice."

"Master, I'm a prisoner of war."

"A stone carver is not a slave or a prisoner of war or a
rich man or a poor man. He is nothing but a stone carver. Do you like carving?"

"When I lost my gaja, I thought nothing could
replace the joy of riding him. But I saw another gaja come
out of rock."

"What are you saying?"

"To make something like that gaja come out of rock
would be a way of feeling joy again."

The silpin nodded. "A way of feeling joy, yes. But also
a way of feeling the cruelest disappointment. Even when
successful, you know you should do better. Any failure of
yours is there in hard rock. It will stay that way when you
are dead and everyone you know is dead and others come
along and look and die and then others come and others
and others, each one of them looking, all of them wit-
nesses to your failure. Do you hear me? You don't seem
to understand."

"I understand, master."

"If you understood, you'd look afraid."

"If one of my carvings ruined the look of a cave,
nothing would console me. But I'm not afraid."

"Then I'm not afraid of bringing you to the point
where you can fail."

That did not quite happen. Before the silpin could bring his new apprentice to the final stages of technical mastery, Arjun was taken from him by Prince Mamalla Narasimha when the northeast winds were sweeping in, bringing cloudless skies and hot days.

The prince's favorite town was named after him—Mamallapuram—although his father had already chosen this seaport south of Kanchi for his own place of worship. Wood, mortar, and brick were all perishable, so King Mahendravarman had decided that the works of devotional art created for him would be cut solely from rock. Not fire or flood or neglect or invasion was going to change what his architects and sculptors created in his name to the glory of the gods.

Situated in a grayish brown countryside, its dull color relieved by the green of outlying fields, Mamallapuram contained administrative offices and royal residences built of timber and brick over stone foundations. Ships from the Orient put in at this port, laden with silks, lacquer ware, sundials, pottery, and metal mirrors, and went out again loaded with spices, copper, oil seeds, ivory, and cotton. But the royal town's most important activity took place a mile inland along a low range of granite hills, where cave temples were being dug.

And not only caves. Mahendravarman had already commissioned an enormous open-air relief which stretched across the length and breadth of a huge wall of sheer rock. Its spiritual purpose was to commemorate divine mercy as described in an old story.

In this devotional tale a hermit wished to sanctify the ashes of his ancestors by putting them into the holy waters of the Ganges River. Unfortunately, the

Goddess Ganges lived in a heavenly realm and refused to come down to earth. Men in those days persuaded gods to help them by practicing self-denial. Standing on one foot for many years with his arms raised, the emaciated hermit finally convinced Lord Shiva of his willpower and sincerity. In response, Shiva commanded the recalcitrant goddess to come down to earth and grant the ascetic's wish. When Ganges protested that she would flood the entire world if she came down, Shiva had her flow first through the twisted locks of his hair, thus breaking the fall of so much water and saving the earth from destruction.

At Mamallapuram a virtual army of carvers had been brought together to create "The Descent of the Ganges." Creatures both great and small were depicted as they gathered to thank Lord Shiva for his mercy. The rock surface was divided by an excavated cleft that served as a channel for water poured from a large basin at the cliff top. When used during rituals, the water cascaded down over a seven-hooded snake. The northern half of "Descent of the Ganges" was occupied by flying gods and animals heading for the central rift, among them two full-grown elephants and four small ones. On the southern face, the ascetic stood on one foot next to four-armed Shiva. Above them sailed a squadron of flying goddesses. On their left was an assembly of humans, lions, and deer. In a niche next to the waterfall sat a monkey picking lice from its mate. Whether earthbound or ethereal, the images flowed unrestrainedly across the immense boulder. Only partially disengaged from rock, they seemed to be in the continual process of emerging from it.

To compete with the accomplishments of his father,

Prince Narasimha extended his own patronage to other artists and brought them, at his expense, to Mamallapuram. And to contrast his own taste with that of the king, Narasimha encouraged novelty. He ordered his array of carvers to make free-standing replicas of wooden temples from a granite outcropping south of "Descent of the Ganges." They had already started to chisel down a hump of rock as tall and long as thirty elephants standing trunk to tail. They went at it like a gardener pruning a hedge into the shape of an animal. Their final goal was to carve out five temples, each with gods set in niches within its shrine.

But the ambitious young prince wanted to do more. Motivated by his competitive spirit, he developed theories about rock carving to contrast with those of his father. He believed that the shaft of a cave pillar should be fluted rather than squared, and feature a corbel and a beam resting on it. A seated lion should replace medallions of flowers and elephants at the base. The lion's teeth must curve backward instead of forward, and its fur should be designed in spiral whorls rather than straight lines. The general idea was to incorporate more complexity into his temples.

Older silpins, disapproving of such bold innovation, worked without enthusiasm. In response, the prince began searching for younger carvers who would view such changes with excitement instead of dread. Although Arjun had not yet been inducted into the guild of silpins, his age was right and his skills too, so in a roundup of new carvers for Mamallapuram he was included.

In the wagon going there, others chosen to work for the prince exchanged rumors and stories about life in the port town of Mamallapuram. Mostly they talked about food. In the royal town almost everything was available: onions, lentils, melons, figs, rice curd, goat meat, and fish—hilsa, which tasted sweet, and mahseer, a fish taken from hill streams. Mamallapuram toddy was by far the tastiest—and strongest—in the land. One of the carvers, a man who had been to Mamallapuram before, smacked his lips and exclaimed, "Spices bought in this town have their own touch of royalty. The cardamon and the cumin and the mustard seeds are so lively, you feel as though a scorpion has stung your tongue!"

Arjun was less eager to get there; he wished he had had a chance to finish his apprenticeship. Having gone through the long process of becoming a mahout, he knew the need for patience, observation, practice. Nor did the silpin make it easier to part. "You should remain with me," the burly man grumbled. "You're not quite ready to wear the hat of a silpin. You're still weak on the use of a small-tooth chisel. And you don't always see well in torchlight. You overemphasize the depth of a plane. Do you understand?"

"I do, master. I still need guidance."

The silpin laughed happily. "Of course you do. But the truth is, you're almost ready." After a pause, he said with a broad smile, "The truth is, you're so close I'd have presented you to the guild shortly. Before another rainy season, you'll be wearing the hat at Mamallapuram." Then his voice became gruff again. "But I hope someone watches carefully when you take up a small-tooth chisel. You need guidance there."

For yet another reason Arjun was not altogether pleased about going to Mamallapuram: He wanted to stay put. Before leaving his village, he had yearned to travel, but travel had led him to suffering and loss. Now, once again, he was on the road, at the whim of an ambitious prince, heading for a new, unknown life.

The first thing Arjun saw was the five temples in various stages of completion. They hugged the ground like huts in a small mud village. Nothing was vertical; the carved rock remained intimately bound to the earth. He had never seen anything like the five temples before.

Nor had he seen anything like "The Descent of the Ganges." As he approached it, Arjun felt the hair rising on the back of his neck. He stood close to the vast canvas of rock for a long time, taking a slow careful journey among the images. Then he focused on the relief's northern section, where the elephants stood.

Under a big male crowded four calves, and behind them came a tuskless female. The bull matched Gandiva for size, though his tusks were not quite as long as Gandiva's. The polished surface of the granite gleamed in afternoon sunlight as the tusker stood like a sheltering tree above his offspring. Moving closer, Arjun touched the cool rock just as he used to touch the warm skin of his gaja. Though the head and face were made of stone, Arjun saw through them into a memory of his dear friend, the long, girlish eyelashes, the wise little eyes, the lower lip coming to a point, the wet, pink gums, the vine-like sinuosity of the trunk.

There was no breath, but he heard breathing. The female was lifting her left front leg forever, following Gandiva. They had four calves, pudgy and content.

Arjun wept openly.

22

THE FIVE SMALL FREE-STANDING temples were called rathas after the decorated chariots used to carry bronze icons of the gods through city streets at festival time. The rathas were in various stages of completion. A majority of workers in this area, at least a hundred, were cutting away the remaining granite that surrounded each temple. Arjun was assigned to this rough work initially; then the supervisor gave him a chance to prove his skill. On a pillar of the largest ratha, the Dharmaraja, so named after a great warrior from the *Mahabharata*, he carved the left front paw of a seated lion.

Having watched the progress of this carving, especially when Arjun used a small-tooth chisel, the supervisor said gruffly, "Now carve the right one."

When this was nearly completed, the supervisor brought him to the architect in charge of Prince Narasimha's projects at Mamallapuram. The chief architect was even smaller and thinner than most Tamils, which made his enormous eyes and prominent nose seem even larger. He was sitting on a boulder with strips of palm leaf by his side. Incised with a stylus and rubbed over with finely powdered lampblack, they were covered by designs and measurements. Looking up from his work, the architect studied Arjun briefly.

"I'm told you have a good eye and hand. Why is it people from the Deccan make good carvers?"

Arjun smiled faintly.

"You may have noticed the large clump of rock next to the Sahadeva Ratha."

Of course Arjun had noticed. Recently, a gang of bull pointers had been swarming over that hillock, hammering away in the first stages of shaping it.

"It's going to be an elephant," continued the architect. "Same size as the bull in the 'Ganges.' I hear you once handled them, so you must know their look. After the elephant's roughed in, you'll be assigned to do fine work on it. Head details. Skull, both eyes, both ears."

He hesitated before going on, as if rechecking his commitment to the idea. "Yes, I mean it," he declared finally. "Few carvers your age get such a chance. But your experience with elephants makes you right for this job. And you'll be in charge of your own work. That means no one is going to look over your shoulder. What comes from here"—he touched his eyes—"will go here"—he fisted his right hand—"then straight into rock." Having picked up the sheaf of palm leaves, the chief architect stared grimly at them. "Our prince wants a lasting record of his piety. The monuments here are to glorify that faith. They must also be the most splendidly carved in the land, unmatched, not even by those his father commissioned. The prince demands it."

The threat and challenge of those words meant less to Arjun than the joy of releasing an elephant's head from rock, of giving life again to the features of Gandiva.

Season passed into season, the wet days becoming cool dry days and then hot dry days and then wet days again. But rain or shine meant little to Arjun, who spent most of every day on a bamboo scaffold, chisel in one hand, mallet in the other. Sometimes he couldn't sleep because his fingers, each momentarily paralyzed into the curve of a hawk's claw, throbbed with pain. Yet the next morning at dawn he would climb the scaffolding and take his position not a hand's breadth away from the granite head and pick up his tools and begin.

As Gandiva's face took shape, Arjun's sense of loss began to fade. The eyes and ears, becoming visible, merged in Arjun's mind with a regained memory of his good times with the great tusker. Long hours of meticulous carving transformed both rock and remembrance into a permanent image of strength and gentleness, of patience and constancy. Arjun began to sleep well; in his dreams he flew between mountain peaks and sailed with long-winged hawks on currents of buoyant air.

Occasionally the architect squatted some distance away to study Arjun at work. Not a word was exchanged. Then one day a silpin unknown to Arjun appeared beneath the scaffolding and shouted for him to come down. No sooner had Arjun reached the ground than the veteran sculptor jammed a white turban on his head. A cheer went up throughout the ratha area.

Arjun had been elected to membership in the guild of silpins.

With it went new privileges. He was paid in coin for his work and given complete freedom to spend his off hours wherever he wished. After so much time in army camps and prison gangs and torch-lit caves, Arjun welcomed the chance to visit the countryside and nearby villages. He began taking walks. Familiar sights that had grown unfamiliar became familiar again. Little tots gnawed on peeled sticks of sugar cane while looking solemnly at the passing stranger. A dog plumped down on its rump to lift a leg and scratch its skinny, flea-infested side. A heavy thud came from a brackish pond where village women were beating wet laundry against the bank.

It was all so achingly familiar that he might have been walking beside his uncle or father or little brother. On the outskirts of the villages, few of which were more than a cluster of huts grouped around a well, were garden patches of onions, cabbages, and mustard plants. The lanes were narrow, dusty, redolent of smoke and chapati bread and fresh spices. The villages reminded him profoundly of home but without imparting any desire in him to return there. This land of the Tamils was now his home.

He dreaded the idea of finishing the elephant because it had become so much a part of his life. The supervisor came to see Arjun after he had polished the entire surface of the head for two, then three weeks. Arguing that it was not quite done, Arjun took another week, and when the supervisor came again, he pleaded for yet another.

Then the chief architect summoned him. He was bluntly told that the elephant was altogether finished, that work of great significance would soon begin in a cave north of "The Descent of the Ganges," that the devout prince wanted this work to overwhelm everyone with its spiritual power. Because of his proven ability, Arjun would have a major role in carving an entire panel.

A silpin accompanied the young carver up a rocky hillside to the cave's entrance. As they climbed, the silpin explained something the architect had not mentioned. The cave had been excavated, leaving panels for carving on the right and left walls. The left wall had already been sculpted by the king's silpins in homage to Lord Vishnu. That meant the right wall must honor Lord Shiva in the name of the prince. The silpin's candor left no doubt in Arjun's mind: This was a competition between father and son.

When they reached the cave, Arjun's experienced eye

took in everything quickly. The left wall featured a large panel of Vishnu lying in a meditative trance on the cosmic snake, Ananta. Attendants and devotees stood nearby. Two celestial beings flew overhead.

In the rear three cells had been carved, each of them empty, and only the left one guarded by a pillar in the shape of a warrior-guard. On the guard's headdress was a discus, meaning Vishnu; an ax would have meant that the sanctum belonged to Shiva. On special days, therefore, a bronze statue of Vishnu would be carried by palanquins into the cave, worshipped, and then removed. Neither the panel nor the sanctum had yet been covered with plaster and painted in bright color. Perhaps the king was delaying completion of the Vishnu part of the cave until he saw what his son would do with the other half.

Then Arjun turned his attention to the right wall, where a large chalk drawing had yet to be incised by chisel on the large gray surface. The drawing depicted a fierce battle between a goddess riding a lion and a demon with the body of a human and the head of a buffalo. The design had been created, explained the silpin, by the great Shiruttondar.

Arjun knew of this famous painter and sculptor. A citizen of the southern Pandyan town of Madurai, he had been given to the Pallavas as a gift of tribute from a defeated king. Living now in Kanchi, enjoying the wealth and status of a king himself, Shiruttondar painted portraits of royalty and contributed designs for Prince Narasimha's rock monuments.

"Have you been told what you'll be carving?" asked the silpin after Arjun had walked around the cave for a while.

"Perhaps the face of the buffalo?"

The silpin laughed. "No more animals for you, my friend. You'll do the entire goddess." And before a surprised Arjun could ask why, the silpin added, "Because you know war."

The next day the young carver was brought before the chief architect again.

The skinny little man was seated within a dimly lit thatched hut at noon. It was hot outside, and so filled with sunlight glare that Arjun could hardly see him at first.

The architect was dipping a chapati into a bowl of spiced curd. Without ceremony he asked briskly, "Well, can you carve a magnificent Durga?"

"Until now I've worked only on animals."

"Does that mean you can work only on animals?"

"It means I lack experience."

"Let me decide what you lack. Did you sleep well last night?"

"No," Arjun admitted.

"Why not?"

"I was thinking of the goddess."

"Of the drawing of her?"

"Yes."

"Not the carving? Was it the drawing that kept you awake?"

"Yes. I'm sure of the carving."

"Ah, so you're not sure of the drawing, even though it was done by Shri Shiruttondar? Tell me the truth."

"I'm not sure of it."

"Good. Then perhaps I've chosen the right man. But there's something else to consider. The prince is devout as you well know. He wants his monuments carved by people who feel the same religious conviction. Shri Shiruttondar, for one, has convinced the prince he has it. So have others, myself included," the architect said with a smile. "So I must judge your spiritual condition. Do you follow Vishnu or Shiva?"

"Neither."

"Don't people from the Deccan worship the gods?"

"They do, but I've been away from it a long time."

"And have no desire to get back to *it*, is that right?"

Arjun said nothing.

"What difference do you find between lords Vishnu and Shiva?"

"Well, Lord Vishnu has love affairs like a man and fights injustices on earth. He's a human kind of god. But Shiva stays aloof even from his wife, meditates in the mountains and spends a lot of time destroying his enemies. Perhaps he's more powerful. Certainly he's more mysterious."

"Anything else?"

"I know people who keep evil away by reciting the names of Lord Vishnu. If snakes pester your house, you write Shiva's name on the wall. The flute belongs to Vishnu, the drum to Shiva. The tulasi plant is liked by Vishnu, the apple-wood tree is Shiva's favorite."

"Are those the differences you can think of? I don't believe you're that simple."

Arjun might have said that his childhood had been dedicated to forgetting most of his lessons as soon as he learned them. But he kept silent.

"Let me ask again. If you must choose, which of the two gods do you prefer?"

"Neither," Arjun said bluntly.

"That's an answer I am glad the prince didn't hear. Let me explain something, Arjun. You'll be working on a panel about Shiva's wife. You must imagine a warrior queen whose power to conquer evil comes from Lord Shiva. Do you understand? It's the depiction of spiritual as well as physical power. You must believe in it. And your belief can't be faked. You must have it in your eyes, your hands, in the deepest core of your heart." The architect dipped a new chapati into the curd. "To that end it's clear you need help. Because the rough cutting of the panel will take some months, you'll have time off, so I'm sending you to a god-man. You'll stay with him. He'll give you the heart to match those eyes and hands of yours."

The rainy season had finished and the northeast monsoon winds were blowing in from the ocean when Arjun reluctantly set out for the coastal village where the god-man lived. Leaving his tall silpin's turban in Mamallapuram, he wore the simple white dhoti of the south, a loincloth with the ends pulled between his legs and tied behind at his waist. Fluffy clouds drifted overhead as he passed woodland and field. It reminded him of the Deccan, even though the plant life was more lushly tropical. He walked beneath coconut and banana palms, wild date trees, and black sandalwoods. Sali rice was ready for harvest, and kalama, planted in early summer, soon would be. Women patrolled the fields, scaring off gluttonous crows by waving bright scarves and yelling at the black birds with wings outspread to land.

The village was a two-day journey south of Mamallapuram. Getting closer to it, he wished the trip was two days longer and two days longer after that. The countryside overwhelmed him with a sense of its timeless beauty, whereas the thought of religious training depressed him. In his boyhood he had endured too many tiresome lectures from the village priest. In the army he had seen men move japa beads in their trembling fingers and mutter long mantras before going into battle and then go out and promptly die. Pain didn't stop because someone hovered over your bleeding body and recited a few slokas from the *Veda*. He had seen enough of war to lose what little faith he had. In Arjun's opinion the gods went their way and he went his.

As he approached the god-man's village, his step slowed. Children crisscrossed his path, chasing one another and yelling in shrill voices. A few huts stood beyond the mud-wall perimeter of the village. Arjun sniffed the pungent smell of spices freshly ground and stared at hoes stacked against a wall covered with flowering creepers. Two women were irrigating a rice paddy from a ditch filled with water funneled out of a nearby stream. They stood apart, each holding one end of a long rope tied in the middle to a large bucket. They dragged the bucket through the water, then with a rhythmic motion swung it up and over the embankment into the field. The day was very hot. Hundreds of crows sat in a single tree, nesting until something unsettled them and they scattered like black pebbles flung angrily into the sky.

All of this was familiar to Arjun, for he had seen the same things throughout his childhood. But now home was far to the west, and he no longer felt like a boy.

Two farmers came along, leading a bullock harnessed for plowing. "I'm here to see the god-man," Arjun told them with a hopeful lift in his voice.

The farmers regarded the young stranger sourly. Although a few days of walking in bright sunlight had darkened his skin, it was still much lighter than usually seen in the south. He wore his hair short in Tamil style, but the scars made him suspicious to the farmers.

"Where, please, can I find him?"

One farmer motioned vaguely toward the village. The other muttered, "Where the old dog is lying."

Arjun entered the village and continued to walk until he noticed an old dog spread out like a moth-eaten rug at the threshold of a hut. Turning off the path and approaching the doorway, he called out, "I've come from Mamallapuram to see the god-man. My name is Arjun Madva."

Not even the dog stirred. After waiting a long time, Arjun decided this was the wrong place, so he returned to the path.

A voice called out, "You! Whoever you are, come in!"

Turning again, Arjun saw a middle-aged man with a big paunch standing in the doorway.

"Whoever you are, come in," the man repeated testily. He wore a topknot and a white loincloth, its front end pulled between his legs and tied at the back. Scratching his ample belly, the man disappeared into the dim interior.

Arjun stepped over the sleeping dog and entered the hut. The man was already seated crosslegged on the hard-packed earth floor. On his left stood a low table with a single cup on it. On the right, occupying a good portion of the small room, was a larger table loaded with offerings of ritual: flowers, bowls of holy water, a pile of coconuts and pineapples. Sticks of incense lent a spicy fragrance to the close, hot air.

The man motioned for his guest to sit down, then pointed to the single cup. "Take this milk. I hope it's still warm. You see, I've had it ready quite some time because I heard a crow cawing and knew you were coming."

Drinking the milk, Arjun found that it was hot,

almost scalding; it had been prepared just before his arrival. How had the god-man timed it so perfectly? Looking up in surprise, he met a cold, hard stare.

"Who are you?" the god-man demanded.

"Arjun Madva from the Deccan country, Swamiji. I carve at Mamallapuram." He wondered if this was the time to hand over the coin pouch sent by the architect. Before he could decide, the god-man spoke.

"So they have ordered you to come here and find God."

"That's true, they have."

"Do you think you'll find God here?" the god-man asked with a frown. "I see from your expression you don't think you will. For that matter, I don't think you will either. But perhaps something will come of your being here. Now who are you?"

"To the best of my ability, I've told you."

"To the best of your ability—well, that's good, very good indeed," the god-man said with a chuckle. "Come on now, recite the Gayatri for me."

The command, at once offhand and implacable, startled Arjun. The Gayatri Mantra, composed of twenty-four syllables, invoked the sun god Savitr. Only members of the three upper classes were taught this secret prayer. When a boy was invested with the sacred thread, a priest whispered the verses in his ear.

"Recite!" bellowed the holy man.

Leaning forward, without hesitating, as if he were a boy again in school, Arjun said in the sing-song voice reserved for such a recitation,

"Tat Savitur varenyam
bhargo devasya dhimahi
dhiyo yo nah pracodayat."

The god-man pursed his lips. "Your Sanskrit is very good. No Kshatriya or Vaishya recites that well. You were taught the Brahman way. You are a Brahman."

"Was," Arjun corrected. "You see, Swamiji, I have no topknot, no sacred thread."

"Did you lose them by choice?"

"No. But I've done nothing to get them back."

"Yet there are many Brahmans at Mamallapuram."

"That's true. I could arrange for a new ceremony. I could recite the Gayatri and wear the topknot and have the thread put over my shoulder by a priest."

"But you choose not to do that."

Arjun said nothing.

"And if Lord Shiva wishes it?"

"Lord Shiva has not confided his wishes to me."

"Ha!" The god-man chuckled. "Thus far I've spoken to you as a Brahman priest. Do you agree?"

"Yes. Like a Brahman follower of Lord Shiva."

"And from your look I see you dislike it. Perhaps you remember a foolish priest from your rebellious childhood. Ah, your smile tells me it's true!" The god-man stared long at Arjun before continuing. "Well, I am indeed a Brahman priest and a follower of Lord Shiva. People are sent to me from Mamallapuram and I teach them rituals and prayers. It's the way I make my living. But with you I'll do differently. I'll speak as a humble yogi who calms the mind and sees within, who seeks the unity of things." His voice had dropped to a whisper. "Every day I ask myself, 'Who are you?' And every day the answer comes back, 'You are that.' But what is 'that'? It is everything that is."

 **23**

A MONTH, TWO, THREE MONTHS PASSED, and although Arjun rarely left the stifling little hut, he often felt that he was traveling farther than the Chalukyan army had marched in its entire campaign. Time here was strangely distorted as in combat, and more was demanded in this dim room than had been asked of him since he left home. It was all because of Bhagavan Nambi's determination to bring him from the outside to the inside.

"Everything outside must be put away," the god-man explained, "including ritual and prayer. They have nothing to do with the inside. Dhyana alone can open that door."

So Arjun spent his days in meditation or in practicing techniques that enhanced it. He learned the difficult and often contortive postures of yoga. Most of all he learned pranayama, the art of breath control.

"Do you think my belly is the result of eating?" the Bhagavan asked sternly. "Of course you do! But the size of it is caused by breathing. Most people breathe from here"—he put his hand on his upper chest. "I breathe from down here"—he patted his belly affectionately—"where the power is." To demonstrate, he inhaled sharply, inflating his gut to the size of a huge melon. "Touch it."

Arjun reached out and touched the round abdomen. It astonished him; a coconut shell could not have been harder.

"Taming the breath requires greater caution," said the god-man, "than taming an elephant. Do it wrong, you can die."

Arjun was soon able to appreciate that claim, as he attempted to master the various exercises: Bhastrika, Sitali, Visama Vrtti, Surya Bhedana, Pratiloma, Ujjayi. Sometimes he felt as though his lungs were bursting, especially when ordered to keep from inhaling long after an exhale. Every exercise involved a precise ratio of inhaling, holding, and exhaling. He began with five pulse beats of inhaling and twenty beats of holding the breath and ten beats of exhaling it. The number of pulse beats was slowly increased, maintaining the exact proportion. Visama Vrtti—irregular action—was the most harrowing and dangerous, because the ratio changed from 1:4:2 to 4:2:1 to 1:2:4, the three making a complete cycle. Eighty cycles had to be completed in one sitting. Watching carefully, the Bhagavan stopped Arjun when he seemed on the verge of fainting. Sometimes he panicked—opening his eyes, gasping, clutching his throat. The god-man only laughed.

For increasingly long periods of time Arjun meditated at dawn, midday, dusk, and evening. The Bhagavan explained what was happening, what was not happening, what must happen in dhyana. He told Arjun that its purpose was to untie the tangled knots within the human heart. Often he posed questions which, clearly, he didn't want Arjun to answer. "Is there anything beyond everything?" he might suddenly ask. "You don't know? Neither do I. What's the use of such a question when the answer is within you, beyond the asking of it?" Another time he came into the room and waited—Arjun had no idea how long because his own eyes were closed in dhyana. Then the god-man said in a voice of utmost tenderness, "What I say doesn't come from me, it comes from your own yearning. It is you speaking, not I."

Such remarks were confusing to Arjun, who experienced none of the yearning mentioned by the Bhagavan. He simply felt he was learning a skill, as he might learn to ride an elephant or wield a sword or use a chisel. After many hours of meditation he detected no change in himself. Dhyana was a calming experience, that was true, but without the joy or revelation promised by his teacher. And sometimes, instead of relaxing him, it made him anxious. One evening he suggested as much to the Bhagavan, who merely smiled as if acknowledgment of failure was the prelude to success.

"When I close my eyes," Arjun confessed, "one thought leads to another and another."

"Find out where the thoughts come from. There's an old poem:

> Return within to the place
> where there is nothing
> and take care that nothing comes in.
> Go down into yourself and find the place.
> where thoughts don't exist.

Listen to me, Arjun. You don't learn anything through dhyana. What you do is rid yourself of what you already know. Don't look so puzzled! Be patient. Watch your breath go in and out like a tide. Stay seated like a rock in the waves and wait for the breaths to grow smaller. They will, you know. They'll become like the surface of a pond."

Arjun and the god-man took meals together, and true enough, the Bhagavan ate sparingly. At such times, after long silences, he would talk to the wall, as if forgetting his student's presence. He said, for example, "As long as I can separate this outer I from the I within, I've not found pure being."

To such remarks Arjun said nothing in return. For one thing, he didn't fully understand them. For another, he had vowed at the outset to be thoroughly honest with the god-man, who was trying so hard to help him. Arjun came to believe that this was what the Bhagavan wanted too.

Once he said, "Some people want everything except God. Others want everything including God. Others want God only. What do you want, Arjun?"

Arjun remained silent for a long time. They sat across from each other in the dim light of a single candle. Winged insects buzzed around it. The old dog, lying in a corner, growled fitfully in its sleep. At last Arjun said, "If I wanted everything, perhaps I'd also want God. But I don't want everything. And I don't want God only."

"A few people, having recognized the divine in themselves, desire nothing any longer, not even God. This, Arjun, is truly the place to be."

He brought out a drawing of Kali, the ferocious aspect of the goddess Durga. Kali stood in a battle pose, with one foot on Lord Shiva's outstretched body. He lay there like a corpse, while she, resplendent in the armor of a victorious warrior, glared down at him.

"Has she conquered Lord Shiva?" asked the Bhagavan.

Arjun studied the savage goddess, her tongue dripping blood, her eyes bulging wildly, a string of severed heads dangling from her waist.

"Yes," he said.

"No," said the Bhagavan. "Birth and death belong to Kali, whose world is outside. Shiva is the spirit inside that allows her to make these things happen. They live for each other as lovers do."

Later that afternoon, Arjun was sweeping the hut. As a disciple he was expected to take care of menial tasks. A wizened old woman came in every day to cook their meager meals, but otherwise Arjun managed the ashram— not difficult, considering that it consisted of a two-room hut and a smaller one where the Bhagavan slept.

Lumbering into the room, the words in his mouth before he had scarcely crossed the threshold, Bhagavan Nambi said, "It is very important to know this. When you find yourself, at that moment you're incapable of remembering your name." Turning, the god-man walked out and left Arjun standing there with the broom poised over a small pile of debris that had blown in from the grassless courtyard.

While meditating, Arjun chanted "OM Namah Shivaya"— Glory to Shiva. "OM" had three sounds to its voicing. After abandoning words and before entering the silence of complete enlightenment called Samadhi, you could still praise God and describe him through the triple-sounded OM.

"Of course you can describe him," said the god-man, "by describing anything at all. It's only a matter of realizing you have come face to face with him. For example, last night while sitting at our meal, I saw Lord Shiva right there." He pointed to the old dog sleeping, as usual, in a corner. "That's him, that's the Lord! Last night, for certain, I saw the Lord as my dog. Yes!" He chuckled and nodded. "My dog was truly the Great One." He ticked off the god's names on his fingers. "Mahakala, Dakshinamurti, Nilakantha, Tryambaka, Rudra, Nataraja," he intoned happily, "the auspicious and divine power of the universe, the celestial Shiva!" Chortling, the Bhagavan slapped his knee. "It's absolutely true! Ha ha ha! It was such fun! The creator of everything curled up in a corner, mangy and snoring! But don't worry, Arjun, I'm not mad! And neither are you for not yet seeing Lord Shiva in my lazy hound."

Arjun was not thinking of the Bhagavan's harmless old dog. He was thinking of all those malevolent dogs slinking through the streets of Kanchi. Were they really the gods Shiva and Vishnu and Brahma? Were they the goddesses Parvati and Laxshmi and Sarasvati? Such an awful possibility upset him until the Bhagavan leaned forward to add in a whisper, "Think only of dhyana. Whereas you're thinking it's ridiculous to see Lord Shiva in a dog. Think only of dhyana. Forget about seeing God in a dog. That will come later, but"—he lifted a finger as if in warning—"it *will* come."

One day he came back from officiating at a funeral. Ashes of the corpse still clung to his white robe. "How have you done today, Arjun?" he asked gently.

As usual, the disciple said, "I have tried."

"Listen to me. I too was in despair because of failing at dhyana. Then without warning it happened. I fixed on a blue dot that came out of nowhere until it fell apart like petals of a lotus flower and left the world totally free of shapes. I saw light jittering like a swarm of fireflies and then streams of it flowed in front of my eyes as molten as melted silver. Out of a terrific brightness came the image of the Mother Goddess. Opening my eyes, I saw her sitting opposite me, close enough to touch. Putting out my hand, I brought it next to her face. My fingers felt the warm breath coming from her nostrils. But she made no shadow on the wall, so I knew her existence was only in my mind. She faded then, yet I heard her running beyond the room, because her anklets jingled. She ran with her hair flying. I saw it here—" He tapped his skull. "Arjun," he said, "there's only one thing you must truly know. He who loses himself finds himself. He who loses all finds all! It's my hope for you, Arjun. Lose all, find all."

Another silpin had been sent from Mamallapuram because he was a drunkard; the chief architect felt he might benefit from religious training. He was a dark, sullen, mustachioed man whom the Bhagavan quartered with neighbors. Managing to get hold of toddy, the drunken silpin caused a commotion in the village, so the Bhagavan brought him to the ashram. Like two puppies, Arjun and the silpin shared the tiny space of the Bhagavan's hut. For the next few weeks the Bhagavan never left the silpin's side. He was not taught meditation or breathing. Instead, the Bhagavan had him memorize prayers and learn the daily rituals of puja with an exactitude beyond that of the most fastidious priest. The silpin had so much to do that he submitted finally to God and even prostrated himself before the Bhagavan, pleading for divine mercy and promising to say his prayers three times a day for the rest of his life.

The Bhagavan sent him back to Mamallapuram. Standing in the doorway with Arjun, the Bhagavan watched the contrite silpin shuffle away. "He'll be drinking soon enough. There wasn't much I could do. You see, Arjun, he lives with bad karma. In a past life he must have encrusted his soul with many wrong actions. Evil surrounds his inner being like the shell around the meat of a coconut." The Bhagavan sighed. "Perhaps what little was done here will help him make progress in the next life. Then he can prepare for happiness in the one after that."

Arjun was having his own trouble in following the dictates of the Bhagavan. During meditation he found his mind wandering more than ever before. Although he was becoming adept at controlling his breath, Arjun sometimes wondered for what purpose, because it failed to bring him closer to the inside. And if his esteem for swamiji exceeded any he felt for other men, Arjun had no overwhelming desire to emulate someone he admired but didn't understand. Nor did the passage of time help calm his doubts. Instead of enhancing confidence, the repetitions of dhyana seemed to break it down. They never brought him the experiences so treasured by his teacher. And then Arjun realized that his growing frustration had little to do with his own performance. He was tormented by the idea of disappointing the Bhagavan.

Perhaps the Bhagavan sensed his disciple's uncertainty. He never let up. When not engaged in priestly duties for the village, he sat watchful and silent while Arjun practiced asanas and breath control. He encouraged his student to work harder, always harder. "The mind is like a pot," he said. "It must be polished frequently. It gets dull unless cleaned by dhyana."

"But what if the pot is made of gold?" Arjun asked suddenly. "Then it doesn't need polishing."

The Bhagavan thought a moment, then guffawed. "That's true, very true. If a man is filled with divine light at birth, he needn't ever meditate. Are you filled with divine light?"

Arjun shook his head. "Not at all."

"But your argument is a good one," admitted the Bhagavan. "I like it very much. And I suspect Lord Shiva likes it too, because the Divine Teacher enjoys debate. Unlike Lord Vishnu, who trusts the heart only." At the time of sandhya, when night met day, the Bhagavan roused Arjun from sleep and lit some candles for puja. "Sandhya is the mysterious hour," he explained, "when the soul feels alone with the Alone. All else is illusion. We seem to be sitting here together, but what is sitting here is only Lord Shiva." From a little bag tied to his dhoti, the Bhagavan took some ashes and mixed them with holy water into a paste. Then he traced three gray lines across Arjun's forehead and chest, then three across his own forehead and chest.

"I consecrate you to Lord Shiva," he said.

Arjun wanted to feel joy at receiving this honor, but what he really felt was dread, especially after hearing the swamiji tell him that he must renounce everything that had seemed, until now, to be the ground of his existence.

"Truth won't come raging in from the outside. It must cuddle up like a little dog in the heart. Soon there won't be an I in you strong enough to suffer." And he went on with the ritual, burning camphor in a bowl, chanting slokas over a jar of water, sweeping the smoky air with gestures of wordless prayer, while Arjun endured the hidden shame of not wanting any of it at all.

On one of his infrequent walks out of the village, Arjun saw a man holding a handful of nooses made of deer sinew used for trapping birds. An older cousin used to hunt like that. Arjun tried to recall the features of his cousin's face, then those of his mother and father and brothers and of Gauri. After a while, they seemed to merge in his memory, leaving the image of people retreating through billows of morning mist.

Coming to the sandy beach, he studied the weighted fish nets drying on bamboo frames in front of weathered old boats. The water stretched unruffled to the horizon. He loved the look of it. All his childhood he had hoped to see the endless water; when he had first seen it, his eyes had been dimmed by the bloodlust of battle. Now he could look at the vast ocean and enjoy a dream coming true. But he felt no pleasure in it. Trudging back to the ashram, he dutifully performed yoga. The Bhagavan came in to watch him do the cobra, the locust, the plough, the head stand. When Arjun had completed his last asana, the Bhagavan nodded approvingly. "You have power and suppleness, Arjun. You are blessed."

Maybe blessed, Arjun thought, but also cursed—something that the Bhagavan didn't seem to realize. Arjun was cursed by a mind that refused to accept the dominance of a power within. Thoughts careened like flotsam in a whirlpool, the residue of memory and vague longing. Often he saw himself hammering stone with a chisel. He simply lacked the ability to surrender. He thought of confessing the depth of his failure, but the expectation of hurting his teacher held him back. Bits, pieces, slivers of idea scattered against the screen of his closed eyes like debris blown willy-nilly in a storm. Arjun sat rock-solid in the lotus position, thumb and forefinger of each hand touching in the curve of the Eternal Wheel, and by this appearance of placid immobility he tried to convince the Bhagavan that his mind was equally calm.

So he was surprised one day when the Bhagavan said, without warning, "You don't want to go farther, Arjun. You've tried hard, but your mind clings to the outside. And I think it always will."

Now Arjun could say it. "That is true, Swamiji. I think it always will."

"A man came to the village this morning from

Mamallapuram. If you feel ready—and if I agree—you can go back there."

"I am ready."

"Arjun, I have my own confession. Pride and stubbornness took hold of me. Because of them, I tried to force you inside. That was wrong, because you belong to the outside." The Bhagavan smiled. "Perhaps I do too sometimes, without knowing it. So I'm ready to let you go."

"The truth is, Swamiji, I want to carve again."

Nothing else was said for a while. Arjun tried to shape his thoughts into words. At last, bowing his head in deep respect, he said, "You've been like a father with a son. You've taught me there's something more than we see. I can't see it myself, but now I know it's there."

"Then that will be enough to go on."

They never stirred until the light failed. Then Arjun rose to light a candle, and his master turned to pet the waking dog.

 **2 4**

UPON ARJUN'S RETURN to Mamallapuram, he scarcely had time to unpack his few belongings before the outside world called on him to make important decisions. At dusk the chief architect himself escorted Arjun up the hill to the cave site where bull pointers had spent the last few months on the right panel—the one dedicated to the Shivaite goddess Durga and patronized by Prince Narasimha.

Holding a torch, Arjun studied the changes made

since he had last visited the cave. Mahisha, the buffalo-headed demon, was already roughed in, along with some of the combatants, but the warrior-goddess and the lion she rode remained in chalk.

"Durga has not been touched," the architect said, "because the great Shiruttondar's drawing displeased you. Does it still displease you?"

Arjun stared at it gloomily.

"Yes? Good. The great Shiruttondar was furious when he heard a young silpin from the Deccan was unhappy with his goddess." The architect chuckled. "'Who is this boy?' he yelled. 'What does a boy know about war?' When I told him you had been a prisoner of war, a handler of elephants, his face turned pale. You should have seen it!" The architect sputtered with mirth. Plainly he disliked the great Shiruttondar. Perhaps he was giving this important assignment to Arjun for that reason. He wanted someone naive enough and brave enough to stand up and criticize the great Shiruttondar, who was a favorite of the prince. Arjun had already considered that possibility, but it didn't matter. In the old days he wanted intensely to ride Gandiva. Now with similar passion he wanted to carve stone again.

By torchlight, Arjun appraised each section of the panel. What he liked best was the rough-cut figure of a man hanging upside down between the goddess and the demon. In this vulnerable pose Shiruttondar had captured the plight of suffering humankind caught between good and evil. No wonder he pleased the prince and other royal patrons, who were artists and musicians themselves.

In the chalk drawing Durga wore a karana mukuta—a towering royal headdress—and a thick necklace, a jeweled belt. That was all right. Her form was elongated, her face heart-shaped. That was all right. Her four arms held weapons as she leaned forward in a fierce charge against the demon armed with a huge club. Something was wrong there.

Turning, he studied the opposite panel, its surface already finished and polished and awaiting a plaster ground for paint. Lord Vishnu, about the length of a tiger, reclined in a divine trance on the giant cobra Ananta, five of whose thousand hoods sheltered the god. The coils of the Infinite One represented the cyclical nature of time. At the end of each cycle, the universe was destroyed, but Ananta held cosmic power in reserve for Lord Vishnu to use. In this manner the world was created all over again and the ages rolled on forever.

The carving was strong, confident, if a little too stiff for Arjun's taste. But King Mahendravarman had been well served by his team of artists.

The architect regarded his young silpin curiously. "Tell me, Arjun, did you learn anything from the Bhagavan?"

"You can't be around him and not learn."

"What did you learn?"

"One thing surely. That I know very little."

The architect smiled. "I hope you still know how to carve. Are you ready to start?"

"Can the work go forward a while without work on the goddess?"

"Are you asking me if you can wait?"

"Yes, I am, Shri Master. I'm not ready."

Shrugging, the architect headed for the cave entrance. He turned there and declared grimly, "I'm putting my faith in you, young as you are. I'm letting you do as you please. But if you fail me, you'll wish you had never picked up a chisel in your life!"

Married Tamil carvers occupied a small village near the beach north of Mamallapuram. Their unmarried Tamil counterparts shared little stone cabins closer in, and silpins of foreign origin lived together in wattle-and-thatch huts west of the rathas. Arjun was put in one of the huts with a taciturn sculptor from Pandya, here of his own choice, and a jolly fellow from Andhra country. As the Andhran explained, his words punctuated with sighs and chuckles, "I was at Pishtapura when your army took it. You had that battering thing—called the Tortoise? Nothing slow about *that* tortoise! Your elephants pulled it right through a shower of arrows and smashed the gate down. What elephants! They won for you. I escaped with Prince Manchanna Bhattaraka, who was supposed to be my loyal patron, considering the fact that I'd served him ten years. Ah, what a patron he turned out to be! Wanting to gain favor with the Tamils and find asylum here, he gave me as a gift to Mamalla Narasimha. The gift was accepted, of course. Narasimha wants glory! And so here I am, working my hands to the bone for an ambitious prince who can't even speak my language. Ah well, perhaps such bad fortune will improve my karma for the next life. God knows it needs improving! What were you in the army?"

"A mahout."

"Ah, then you might have ridden one of the elephants who pulled the Tortoise! But that isn't possible," the Andhran said with a grimace. "The world's not so strange that it would put such a hero in this lousy hut with me."

Remembering his friend Manoja, who claimed to

have seen most things and heard of the rest, Arjun could have made a good case for the world being that strange. But he said nothing.

It was the convivial Andhran who rushed into the hut soon after Arjun's return and called out gaily, "Come with me and see the saint! There's a band of them dancing and chanting down at the beach. Come along! Have you ever seen a saint?"

"No," said Arjun with a laugh.

"Well then, here's your chance," the Andhran said, pulling Arjun's arm.

As they headed out, the Andhran, who seemed well informed about such matters, explained a new fashion in communal worship. "They call it Bhakti, complete surrender to God. Both the followers of Shiva and Vishnu practice it. I think the cults agree on only one thing, their fear of the Buddhists." He laughed heartily. "Each cult follows the leadership of a few saints. Oh my, there are more than a few. Just for the Vaishnavas there's a lot. There's a woman from Karaikal whose name I can't remember. There's an outcast they call Nandanfrom Adanur who comes from I don't know where. The Tamils say there's a general who gave up war for God. And there's Appar from Triuvamur. After being tortured for undermining the government, he convinced Prince Narasimha of Lord Shiva's power. That's why our ambitious prince has become a devout Shivaite, did you know that? Isn't it remarkable? First you torture someone, then venerate him!"

The Andhran kept up his talk as they walked, "And there's a Brahman from Tanjore who, at three years of age, drank the milk of knowledge from the divine breasts of the goddess Parvati and was carried in a pearl-studded palanquin throughout the land and defeated scholars in debate by the time he was six. Someone told me this fellow had no past to regret but was utterly pure—whatever that means. And there was Tirumalishai. At birth he was a shapeless mass of flesh who was abandoned by his embarrassed mother, then brought up by an outcast woman. I think he wrote poems. And another was a highwayman who turned to God after a robbery victim forgave him. And there was Tiruppan, a minstrel of the lowest standing, who became famous for composing songs anyone could sing. He, this Tiruppan, was the one whose disciple is the saint we'll hear today, one of the twelve alvars who go about the land praising Lord Vishnu. Somewhere in *that* mob!"

During the rambling speech about Bhakti and its cults, he and Arjun had come to the beach. The Andhran pointed at a mass of people crowding around someone seated in the sand. Arjun had a glimpse of flowers plaited in a woman's long hair and bangles on her thin arms darkened to a chocolate-brown color by sandalwood paste. Before he could get a better look, three dancers separated from the milling throng, their bodies shaking violently as if their bones were unhinged. As they danced, the onlookers roared approval. Drums banged, a flute played, and the dancers, thumping the sand with their feet, made hand gestures of spiritual meaning: adoration and reassurance expressed by fingers and palms held in the various positions of ahbaya and chinmudra and bhumisparsha and karana.

Spectators were swaying happily when the dance finally ended.

The flute sounded again, a long, wavering note that lifted like smoke into the twilight air. The crowd became abruptly quiet.

Then a voice began singing.

Arjun froze.

"What's wrong?" his companion whispered. "What's wrong with you? Arjun? Arjun! You look so—"

Arjun was pushing through the crowd.

That voice—could it be hers? The memory of Gauri's voice was so vivid that he might have been standing beside the village pond many seasons ago, hearing the sweet sound in the distance, as farmers turned to it from driving their bullocks home and women halted at shelling peas and children ceased playing ball.

Having struggled to the front, Arjun stared down at a forehead bearing a straight red line of kumkum powder in honor of Lord Vishnu. Two eyes met his without recognition.

Arjun turned away and moved out of the crowd. The Andhran rushed to his side and touched his arm. "For a moment there I thought you'd gone mad or joined the saint's followers, which is maybe the same thing. But you're all right now, aren't you?"

Arjun nodded.

"I thought maybe you knew the woman."

"I thought I did."

The Andhran sighed. "People like me and you, we move so much through the land that it seems we have many chances to meet old friends and family. A face here, a face there comes out of the pack and for a moment we live in memory. Then we know better. It hurts to know we've been wrong."

Arjun turned to look at the Andhran. "You have just spoken as much truth as I have ever heard."

◆ ◆ ◆

That night he lay awake and imagined a different outcome to what had happened. The wandering saint had actually been Gauri. They had sat together on a piece of driftwood and looked out at a full moon scattering light across the waves.

She confessed that she had always possessed the power of speech, but she had been waiting for the right moment to say something. When it didn't come, she had remained silent. She had refused to talk even after the dacoits sold her to a rich house, where she swept the floors and weaved cloth. Then a man came along one day, singing. She had gone to the road and watched him pass. He wore a loincloth and carried a walking stick. Children followed him, circling and laughing and singing. She followed after him, and when night fell, she was still following. He offered her food, and the next morning, when he arose singing, she sang too—a song with words, his words, a song praising Lord Krishna. So she had followed him all this time, and when he died, she had continued to go his way, seeing what he had seen, praising what he had praised, singing his songs, teaching the ecstasy of surrender to God just as he had taught. And she would go on this way for the rest of her life.

He would have then flung himself at her feet and asked her blessing, for she had located the divine self within. Then she would leave him on the beach and join a knot of devotees patiently awaiting her. And he would never see the saintly Gauri again.

Finished with the vision, he felt tears in his eyes. It was an imagined encounter to be cherished, but Arjun knew that the Bhagavan would have laughed at it.

"The foolish dream of a boy," the master would have grumbled. "Think only of dhyana."

But he was thinking of something quite different. Spiritual devotion and rigorous meditation had little to do with him. They were not his way. He didn't even know what the way should be for. And from that moment, his attention shifted like an immense rock into a sturdy place, unmovable, in his mind. All he thought about was carving the goddess Durga out of stone.

 2 5

THE TRUE GURU, without help of words, can enable an attentive soul to hear endlessly but soundlessly the mantra "Tat tvam asi"—you are that—which links the consciousness to everything in the universe.

So the Bhagavan had told him.

But Arjun had never felt the truth of it, especially not now as he ascended the hill to the Durga cave. His consciousness was linked to one thing only—a wall of rock. Bull pointers were already at work, sending up swirls of dust and clanging their chisels noisily. To the left, as he entered, the god Vishnu lay in a trance, awaiting the proper time to recreate the world. On the opposite wall the goddess Durga must conquer a demon so fearsome that he had driven the gods out of heaven. A figure hung downward in a pose of helplessness, which emphasized the tyranny of evil and the human need for divine help. Durga's attendant warriors were short, fat creatures. One of them had already fallen; the others soon would. Mounted on her lion, Durga must herself defeat the buffalo-headed Mahisha. Shiruttondar had given her four arms, each hand of which held a weapon: a discus, a dagger, a sword, a trident spear.

To aid his thinking, Arjun left the cave and walked down to the ocean, where he stood a long time looking out at the blue water.

Staring at it, Arjun began to see nothing but men in battle, their bodies contorted in the act of striking and being struck. The demon leaned away from the advancing goddess, but the huge club in his hands was poised to swing. Arjun had seen this defense stance taken many times. Defeated warriors turned for a last wild swing before bolting in panicky flight. The panel was about the tumult of war, the excitement of pursuit, the bleakness of retreat. He recalled his own strange ecstasy when going into battle. Durga must seem equally serene and fierce and joyful as she advanced against an opponent who had turned for a last desperate stand.

Serene, fierce, joyful. All at once. She must have the supremely confident look of a great warrior.

He felt free of the past, to think only of Mahishasura-mardini—crusher of Mahisha—the warrior-mother who restored heaven to the gods.

It was all suddenly clear to him.

Durga needed more than four arms. She needed four more. She needed eight altogether to demonstrate her divine power. A corona of eight arms, whirling around her like a ring of fire.

Flinging his own arms wide, Arjun shouted at the cloudless sky. People strolling down the beach stared in astonishment at the young man running wildly toward the granite hills west of town.

During weeks and months, during a year, during two whole years, Arjun devoted himself to the vision that had come to him on the sandy beach of Mamallapuram.

To give himself privacy, Arjun slept during the day and worked at night. In the early stages he had an assistant swing the heavy mallet while he held the chisel. Later, finished with the rough cutting, he carved alone, wielding a small mallet and a point tool to chip away bits of stone and bring each plane from the wall. Then, for the fine work, he shifted to claw chisels and tooth chisels. Struck through endless hours, they slowly but emphatically released the features of a life-sized goddess. Silpins and cave sweepers began coming around to watch silently, awed by Arjun's implacable concentration, while a Durga both fierce and serene emerged from the torch-lit gray surface.

Two of her eight arms were put into deeper relief than the others and therefore imparted a stronger visual reality. A prominent left arm, stretched to full length, grasped a bow. A right arm was drawn back as if to loose an arrow. Neither the arrow itself nor the bowstring was shown. The other six hands held a trident spear, a bell, a dagger, a piece of rope, a discus, and a sword. He had positioned her on the lion like a Chalukyan cavalryman: back arched, thighs gripping the animal's muscular flanks.

When not working or sleeping, Arjun meditated, practiced yoga, and controlled his breath. He did this not to find the inside but to strengthen contact with the outside. The deep silence, the intense focus, and unremitting discipline refreshed his mind and body each time he went to work.

The chief architect came around often to study the panel. Sometimes he would mutter to himself before going away.

Arjun began dreaming of Durga, whose arms multiplied into dozens of waving branches like those of a huge tree in a storm. Sometimes the goddess possessed sweetness, but sometimes her face, looming out of a nightmare's darkness, reminded him of men dying in battle, so that he awakened abruptly, surprised by the sound of his own sobbing.

Even so, he worked on with demonic energy.

Arjun had reached the polishing stage when an unexpected visitor appeared one morning just after dawn. Bent over the hand of Durga's that held a sword, Arjun was working an abrasive flint of quartz across the clenched fingers.

Hearing a rustle behind him, the young silpin turned to find a small, dark, wizened man squatting in the entrance. When the man failed to identify himself, Arjun turned back to his work. He had nearly forgotten the visitor's presence when a keenly sharp voice said behind him, "There's no arrow or bowstring for the bow."

Arjun turned to look at the squatting man.

"You left them out and I know why. They'd detract from the look of the bow being drawn taut."

Arjun put down his quartz flint and sat on the ground with his back against the cool rock of the wall. "Who are you?"

"A man from Madurai in Pandya."

Arjun had already guessed that this might be Shiruttondar, the precious gift from a defeated king to the Pallavan court. He steepled his hands in respect. "Welcome, Shri Shiruttondar."

Thus acknowledged, the artist began pacing in front of Durga. "I was not happy to hear of you altering my design. But you must know that."

Arjun nodded.

"I was angry to think someone so inexperienced, hardly more than a boy, would dare to correct me. Then I began hearing things about your work, so curiosity has brought me here." He said nothing more for a long time but shifted his acute gaze from one section of the carving to another. With an abrupt sigh, he turned to Arjun and declared harshly, "The king won't like it." Once again he studied the rock.

Arjun waited calmly for the upcoming judgment.

Suddenly the critical man from Madurai threw up his hands. "The air around her arms is full of thunder!" Turning, he smiled at Arjun. "You honor the stone. It was right to add four more arms. Your Durga is very wonderful. Her body is fierce as it goes forward to battle evil, yet her expression is one of joy. The king won't like it, because it makes the Vishnu carved by his silpins look dull and lumpish. But the prince will reward you. Make no mistake about that. You have given him victory over his father." Placing one finger against his lower lip, Shri Shiruttondar regarded the sculpture one last time. "Who is she?"

"I don't understand," said Arjun.

"The model for your Durga."

"There is no model."

Shiruttondar frowned. "Oh yes, there is. But perhaps you don't know it. You have put in hard stone a fleeting smile. You have caught in it a face of mystery. No one will ever stand here without wondering who this woman was. You did that, silpin. So don't tell me there wasn't a model."

Long after Shiruttondar left the cave, Arjun studied his work. Was the face of Gauri in the face of Durga? He wasn't even sure that he could pull from the bog of memory a single feature of his sister's face.

But now as he regarded the stone, Arjun could see something that he had not consciously put there. It was not remembrance but creation, a vision as unique and transitory as a buffalo standing knee-deep in a pond, a flock of crows rising in a black cloud from a field. In the Ajanta cave, watching an artist at work, he had said to his friend Karna, "What was not there before is now there. And what is there is not like anything else."

Walking up close to the sculpted wall, Arjun looked carefully at the goddess Durga. Satisfied that his carving had changed this little part of the world, aware finally that it was what he had been working for all the time, Arjun picked up the quartz flint and continued to polish the stone.